AN ITALIAN LOVE STORY

By Ida Maddalena

Published by New Generation Publishing in 2017

Copyright © Ida Maddalena 2017

First Edition

www.newgeneration-publishing.com

New Generation Publishing

Chapter 1

This is a story from the beautiful mountain of Cesena, in the south of Italy. I am sitting on a small, wooden, dusty seat that has been left outside my grandfather's farm. I am imagining grandfather with his strong arms and his deep laugh. He is twirling a little blond-haired girl around in a circle. Angelina was my mother and Beatrice was my mother's cousin.

After grandfather's death my mother told me about her life on the farm with her loving, caring family.

There was a big wooden gate at the entrance to the court yard and a long flight of steps up to the family residence. Next to the steps was one big door and another of normal size. Behind the big one there was a room for making cheese, salami and ham and an oven to bake the bread. The other door led to a washroom and toilet for the family use.

There was a cowshed and a much bigger shed for the flock of sheep; also a stable for the horses and other livestock including hens. The family lived upstairs, where there were four bedrooms and a dining room. The bedroom where my mother and her cousin slept had a French door opening onto a big terrace. In summer the whole family would often have tea there whilst enjoying the gentle breezes and sometimes Grandfather played the accordion. At other times they would all dance together.

During the long winter evenings they would all sit in front of a big charcoal fire and my mother would ask her father to tell them some of his fairy tales. He knew so many of them.

In springtime her poor father became very tired because he needed to work so hard. In those times all the farm work was done manually. My mother told me that she remembered one day, when it was very hot, her father was resting under a big apple tree for a bit of shade. She and

1

her cousin Beatrice kept annoying him, saying, 'Will you tell us a fairy tale?'

He had shouted at them to go away saying, 'Not today. It's very hot and I'm tired. I need some rest. Why don't you go into the woods and look for some treasure?'

The girls had looked at one another and thought he wasn't being very nice today. Sometimes he was very silly.

Angelina had shrugged her shoulders and said to her cousin Beatrice,

"Why does he want us to go to the woods? What kind of treasure can we find in the woods today?"

"Never mind" said Beatrice, "We'll go and look and maybe we will find a surprise."

Holding hands, they made their way towards the woods. As they wandered among the trees, they heard the cheep cheep of a little robin and had stopped for a moment to listen. Then they saw him on a branch of an oak tree.

Between the shrubs and the fern, Angelina found some strawberries, then more and more. They were small, but sweet and scented. Angelina picked the strawberries but didn't know where to put them. Then Beatrice, who was older and cleverer, said, "Don't worry, Angelina, we can find something."

They made a little basket with some stems of broom. Then Angelina said, "Now Beatrice, let's go and find some pines."

Not very far away they spotted a big pine tree. As they got nearer to the tree they saw a squirrel jumping from one branch to another. They thought the little rascal had eaten all the nuts, but at last they found a few. They sat down on a big stone and smashed the nuts, eating some and putting some in the basket.

Then Beatrice said, "We must go back and find uncle. He must be very worried about us by now. I hope we'll be able to find our way back, otherwise we shall be in great trouble."

Angelina replied, "Oh no, we won't! After all, he was

2

the one who told us he needed some rest, and to go into the woods to look for treasure. We didn't find any treasure but we have found strawberries instead ha... ha!"

They had continued to wander through the woods, trying to remember the way they had come but the more they tried the more difficult it became. Angelina and Beatrice began to shout, "Uncle.., Dad... we are here, please come and help us!"

Angelina's father heard the girls shouting and when he realised they needed help, he immediately went to look for them. He saw some movement in the bushes and again he heard their voices. He ran to embrace them both saying,

"This won't happen again, because from today on, I won't ever be too tired to tell you a fairy story. If I do then I will be like Pinocchio, and my nose will grow and grow just like what happened to him when he lied to his father, Geppetto."

Then Angelina and Beatrice had burst out laughing, and were eager to reach home and show Angelina's mother the lovely strawberries they'd found in the woods.

Angelina's father was always very busy and the girls kept away from him but after a couple days he called to them and said,

"Children, tomorrow I will take you both to see a play about the children who are helped by the Dominican Sisters, and then I will buy you both either a box of toffee, or anything else you like."

They were very happy again, because they realised he had never stopped loving them, even when they demanded too much of him.

Next day the father was singing a song that Angelina and her cousin couldn't understand, and Angelina had asked,

"Dad we don't understand you, but we like the tune of this song, what is it?"

"Ah, you don't understand because the song is an American one." he answered.

"But what is America? Angelina had asked. She was

always so curious and asked a lot of questions.

"Well......," said her father,

"America is another country, and you are much too young to understand, but let me tell you both something. You will learn all these things when you go to school, and learn geography."

"America was discovered by Christopher Columbus who was born in Genoa around 1442 and who had a passion for geography. He was persuaded that the planet earth was round and that if he left Gibraltar in a boat and kept sailing in a straight line, he would return to the same place he had left."

"He went to tell the Italian King, who told him he was crazy."

"But Columbus didn't give up. He went to Spain and asked Queen Isabella if she would help him. She gave him three small ships named, Nina, Pinto and Santa Maria, crewed by 150 men who had been condemned to death."

"Sometime later this same exploration was repeated by America Vespucci, who named the continent America."

"But Dad...we still don't understand", said Angelina.

"As I already said to you before, you are much too young to understand the history," said her father impatiently.

Still persisting, Angelina said, "Can you tell us tomorrow, Dad?"

"Yes", said her father, "But remember, tomorrow we are going to see the play. There'll be no time for anything else, do you understand?"

He continued, "Now, listen to me. You and your cousin need to go to bed, because tomorrow you need to get up early."

So Angelina and Beatrice had gone to bed.

Angelina was very restless and kept looking for the early morning light coming in through the French doors. She was thinking about her father's promise to take them to see the play. He'd also said that if they were good girls they would enjoy themselves and have a lot of fun.

At last she began to see the light appear.

She jumped out of her bed, and began to shout,

"Beatrice, wake up.... we must get dressed now! The special day has arrived."

But Beatrice continued to sleep and wouldn't wake up.

Angelina ran to her mother and father's bedroom, shouting, "Mum, Dad soon it will be daylight and Beatrice won't wake up."

Her mother said, "Angelina, go back to your bed, it is much too early. The play is not until this afternoon."

Angelina began to stamp her feet and make a lot of noise.

"That's enough!" Her said mother sharply. If you wake your father he might change his mind and you won't go anywhere. Do you understand?"

Despite her mother's words, Angelina continued so loudly with her tantrum that she managed to wake her father and he was very angry.

"If you don't do what your mother said, Beatrice will see the play this afternoon, but you won't. Do you understand?"

Angelina returned to her bedroom sobbing and whining so loud that she woke her cousin.

Beatrice said, "We must be good girls, otherwise uncle won't keep his promise for this afternoon."

Angelina, looking shamefaced, said that she would be quiet until her mother came to tell them to get up. She gave her cousin a cuddle, and said she was sorry to have made such a fuss. Then she went back to sleep.

Later, her mother came to see the girls and found them cuddling one another. A tear fell from her mother's eyes. She remembered they were only two little girls, always wanting to know and learn more, after all. The mother touched the little girls very gently and said,

"Wake up little angels. Now it is time to get up and I will give you both a good wash and comb your hair. Then I will put pink ribbons in your hair to match your dresses. You'll be the prettiest girls there."

Angelina had jumped out of bed and run towards her mother, closely followed by Beatrice. She embraced her mother, saying, "I do love you and Dad, you're the best Mum and Dad in the world." And Beatrice agreed.

Renato, hearing all the fuss, gently opened the door and said, "Can I join the party here?"

Angelina was bubbling with excitement.

"Oh Dad, Mummy is going to put ribbons in our hair, to match our new dresses that were made for us. We shall look so pretty, just like the others girls in the village who are coming to see the play."

"I agree with your mother," he said.

Then Renato turned to his wife and said, "Mary come into the kitchen, I need to speak to you."

When they were alone, he said,

"Make sure the girls eat well before we leave the house, otherwise in the middle of the show there is a chance they may became very restless, like children always do when they need food."

"Oh, don't worry Renato," she assured him, "I will make sure they eat well and I will also make a snack just in case the two girls see other children eating and feel left out, especially Angelina."

Angelina heard her parents' conversation and she started, as always, to stamp her feet saying, "But Dad, you promised to buy us a box of toffee while the show is on."

"But of course my pretty girls, you know I always keep my promise, but what will happen if there is nothing to buy? And, remember," he said, "That the pair of you have both promised me you will behave during the show."

"Of course, Dad, we will both be very good girls, won't we Beatrice, but sometimes you get a bit annoyed with us", said Angelina with her head down.

"But most of the time you keep asking me questions when you know I'm very busy," her father pointed out.

Angelina ran towards her father and embraced him, saying, "Sorry, Dad. From today on I will only ask a question when we all sit near the fire."

6

"Thank you", said her father smiling.

Chapter 2

Soon after dinner, Renato went downstairs to prepare the horse and carriage to take the girls to the village. Meanwhile his wife gave the girls a good wash and combed their hair, putting in pink ribbons to match their beautiful dresses.

Angelina and Beatrice looked in the mirror and became even more excited.

"Thank you Mum", said Angelina, "We will never forget this day. We both promise to always obey you and Dad and we will try to love our brothers, and our uncles and aunties."

Her mother smiled and kissed them both.

"Your father won't be long now," she said, and a few minutes later they heard him coming up the staircase.

"Come on girls, the carriage is ready and the horse is getting impatient," he said in a loud voice.

Angelina danced up and down in excitement. "It's time to go", she said to her mother, and both girls embraced and kissed her goodbye.

Beatrice gave her aunt an extra hug, and said,

"I love you more than I can say and I'm so grateful to you, and Uncle Renato for letting me stay here with you all. In my house there are so many children and it's not easy for our mother to give us all the same attention that you give to all your three children and me."

Mary smiled and thought 'I know jolly well that it's impossible for my sister, Giovanna, to look after all her ten children and that was the reason I decided to take Beatrice under my care. It is also good for Angelina. With two older brothers, she didn't have anybody to play with her.'

Mary was touched to see the two girls so happy together. She kissed them both again and said, "Hurry up, you two, he's waiting for you."

"How right you are Mary," said Renato. "I'm getting very tired of waiting for these two girls. If they don't make a move soon the horse will start galloping off with an empty carriage."

The two girls ran down the staircase as fast as they could and jumped into the carriage. Renato took the reins and commanded the horse to go as fast as he could or they might not have a chance to sit in the front seats for the best view of the show.

In fact when they reached the village a surprise was waiting for them.

There was a long queue of people waiting to go in and a young lady was shouting,

"Is Mr Renato here, with his two girls? Please put your hand up."

So he did.

"I'm Renato with the two girls but what is wrong?" said Renato.

"No sir, there is nothing wrong. Your two young sons came here early and booked seats for you and the children."

Renato was speechless.

"Well, well, this is a surprise! Not in a million years did I expect that from my two young sons," he said.

He put a ten lire note in her hand and the young lady blushed and said,

"Oh thank you sir, very much, this is a surprise for me too. No one has ever given me such a large tip."

Then she went away to help the next customer.

Chapter 3

After she had gone Renato turned to the girls saying,

"You both complain about the boys, saying they never have time for you but as you can see, they are not so bad after all. They came early to make sure we had the best seats to enjoy the play."

The girls looked at one another and giggled.

Not long after they sat down, the big screen opened and they saw the scene of a building surrounded by beautiful countryside and monks working happily in the fields. Suddenly they heard a faint voice crying in bushes not very far from them. They stopped work and looking at one another, they said, 'Let's go and investigate.' So they did and they found a frightened little boy crying. His little body was covered in mud and his cheeks were glowing and bright red with sunburn.

The monks picked him up and took him to their monastery. They gave him a good wash and some food and attended to the sunburn on his face. Then they asked him what his name was.

He told them his name was John.

"And how old are you? The monks asked.

"My auntie says I'm four years old" he whimpered.

"Where are your parents now?" The monks asked.

"My Mummy and Daddy are both in heaven. That's what my auntie said."

"Where is your auntie now?" The monks asked anxiously.

"In the little house in the village" the child answered.

"Can you take us there?" they asked.

He boy nodded his head.

"Shall we go to see her now?" asked one of the monks.

John nodded again.

"Your aunt will be very worried about you by now", they said.

Brother Dominic and John followed a footpath through

a green shady meadow that gently sloped down the hill, and came to where there was large flock of sheep vigorously nibbling the green grass. Then as the way became smoother the village came into view.

They hadn't gone far when John pointed his finger at the house where his auntie lived.

"Your auntie will be very happy to see that you are safe", said Brother Dominic.

John nodded his head but then began crying. Brother Dominic couldn't understand why and suddenly, he became worried about John's situation. He asked himself, what could be the reason for the child to be crying.

He was still wondering and asking himself why the child was crying when they reached the auntie's house. He knocked on the door and soon became aware of the problem. The door was opened by an angry woman who glared at him.

"Go away", she said, "We don't have anything to give to you."

"But I don't want anything from you." The monk told her. "I believe this child belongs to you".

She threw her arms up in air, shouting and yelling.

"Listen to me, dear monk. We have ten mouths to feed and my husband is very ill. We don't have any space or food to care for another child so you can take him away and do what you like with him."

She slammed the door in his face and Brother Dominic was shocked and at a loss to understand how an aunt could treat her little nephew so badly when John was such an adorable little boy who just longed to be loved. On the other hand he did understand the desperation of a mother with a lot of children and no food to give them. She was obviously barely providing the essentials for survival.

He took John in his arms and said gently,

"Don't worry little one, we will take care of you. You will have many uncles to make a fuss of you and love you as you deserve."

John put his little arms around Brother Dominic's neck

and kissed his face. Then the monk hugged the child, took his hand and together they went back the way they had come, to the monastery.

The other brothers saw Brother Dominic return with the child and were curious. They gathered round him and Brother Simon asked what had gone wrong. He started to tell them what had happened in the village. With tears in his eyes and the frightened child still in his arms, he tried to explain the heartache of a woman unable to feed her own ten children. Sadness settled on all of them. They all agreed to give John all the attention they could in order to provide him with a good education and every help possible for him to become a young man of good character with prospects for a promising future.

The next day the monks had a discussion to decide which brother would be responsible for the child's welfare needs. Later they would arrange the right school for him to attend in the neighbourhood and then he would be able to mix with other children of the same age.

Brother Dominic put his hand up and said,

"I'm the person who found this little boy and I would like to be the child's guardian. I will give him all the love a child of his young age needs. As you see, he already knows and trusts me and I will do whatever it takes for him to feel loved and secure now and in his future."

"I will support you in any way I can, when you need help," said Brother Simon.

Then the Father Superior spoke and said,

"Brother Dominic, if you think you can manage to look after and love this little boy, we all appreciate and understand the responsibility you are prepared to take on. We can't say anything else but congratulate you for the courage and love you have shown for the child's welfare."

He gave a sign to the other brothers to agree with him. All the brothers clapped their hands and smiled. Then one by one they embraced Brother Dominic, who then asked the Father Superior if he could have an extra bed in his room, so that he would be able to assist the child in his needs and give him all the love his own father would have done.

The father Superior said he could and told him that from that day forward, he would be John's guardian and would have all the support he needed to care for him.

"He will be able to grow up like any other child in the village." he said.

This is was the end of the play's first act.

Chapter 4

During the interval some people stayed in their seats while others went outside for a breath of fresh air. Some went to the theatre's restaurant for refreshments.

Angelina looked at her father and said, "Daddy, didn't you promise to buy us some sweets?"

"Yes, I did, but since your mother has made some sandwiches, I thought that was more than enough." He gave her a smile.

"But Dad," she said, "Sandwiches aren't sweets, are they? After all you did promise." Angelina finished, in an annoyed voice.

"All right, girls but will you please remain in your seats while I go to buy them," said her father.

By the time he returned, the second part of the play was already starting and the girls were so engrossed in the play they didn't even notice he was back and sitting beside them. He had purchased two large packets of sweets and he tried to give them to the girls, but they didn't notice. They were so engrossed in the play that they'd forgotten all about the sweets.

Then Renato said "After all the fuss you both made about those sweets. Now you both look as if you don't really want them."

"Be quiet Daddy, said Angelina, "Can't you see the play is on?"

Renato was not amused at his daughter's behaviour.

The play continued, telling the story of the little boy found in the bushes by the monks, and tears came rolling down the faces of the two girls at the sight of that little boy among all those monks.

It seemed that Brother Dominic himself was beginning to realise that the monastery was no place for a child of that age and he didn't know what to do. After the prayer meeting he went for a stroll round the monastery grounds. While he walked, he lifted his hands up in the air saying,

"Oh Lord, give me a vision of how I can I bring up this little child. He needs his mother and father, but you know Lord they are no longer with us. I want to do the very best for him but even with all my good intentions, I am only a monk and I don't know anything about children."

The stress overcame him and he fell onto the ground. He lay there and he couldn't stop crying until eventually he fell into a deep sleep. In his sleep he dreamed that Jesus said,

"Brother Dominic, don't worry about the child. Everything will be according to my Father in heaven."

Still on the ground he heard a human voice calling his name. He scratched his head and wondered what had happened to him. When he saw Brother Simon looking down on him, he realised he had slept for long time and the other monks were walking round the grounds looking for him.

"Brother Dominic, what has happened to you?" asked Brother Simon. "John has been asking for you, and he won't let any one of us near him. You are the only one he wants and he keeps crying for you."

Disturbed by the voice of Brother Simon, Brother Dominic jumped up saying, "Where am I? Where am I? What happened to me?"

"Calm down will you", said Brother Simon, "You are not the only one who has had a shock. When you jumped from the ground and began behaving like a lunatic we all wondered what had come over you."

Brother Dominic, still in state of shock said, "I'm sorry Brother Simon, but I don't know what came over me."

Brother Simon tapped him gently on his shoulder and said,

"Don't worry, you must have been very tired, and you stretched out on the long green grass and had a good sleep. But now it is time to come home because the child needs you, and you are the only he wants. He won't let anybody else near him and he has been calling for you for a long time".

On the way home Brother Dominic said worriedly,

"Poor child, it is very sad that he needs to stay amongst old monks like us. I asked myself what kind of place is this for a little boy like him."

Brother Simon tried to reassure him by saying, "Yes, but he will go to school when he is six, and then he'll be among other children of his own age."

Brother Dominic gave a big sigh, looked at his friend and said, "I know, but until then the boy will have no chance to develop his potential."

"Why don't you consult with the other brothers?" suggested Brother Simon. "Some of them come from a big family and they know something about what it means to have many brothers and sisters. They have much more experience than us."

"Yes, I will," said Brother Dominic,

"This afternoon, after our prayer meeting, I will talk to Father Superior about my worries. I will tell him the concerns I have for the little boy, and ask what advice he can give me as to the best thing I can do for poor little John."

Brother Simon nodded his head in agreement, "That's a good idea, but before Prayers, go and spend some time with the child. He really needs you now, more than you can imagine."

"Yes, I will," said Dominic, "Thank you for your advice. You are the most trusted friend I've ever had, and I appreciate that. After the prayer meeting I will explain everything to the Father Superior. It's the sensible way to go about things."

After a few days later a meeting was held in the conference room. Every brother spoke of his childhood, but none of them came up with a solution, except as always, Brother Simon.

He said, "I have noticed that not very far from the monastery there is a little cottage, and there is a little boy there. I believe he lives with his mother and an old lady, who must be the grandmother of the boy. It seems to me that he is always very lonely, except when he is with his goats and some sheep. I dare say if we go to see the mother of the boy, and tell her about John's situation, she might understand and agree to let the two boys play together. Maybe they will become good friends for life. Certainly we can't expect them to play by themselves without any supervision but there is his mother there and the old lady and the old people are often much better with young ones."

"Right" said "Brother Dominic, "We will approach the family in that little cottage, explain the situation to them and hope that they will let their little boy play with our little John."

"We need to have the right approach, otherwise there is a chance they won't even let us go in, never mind talk to them. You know they always think monks only go calling to beg for food," said Brother Simon with a smile on his face.

"Yes, yes, I know, but this time we don't go there begging for food. We're begging that they let our little boy play with their little child." Brother Simon said.

Chapter 5

A few days later, the monks noticed some goats in their fields and they were happily eating the young trees they had just planted. Then they noticed a little boy and an old lady shouting as they tried hard to remove the goats from the monastery grounds before the monks saw them.

The little boy began to cry saying, "They're my goats, and I look after them. My Mum is in the kitchen making tea for me and my Nana."

The monks went back to the monastery and told Brother Dominic, saying, "There's a little cottage in a beautiful meadow of very short grass and surrounded with many fruit trees. It's beautiful, but also very sad. There is a little boy living there with two women. He really needs the company of other children like John."

Brother Dominic said, "Yes we know all about them and we're thinking about paying them a visit this afternoon."

Later that afternoon, Brother Dominic and Brother Simon set off towards the cottage. When they arrived they tapped on the door and an old lady came to open it. She saw they were monks and immediately said,

"Listen, you two monks, if you have come here to ask for a donation for the monastery, I am telling you that we haven't anything to give to you. We are only two women with a young child to feed and we are poor like you are."

"No, no" said Brother Dominic, "We don't need any charity, but we wondered if it is at all possible, for the little boy we have in our care to come here and play with your little one."

The old lady burst out laughing, and called out,

"Mary, listen to these silly monks. They are saying they don't need charity but are asking if we will let a child in their care come here and play with our boy. Ha...ha, this is news to me. I've never heard that the monks have a child in their care. Tell me Mary, what mother in her right mind would ask a bunch of monks to care for her baby?"

"Mother, behave yourself, and let them come in." the daughter told her sternly.

"You are a silly woman to let two monks enter into our cottage. You are out of your mind, but as always, you do what you please." Spat the old lady ungraciously.

Laughing bitterly, she moved away from the door, muttering so that only her daughter could hear. "I've heard of men dressing up as monks to get into people's houses."

The daughter let the monks come in, and said,

"Please forgive my mother. She is an old woman and she doesn't trust anybody, but she is harmless. Believe me, she wouldn't harm anybody, and she likes children very much. Will you come in and sit round the table near the window. I will ask mother to make us a cup of coffee while we talk."

She looked round the room but her mother was nowhere to be seen. She sighed and said, "Lately, Mother has been having little outbursts and then she goes out to see if the child is alright."

Brother Dominic apologised, saying,

"We are sorry to come and disturb you and your mother, but as you know we are not very far away from you. We often see your little boy looking after the goats and sheep and most of the time he is by himself. We wondered if you would like the little child in our care to come here and play with your little one."

The lady explained their situation, saying,

"Well Brother, our little boy, with Mother's help, enjoys looking after the animals while I do other jobs. You see my mother is an old lady, and we don't have any other food except a little milk and cheese that the animals produce for us, together with the fruit and vegetables I grow on our land. Also, the village people often come to and ask for my services as a dressmaker."

Brother Dominic said, "Now we understand your position I wonder if it would be of any help to you if your family allows our little boy to come here and play with your child. We found him in the bushes, not very far from your home here and brought him to the monastery. After we had washed and fed him, we asked him where his Mum and Dad were. "He told us, that his aunt had told him that both his Mum and Dad are in heaven. We understood that the little boy is an orphan and left alone except for his aunt. We went to see her, but she said that she was not in a position to look after her nephew, having ten small children of her own to feed and her husband very ill with TB. She just couldn't cope with another mouth to feed so she had abandoned him in the hope that somebody would find him and take care of the poor child."

"We then had no other choice but to take him to the monastery with us, and see what we could do for him. Now I have been made a guardian of the child, I am concerned like any other responsible person that I do the utmost I can for the boy in my care. Not just wash and feed him, but give him the opportunity to grow up like every other child of his age with a proper family. This would not be possible in a monastery."

"But brother, I don't understand you. How can I be of any help in these sad circumstances?"

"Please forgive me my lady, if that is too much to ask, but since you are a mother, and have a little boy, we wondered if it was at all possible for John to make friends with your little boy, and together they could look after the goats and sheep under the supervision of the old lady. We are prepared to give some money to the old lady, which would help your family and help us in this desperate position of an innocent child, who for no fault of his own has lost his Mum, and Dad."

"Brothers, I need to have a consultation with my mother, and then I will give you an answer. I know where you live, and we will contact you as soon as a decision is made."

The Brothers were happy at the outcome of their visit to the boy's mother. They shook hands and then went back to the monastery. Not long after the monks had gone the old lady returned. She called out and with a hysterical laugh said, "Mary, did you enjoy the chat you had with your two silly monks?"

"Mother, sit down and listen to me!" Mary, was becoming exasperated with her mother's behaviour.

"They are not silly monks, and they behave much better than you ever do."

Her mother replied, "Yes, yes, I know you will never change your soft approach to anybody who comes to you crying for help, when you jolly well know there is not much to give."

Mary looked at her mother and said firmly, "But mother, this time the monks didn't come to ask for anything but to give."

The mother looked at her daughter in very peculiar way, "Mary, I have never in my long life heard such a thing.''

"Well mother, I don't expect you have ever heard of it before but such things do happen very often. We live in this little cottage, and we get to know very little of what is going on around us," said her daughter sadly.

"Alright then... tell me what the silly monks wanted to give to us," demanded the old lady, as she started putting some logs on the fire.

"Only if you sit down, and listen very carefully, without making any silly remarks, as you usually do." said Mary.

"Listen, my darling daughter, I only make silly remarks when I know what you are telling me is not serious. But this time, looking at your face, it seems to me you are very concerned about something the two monks have said to you. Come on daughter, spit it out," said the old lady with an expectant look on her face.

"Mother, did you not know that Mr and Mrs Simpson died?" Mary asked.

"Oh no, I can't believe it. When did it happen?"

The old lady was obviously shocked.

"Only about a month ago, that's what the monks said,"

said Mary realising that the old lady was very upset.

"Oh! Dear me. What happened to their little boy John?" The old lady had tears in her eyes.

"Mother, this is a very sad story. You remember Giovanna the sister of Mrs Simpson? She has ten small children, her poor husband is dying and she just can't feed and care for another child. So she took the poor little boy into the woods and prayed that a kind person would find him and be able to give him a better home than she could. The monks, as always, were in the forest to gather wood for the fire, when they heard a whining sound which could have been an animal, or a bird. They went to investigate, not for a moment expecting to find a little boy covered in mud. The monks took the child into the monastery and looked after him. After a few days, they began to ask him his name, and the reason he had been abandoned. Now, mother, the monks came here today to ask us if was at all possible for John to come here and be friends with our little Peter, and together they could look after the goats and sheep under your supervision. The monks would give us money in recompense."

The daughter knew her mother would in no way refuse to help a little child at any cost.

"Listen to me Mary," said the old lady. "I would do that and more to help that little boy but we don't need the charity of the monks in this house. We will manage to give the poor child a better home than the monastery can give him."

The old lady was quite emotional.

"Mother, one step at time, but I knew in these circumstances you might be more than willing to help a child in need."

The mother answered, "You're right, my daughter. The only thing decent people can do, is never to abandon a child in need, no matter how poor they are, there must always be a place for a child like John."

"Yes mother, I know you. Although on the exterior you seem a tough old bird, underneath you have a heart of gold, and you've just proved that now."

Mary couldn't hide her emotion towards her mother for the love she had for this child.

The next day Mary made an appointment at the monastery to have a word with Brother Dominic. The day couldn't come soon enough for Mary to give the good news to Brother Dominic.

It was a relief for Brother Dominic to receive a message from Mary. He went into fields where Brother Simon was working with the other monks and said,

"Brother Simon, as you know, Mary from the cottage told us she would let us know what she and her mother had decided was the right thing for both children. Well, this morning I received a message from the lady inviting us to have a further chat to see what is the best way for these two children to spend some time together and to see how they get on."

Brother Simon smiled and then said, "Well Brother Dominic, I'm sure the good Lord will bless you for the love you have shown for this little boy, and it is an honour for me to take part in this project."

The next morning Brother Dominic went to the child's bed and gently touched his face, saying,

"John, wake up. Today we will take you to meet another little boy like you, and you can play with him. Would you like that?"

As the little boy opened his eyes, a gleam of sunshine came through the little window of the room where his bed was.

The boy asked, "But do you still love me?" and he started crying "I want my Mummy and my Daddy."

Brother Dominic realised that he hadn't ever lived with anybody for more than one day at time.

"No, my little one," said Brother Dominic, "You will just go to play with another little boy like you, and later on I will came back to get you and bring you back here with me."

John stretched his little arms towards the monk to be

lifted up, and threw them around his neck, and began to kiss him until Brother Dominic said,

"It is okay, John. I will always be your best friend now and forever."

He put John down, then took him by his hand, and said,

"Come now. I will wash you and make you smart. We will take Brother Simon with us, and on our way we might see some swans, and little rabbits, and lots of little birds in the trees and fields, singing cheep, cheep. They'll be so happy to see a lovely little boy like you."

John saw Brother Simon coming, and pointing a finger towards Brother Dominic, he shouted,

"We are on our way to meet another little boy like me, and we will see many little animals. But what I like most is that the birds will sing in the trees for me."

He then took his little hand away from Brother Dominic and began to run until Brother Dominic called out, "John, wait. That isn't the right way, it's this way."

He pointed his finger to the left side of the field. Then Brother Dominic and Brother Simon walked either side of John, gently taking, his hand, and jumping him up and down until they reached the little cottage. Then they heard a small voice saying,

"These are my goats. That one," pointing with his finger, "Is the big goat. Her name is Snow White and that is her little kid. I named him Capretto and all the others have names."

He stopped talking because he realised that his grandmother was looking down from the upstairs window of the little cottage. The old lady immediately rushed downstairs, recognising the two monks. She let them in and with a lump in her throat, she said, "Ah, this must be the lovely little boy you spoke about to my daughter."

She turned round to her grandson and said,

"Peter dear, take the little boy with you and tell him all about your lovely animals, while the two monks come in and have a cup of coffee and wait for your mother."

Peter nodded his head towards the boy and said,

"What's your name?"

The little boy answered, "My name is John."

"My name is Peter. John, come with me up the hill and help me bring the goats together and look after the animals."

Brother Dominic turned to the grandmother and said, "Peter is a lovely little boy. You must be very proud of him."

As the monks had entered the front room they noticed some floral material, a pattern and some scissors on the table, ready to be cut for ladies dresses.

The old lady said, "My daughter won't be long now. Early this morning, she needed to rush to the village shop to buy some cotton so that she can start to making a dress for a customer. I will go and make you both a cup of coffee while you wait."

Happily, the two boys climbed up the hills where many blue and yellow flowers were opening their buds and seemed to smile at the two children. They picked a big bunch each and Peter said to John, "Now we can run back to the cottage, and take the flowers to Mummy and Nanny."

He looked in every direction, trying to gather the goats and sheep together again, shouting and whistling, but the big goat with her little kid were nowhere to be seen. Peter became exasperated at not being able to see them. Then John spotted them. "Oh, look Peter," and he pointed a finger towards a big oak tree.

"Oh thank you," said Peter. He ran towards them, brandishing his stick at the goat which was munching the green leaves on one of the branches of the oak tree.

John felt very concerned for the goat and her little kid and began crying and shouting, as if singing, "Corri capretta......corri capretta col caprettino......corri capretta ...non ti arrestare sull'erba molla tu devi saltare."

"Run big goat, run, with your little kid. You will find that you must jump on the soft and beautiful grass."

Peter was flabbergasted to see and hear John crying and

singing at the same time because he thought that Peter with his stick, was going to strike the little kid and the mother goat.

Peter said, "I only have a stick to show them the way we want them to go, but I wouldn't do any wrong to my goats."

John stopped crying and slowly they made their way back to the cottage. John and Peter together presented the flowers, one bunch to the mother and one to the grandmother, saying, "We picked these flowers especially for you."

The mother and grandmother, both with tears in their eyes thanked the children for the flowers and remarked how beautiful they were.

"While you were picking flowers for us, we had a long chat with Brother Dominic, and Brother Simon," said Mary, and they asked if we would take John here, to play with you, Peter. Would you like that, children?"

Both children jumped for joy and together answered, "Yes," in unison.

Brother Dominic said to Brother Simon, "This is certainly a good thing for both children. We should feel very proud of what we have achieved today."

They both turned to the ladies of the house and thanked them for their hospitality and better still for allowing John and Peter to play with one another, hopefully for many years to come. Then Brother Dominic picked John up in his arms and said, "Goodbye little friend. We will see you later." Then away they went, back to the monastery.

The next morning John was not able to lift his little head from the pillow. Brother Dominic touched his head and realised the little boy was very hot and sweating. He immediately alerted the Father Superior, and the doctor came to examine the child.

After the doctor had given the child a good examination, he shook his head and made them understand that he needed to speak privately to the person who was responsible for the wellbeing of the child. The Father

Superior and Brother Dominic both replied, "The little boy is an orphan and we are the people who care for the little one."

The doctor said, "I'm afraid this little boy is very ill. He will not be able to play now, or when the time comes to go to school. There is nothing that can be done for him. What I recommend to all of you, is to be kind to him and look after him. Give him a lot of tender loving care, as much as you can."

He shook hands with the Father Superior and he went to his carriage which was waiting for him.

As soon as the doctor had gone, Father Superior asked all the monks to go to the chapel and pray for the child because he was very ill.

The next day Brother Dominic went to see Mary and the old lady to tell them the bad news. He recommended that they tell Peter that when John was better he would come and play with him again. The news shocked Mary and the old lady.

Mary said. "Please don't worry. We are quite sure he will get better soon. When he recovers he'll be able to come to us, and he and Peter will be able to run in the fields and pick flowers for us."

Brother Dominic looking very sad said, "But the doctor said there is no hope whatever for him and he won't be able to play or do anything else."

"Listen to an old woman," the grandmother said. "In my life I have seen many children very ill, when the doctor said they had no chance to recover, but often young children get over a nasty fever and grow up to be very strong and healthy, even more than before they had been before they were ill."

The old lady patted Brother Dominic's shoulder and continued.

"Never mind what the doctor said. Isn't it right that our God can change anything?"

Brother Dominic's eyes glistened with tears. He looked at the old lady and said, "How comforting your words are to me! You see when Brother Simon and I found this little boy in the bushes we tried our best to find his parents. With great sadness we heard they had both passed away. Immediately a great joy came over me when I was made his guardian. I thought God wanted me to look after this child and bring him up as good person, and now? I must go now. John may think I have abandoned him."

Chapter 6

Brother Dominic left the cottage and remembering the words of the old lady, he began to sing on his way back to the monastery.

"How great is our God.

How great His name.

How great His love,

Forever the same.

He rolls up the water

Of the mighty Red Sea

And he says I will never leave you.

Put your trust in me."

As soon as he reached the monastery he pushed open the big door and went upstairs, where he knelt down beside John's bed, and he said, "My dear precious child, all the monks and Mary and Peter's grandmother are praying to the Lord for you to get better very soon and then you will be able to go down to the cottage and play with Peter."

Brother Dominic with great amazement saw the child jump out of the bed and throw himself into his arms putting his own little arms around his neck saying,

"Brother Dominic, I have seen my mummy, and daddy. They looked beautiful and they held me in their arms and told me I would soon be with them forever."

Brother Dominic couldn't hold back his tears. He said. "This is wonderful."

He put John back into his bed again thinking, 'I'm sure the high fever made him very delirious.'

Brother Dominic went downstairs to get a sponge and lukewarm water to sponge his little body and help to bring the temperature down. After a while the child appeared much better and he slept for many hours.

Brother Dominic sat down beside John's bed all night praying and hoping that the good God would take away the high temperature, so that he would be able to go to the cottage and play with Peter.

The next morning, John looked even more poorly than ever but Brother Dominic knew the medicine given by the doctor would take some time to work. He very much hoped the doctor was wrong about his diagnosis. The boy only had a fever that children of his age sometimes have. In fact the following morning John seemed to be a little brighter in himself. And he was able to sit up in his bed, and ask questions about his mother and father.

Brother Dominic reassured John that his mother and father were in Paradise looking down and praying for him. The child tried to skip round the little room chanting, "I will soon be able to go to the cottage and play with my friend Peter."

That pleased the monk immensely and he felt he was right, and the Doctor had got it all wrong. He ran round the monastery to tell the good news to the rest of the monks who were in residence at that time of the day. However, Brother Dominic's excitement didn't last long. When he returned to the boy's room he wasn't skipping round any longer, but lay on his bed, almost unconscious. Brother Dominic was shocked to see the unfortunate child in such a poor condition. He ran to the Father Superior to seek his help and was almost hysterical with his arms waving in the air and shouting.

"Help, Father, help! Please come and help. The little boy is very ill indeed."

Father Superior spoke calmly and reassuringly.

"Brother Dominic, compose yourself. This is not a sensible way to help that poor child."

The Father Superior sent for the doctor immediately, and a short time later, the doctor arrived at the monastery door. The monk who opened it said, "Thank God you are here doctor, because the boy is very poorly."

The doctor said, "I'm afraid this little child needs to be taken to the Baby Jesus hospital."

Brother Dominic said firmly, "Doctor I'm his guardian, and this child will go nowhere, because he will not be able to survive without me."

The Doctor replied, "You are his guardian, but I am the doctor and I'm the one who will decide the wellbeing of this child. This is an emergency. He needs to be taken to the hospital now, where a doctor and nuns who are nurses are there waiting for him, knowing he is very ill."

Brother Dominic couldn't sleep at all that night. Very early in the morning, he went to the hospital, to find out if the child could return with him to the monastery.

The doctor in charge of the hospital said, "I'm very sorry Brother Domenic, we will do whatever is possible, but you know this child is very seriously ill. Only the Lord will decide if he is to remain a part of this world or go to the little angels in paradise. You need to leave things in His hands, and there is nothing else you can do."

The monk looked at the doctor with tears in his eyes and said, "It's not easy for me to accept the situation I'm in."

The doctor shrugged his shoulders and said," Brother Dominic; you need to take care of yourself. Leave it to the sisters to stay with the child, so that you can have some rest. The child will have every attention he needs. You can visit any time you want. As you know already, God works in mysterious ways."

After a few days the child appeared to be a little better, but strangely one day the sister noticed that the child had disappeared from his bed, and nobody knew where he was. She decided to hide in the corner of his small room and she saw him go to the hospital chapel. Without him knowing, she followed him. She saw John kneel in front of the statue of Jesus. Underneath it was written 'Suffer little children to come unto me, for theirs is the Kingdom of Heaven'. He was asking Jesus if his mother and father were together in paradise, and if so, when would they come back for him. Then very slowly he returned to his bed, and was soon fast asleep. This continued for a short period of time, until one day the sister noticed that the child hadn't returned to his little bed. She didn't have any choice but to go and see where he was and why he hadn't moved away from the statue of Jesus.

For Brother Dominic and Brother Simon, and for Mary and her mother, and all the other monks of the monastery, it was a very sad day.

John was longer an orphan. He had been reunited with his mother and his father.

The curtain closed and the audience was left sitting in their chairs, weeping.

Slowly they all went home. Angelina and Beatrice were grieving all the way.

Chapter 7

A few days later there was great excitement around the house. Angelina had overheard her mother say to her father that she needed to go to the shops to buy material to make smocks for the girls, as they would soon be old enough to go school.

The girls skipped and jumped round the house, singing and shouting, "We're going to school. We're going to school."

Renato, letting out a heavy sigh said, "Listen, little ones, will you both please go outside and play. I need to have some rest and it's impossible while you are running about, making such a racket."

The girls did go outside giggling and Angelina chanting, "Ha. Ha. My father is a grumpy old man. He doesn't like it when we make a noise."

But Beatrice said, "I can assure you Angelina that your father is kinder than mine. My father doesn't grumble. Instead he runs after us with a stick when we upset him."

"Never mind," said Angelina, "We are soon going to school and we will have much more fun there. There will be many more children to play with and my brothers say that we can make as much noise as we like in the playground."

A few days later, the mother came rushing into their bedroom and said, "Wake up children. Today is a special day for you two, because you are both going to school and you must both promise to be good girls."

"Yes, we will." They answered in chorus. However, the excitement soon disappeared when Angelina and Beatrice entered the schoolroom. There were many benches and each bench was made for two children to sit on. Many double desks were there, with the ink pot in the middle and each pupil had a separate space to keep their books. Most of the children were boys, with only a few girls. The teacher was a man with a beard and moustache and a long face. They were frightened and began crying for their mother. For a few days the two girls were unsettled, but they soon found that the school was a way of life.

Angelina liked History and Geography. They were her most interesting subjects.

She never forgot hearing her father sing 'Oh When the Saints Go Marching in' and she heard her father speak many times to her mother about the way of life in America. It was winter time and it was very cold. Daylight was very short and they all sat round the big fireplace.

Angelina didn't ask for fairy tale stories any more. She was more interested in the history of Italy. "Daddy," she said one day, "In school today, we learned about the Unification of Italy, but I didn't understand what it really meant."

The father answered, "Now, listen Angelina, I will explain it to you the best I can but not now – maybe tomorrow."

"No, no daddy now," She insisted.

Renato was annoyed, but he knew she wouldn't stop until he did.

So, he began to tell the history of the Unification of Italy.

"The 17th of March 1861 was also the breakdown of the feudal system which had survived since the Middle Ages. History tells us about that people's lives changed dramatically as most of the land was allocated to the king, the aristocrats and the church. Small farms were left for the common people. The farming population increased and so the plots were divided amongst their heirs. That made the farms very small and unproductive. Therefore, people began became lawless and there was a lot of suffering, violence and strife amongst them. Now that is enough for today."

"But dad I want to know more," protested Angelina, banging her feet down on the floor, but her father walked out of the room. The next day the weather was awful. It didn't stop raining, and it was also very, very cold. As always, her father sat down near the open fire. Angelina didn't waste any time. She immediately asked her father to continue with the story of Italy.

"All right," agreed her father.

"The aristocracy and the wealthy had little knowledge of how to govern big estates with a lot of land. They needed servants, mostly men and a few women. The servants suffered badly, not only from the proprietors but also from supervisors, who were employed to look after them. They employed men to cultivate the land, some to supervise the labourers in fields and others to supervise the planting of the orchards and vines. As the rich owned lots of land with big farms, men were needed to work on them. The labourers were to work without much rest for long hours as well as being under a lot pressure. They mostly lived in fear and suffered a lot of abuse from the patrons and the supervisors. However, this didn't stop them having large families. Thus the population grew."

Chapter 8

"Around the year 1870, poverty increased. Along with other men of our village, we were convinced that the farms with small plots of land weren't big enough to produce enough food to support our families. We had little choice but to emigrate from here to countries which offered us a chance to improve our lives. Most of us went to America, others went to Britain, France and other parts of the world."

"At first, only a few of us left Italy but in the 1880's two or three ships a day were leaving the port of Naples. Most of the migrants were men with only a few women and mainly from the rural villages of the south of Italy. We all went with the hope of making some money and then returning to the family we had left behind. Only a small number of men and women came from the northern region."

"As we sailed from the port of Naples, we Neapolitan people, sang 'Partano...I bastimenti ..E... vanno assai lontano...... cantono accor de sol Neapolitan'."

"On the ships we tended to socialise with those who more or less came from the same district of Italy. We all hoped to return to our beloved families we had left behind. Migration was slow at first with only a few people leaving Italy but later, in the 1880's, massive numbers of Italians arrived in America. It made the Italian economy very unstable and it was difficult for those left behind to survive. It was necessary for them to follow friends and relatives, with the hope of finding a job and improve the lives of the Italians left behind. At times there was hardly any schooling for the poor, some for boys but nothing at all for girls. The best education was for those who were well off."

"In America the only work available for the migrants was manual or working in the fields. Most were sending money back home to Italy. Some of them settled in cities, others bought fields and settled down. They made sure that the new arrivals who were employed came from the same district so that they would be able to understand one another. Many of them couldn't speak the official Italian language, only the dialect from their original villages. It made it very hard for them to be understood. Few of them were literate, unable to read or write in either Italian or English. They made every effort to overcome these problems by learning to adjust to the American way of life. Social life flourished among the Italian and American neighbours and others who came from the same villages and provinces, and so a kind of little Italy was formed. Some of them made great progress, settling down well and in no time began to prosper and provide good food for Italian shops and restaurants. Some of the Italian people only wanted to emigrate for a few years until they had earned enough money to enable them to return to their families and buy land to farm. I was one of them. But some of them had big ambitions of starting a business when they got back to Italy. My ambition was to return to the lovely family I had left behind, and if I had a chance to buy myself a farm, I would do just that."

"Most of us achieved our goals and we returned to the homeland. But two percent of the men didn't bother anymore about the wives or the children they had left behind. They decided to stay in America and start a new life. When I and others tried to remind them about the obligation they had towards their family, the answer was "mind your own b... business.""

"As the First World War approached, it soon wouldn't be possible to leave America neither would it would be possible for people to emigrate anywhere in the world. Thousands of young Italian men decided to stay and support America and went into the armed forces while others took jobs in arms factories. Many of us decided to return to our homeland, but many more decided they would have a better chance to continue the progress they had already made for the future of their families, so preventing the Italian government from forcing them to join the Italian army, as rumours of a World War became more and more of a reality."

"Some Italians began to purchase bonds and supported American patriotism; others became richer by producing more and more good food from their farms, also supplying other Italians, as well as restaurants and many other businesses. The situation of the men returning home changed dramatically in Italy as all over the world. Lives became very unsettled with many distractions, but people always do their best to survive. I and a few others returned from America to the little village of Cave in the province of Campania. Despite what was going on in the world we didn't seem to find any difficulty in settling down again. We were just glad to be home, with our beloved families".

"And now, my dear children, I'm tired, so I will continue to tell you the story another day."

A few days later Angelina said, "Dad... today, our teacher would like us to write an essay about how difficult it was for you to settle down again in the village after you had been in America for ten years."

Chapter 9

"My dear little child," said her father, "I tell you, I soon began to think of what was the best way to invest the money I had earned in America. With a lot of sacrifices, I decided to take a long walk around the district to see if I could buy a farm, or rent one. I came to a path leading through to a beautiful, green shady meadow pasture with a gently sloping footpath going up the hill. This led to the mountain of Cesena, which has a majestically high waterfall. The water crashed down making many plants grow in the valley below. There was a fragrance of many fruit trees and it filled the air. As I walked on, the footpath became more and more rugged as it rose steeply towards the Alps. I think that is enough for you to make a good composition."

Angelina smiled, "Thank you Daddy" she said, "I will try my best." Then off she went to play with her cousin Beatrice.

Two days later, Angelina came home from school skipping all the way.

"I'm so happy," she said, "The teacher liked my composition, and she wants to know more about your progress as the time went by."

Her mother said "Your father needs to tell you more about life on the farm then. After all that's where the progress was really made."

So Angelina ran to her father and said, "Dad tell me more, tell me more. What did you do after you came home from your long walk?"

The father looked at his little girl and didn't know what to make of her. Again, he had no choice but to start again from where he had left off.

"Okay", he began. "When I turned back towards home, I couldn't wait to tell your mother about the beautiful waterfalls, the shady green meadow and the fruit trees, which at that time of the year made the valley at the foot of

Mount Cesena so lovely. And it was not that far from our house."

"My dear Mary" I said to your mother, "I went for a long walk and I came to a huge waterfall, which ran from the Alps of Cesena to a beautiful meadow below. It was a magnificent sight. I've never seen anything like that before."

Your mother said, "But Renato, I'm surprised you hadn't noticed that before. After all, it's a very big mountain and even a blind person could hear the noise of the waterfall running down with such force, even if he couldn't see it. Just the crashing noise would have made him realise that there must be a waterfall not very far away. In fact it has always been there." Your mother finished.

"Mary," I said, "I wasn't interested then because I didn't have the money for any project of this kind, but now is the time for me to invest the money I worked for and earned with much sacrifice. I would like to buy a farm house and maybe also some of the land close by. That is if we are lucky enough to convince the Duchess of our good intentions. Now is the time to approach the land agent. He may be able to give me an idea of how I could negotiate a good price."

Renato had a sparkle in his eyes as he continued. "Your mother said, "Oh well Renato, you know as well as I do that the Duchess's land agent is not well thought of. There is a rumour about him that says he is far from reliable. The wise thing to do is to take a friend whom you can trust and both of you to go to see the Duchess."

"I knew she was right and I told her so, "Well Mary, you know more about these people, much more than I do. I've been away in America for so many years. I've lost touch with the ways of the people of this village."

"Then I put my jacket on and went out for a stroll around the village hoping to find out more about this particular land agent to see if I could have a chat with him about what he had in mind. After strolling around the village, I didn't meet the man I was looking for, but only some men playing boules. So I thought 'this is no use. I must return before your mother wonders what had happened to me'. Slowly I started to make my way home to our house and on the way I met an old man called Pasquale and I stopped to chat with him."

"He looked up at me, and he said "Goodness me, Renato I'm not dreaming or am I? You must be that young man who went to America a few years ago."

"Indeed I am that young man, and as you see, I haven't changed that much. I can't understand why you had a job recognising me, even if I've been away for quite few years." I replied."

"Yes, yes you're right, my friend, you haven't changed much. But I'm an old man" Pasquale said.

"You don't look an old man and anyway you are only as old as you feel! Are your family alright?" I asked him."

"Well, all my family have grown up no and they've left the nest. Now it's just my wife and I left alone at home." said Pasquale, looking sad.

"Well that's life! It comes to all of us sooner or late," I told him. "Some of us get old more quickly than others. It's a road we all have to take. As long as you keep well, that's all that matters."

"How right you are my friend. I expect you've heard the news." Said Pasquale, changing the subject.

"Depends on which news you're talking about." I answered.

"Here in Italy, everyone is talking about a great war and saying that soon the ships will not be able to sail and so, my dear fellow, that'll be the end of emigration," said Pasquale.

Chapter 10

"Oh yes, I know all about that." I replied. "That's the reason I came back home early. Perhaps the Italian government might recruit me to join the army. I wouldn't like that at all. I sincerely hope that doesn't happen. I've returned to Italy with only one thing in mind and that is to be home with my beloved family. I hope to meet the land agent who is working for the Duchess, to see if there is a possibility of making a deal. What I would like to do, is to buy or rent one of her farms, actually, the one that is not far from Mount Cesena." I told him.

"Well, I've known that man long enough and my advice to you is that you need to have a mediator to enable you to make a deal with the land agent and to see the Duchess." Pasquale advised.

"Okay, I agree with you Pasquale, but now I need to go home, because my wife and children will be wondering what has happened to me. I'll follow your advice and get legal counsel before I make a move. Goodbye my friend."

"And with that I left Pasquale and carried on towards our home with a sense of satisfaction that I had had a good chat with an old friend from the village. I opened the door of our house and called for your mother." Mary where are you?"

"I'm in the kitchen, where else would I be?" She answered.

"Oh, I met Pasquale and I had a good chat with him." I told her. "You know what Mary, he recognised me." I said.

"I'm glad you met Pasquale. I expect he told you some local gossip."

"No, no he didn't say much, but he confirmed what you already told me about the land agent. I assured him I would seek legal advice before I go to see him."

Your mother asked if he'd said anything about his family.

I said, "He told me his family had now grown up and left home. He doesn't find life easy without them."

"Well," she said, "Pasquale had two sons. Both were very musical .They kept the village well entertained with their music. The second son, who was called Little John, wrote some fantastic songs. He was a very good singer, tall with lots of black hair brushed back. He had very dark eyes, wore very fashionable jackets and trousers. All the girls loved him and most of time he made them believe that he loved them too. But he made a lot trouble for his parents. One evening he was invited to a feast underneath a balcony and he realised it was the house of a girl he had once been out with. He had left her with a bitter taste and very disillusioned. Before he could run away the girl threw a bucket of cold water over her balcony onto him. He returned home, locked himself in his bedroom and for a few days he behaved very badly. That didn't please his parents very much," your mother finished, laughing.

I said to your mother "Well, now I understand why he and his wife missed their children so much; they must be feeling lost now that they haven't anything to worry about! But I sincerely hope this cloud of war doesn't come to anything. For the young people and some of us as well, there isn't much to look forward to. My only hope is that the war never materialises, for all our good."

"Well my dear husband, we do hope and pray that eventually everything will be ok. With God's help, our children will grow healthy and strong, and as they grow up, they will able to help us to run the farm." Your mother pointed out.

"So, my dear wife I need to go and get advice from the right person who would be willing to come with me and help negotiate a deal with the land agent and the Duchess. But for now I'm tired and what I need is a good supper and a long sleep."

"Yes, I can see that," she said. "I have prepared a good, tasty supper for you and our two lovely children."

''That's a good thing after having to eat all that junk

food while I was in America." I told her.

Next morning, the smell of bacon and coffee, made me jump out of bed and run into the kitchen with very few clothes on. I sat down and Mary, your mother, shouted loudly,

"Renato, what are you doing?"

I was surprised. "Well what do you expect me to do? I came to join you for the breakfast you've been cooking for me. What else?" I said laughing.

Your mother was furious. She began waving her arms up in the air. "If you think you can come here and eat your breakfast without washing and dressing yourself properly, you have made a big mistake."

I got up from my chair in a stroppy mood and said, "Alright, alright," I told her, "I'll go and get washed and shaved and brush my teeth as well. Perhaps that'll satisfy you."

Your mother replied. "And you'd better put on your best suit. Remember, you need to go to the village. Only then will you know if the lawyer can advise you if there is any chance of buying the farm you've always wanted. If so it will be a reasonable investment for our future."

So, I went back to our bedroom and emptied the water into the washbasin from the jug already prepared for me by your mother before I got up. I washed and shaved thoroughly and then I put on my best suit just as I was told. I came out of the bedroom, thinking I must look a very sophisticated man.

When Mary, your mother looked at me, she said "I remember the day we first met. You came up to me and we began to chat, and you said, "Mary you are a very beautiful woman and I would like to meet up with you again". And I turned round as I said "Why not, as long our parents don't know about our meeting."

"Not long after that, we did meet, but if I remember rightly, what a battle we had. Our families had never liked one another. It seems to me they fought like cats and dogs but at the end of the day we won the battle."

Mary finished the story with a big smile, saying. "And now my dear husband here we are now."

I told her. "It was really true love Mary."

Your mother threw her arms round my shoulders and said; "Let's sit here together and enjoy the breakfast I cooked for us and the children."

When I'd finished I got up from the table, and announced, "Mary and children it is the time for me to make a move. I hope today is the right day to see the lawyer and make a deal."

"Well Renato, you look very smart, she said. "I'm sure the lawyer will be very happy to meet you and listen to the plans you have about the farm. Let's hope that everything will go the way you always wanted .Good luck for today," she finished.

I embraced and kissed your mother and the children and ran down the staircase. I hurried down towards the village square, hoping to find a bus to take me to Tora village, to see if it was possible to meet with the lawyer. After a few minutes I had reached the village square and found out there was no transport at all to go to Tora village. The only way was to walk."

Chapter 11

"The path I needed to take was a rugged road which rose steeply up the mountain of Pitiano. As it was such a beautiful day I felt sure the long walk would be good for my body and soul. As I was walking, I was enjoying the panorama of the mountain and the fresh air of the chestnut trees inside my lungs. It was hard to climb up the mountain path, right up to the peak, but easier as I started to go down. The path was just as rugged, but soon I reached the village of Tora, which lay at the foot of the mountain of Pitiano. The rugged path took me to the village square. It was pleasant and in the middle it had a fountain for people to collect water for domestic use. I stopped to ask people in the square for directions to the house of the lawyer Falciano.

A young lady said, "Yes sir, it's not very far from here. If you like I will take you there."

"That is very of kind of you. I would like that very much." I said, smiling. After a short walk we arrived at a beautiful villa with a big iron gate. The young lady said; "There you are sir, this is the villa of the lawyer Falciano."

"Thank you, young lady. I'm grateful for your help" I said. Then I shook the young girl's hand and gave her 3 lira. The girl was over the moon, for she didn't expect any gift. She said, "Thank you very much sir, I didn't expect anything. But the money will help me to buy myself a new pair of shoes."

She went way skipping and singing towards the village square, full of joy.

Now that I had reached the big Iron Gate, I hesitated for a minute or two. Then I went forward and knocked on the door. A couple of minutes later the door was opened by another young girl.

I said, "I would like speak to the lawyer Feliciano if it is at all possible."

The young girl said in a very low voice "May I ask

your name sir?"

I answered. "My name is Renato." The girl smiled and said, "Will you please follow me, sir."

I was taken into a very large room and shown to a chair near the desk.

The girl said, "Will you please take a seat. Falciano's secretary won't be long." Then she went out of the room pulling the door to behind her.

And she walked along the corridor she spotted the secretary talking to one of the ladies who worked in the kitchen. She waited until they had finished talking, then she said, "Miss Catherine, there is a gentleman in the waiting room, and he would like to make an appointment with the lawyer Falciano." "Thank you Valery," she said with a smile.

The secretary entered the room and coming towards me she said, "My name is Catherine and I'm the secretary to the lawyer Falciano."

I stretched out my hand and said, "How do you do Miss Catherine? I have come here because I need to make an appointment with the lawyer Falciano." The secretary looked at me, and said, "Will you make yourself comfortable, and then you can tell me why you need an appointment."

"Well, Miss, I would like to make an investment, and to do that I need advice from the Lawyer Falciano." I said, with apprehension on my face.

The secretary realised I was very nervous and she said, "Make yourself comfortable while I look at the lawyer's diary, and I will see how he can help you."

"I do appreciate your help, Miss."

The secretary went out pulling the door behind her.

A few minutes later the lawyer Falciano himself entered the room. He stretched his hand out to me saying, "I'm pleased to meet you Mr Renato, how can I help you?"

"Well sir, I would like to make an investment, and for that I really do need your help."

47

"What kind of investment do you have in mind?" the lawyer asked.

"Well sir, I went for a long walk, and I came to a majestic waterfall from the mountain of Cesena, looking down onto a beautiful meadow in the valley. To me it is the most magnificent sight I have ever seen, and I have decided I would very much like to buy the farm there. The farm belongs to the Duchess who uses an agent to administer all her property." I told him.

"Well Mr Renato, first we need to approach the land agent and then we will take it from there. Is that what you want?" The lawyer asked.

"Yes sir. That is what I would like." I felt a sense of relief.

"Well Mr Renato, I will do everything in my power to achieve the purchase of this farm for you, as long as the Duchess is prepared to sell you the farm."

I shook hands with the lawyer and off I went. I was very happy and I couldn't wait to arrive home and tell the good news to my wife and the children. I thought how happy my family would be to know that the Duchess would sell the farm and that it would be done professionally. I began to make my way home and, as before the footpath sloped gently upwards on the mountain. The fragrance of the short grass and vigorous chestnut trees filled the air and I began to sing the songs about the Unification of Italy until I reached home. Then I ran upstairs shouting, "Mary, children, where are you all?" I have such good news to tell you all."

Mary came out of the kitchen and said, "Renato, whatever is the matter with you, why you are so excited?"

"Well Mary, the lawyer said he will contact the Duchess himself, and he will do what it takes to see the project is completed. He will do his very best to make a good deal for us. And when the time comes he will let us know if we can afford it." I said.

"This is indeed good news." Mary said, smiling.

"But now we will celebrate our future with a glass of

red wine, even though we do not yet know the outcome," I said, rubbing my hands together.

Then I went down to the cellar to fetch the best wine we had, and Mary went into the kitchen to prepare ham and cheese sandwiches and we both went onto the terrace of our house with the children and all enjoyed the tasty sandwiches with a glass of our best wine. I said, "Oh Mary, just think, if we manage to buy the Farm, how happy we shall be in the future, with the children playing happily in the fields while we gather the grapes. We shall make a lot of wine and maybe even sell some of it."

"Renato, don't count your chicks before they hatch." Mary warned, laughing. She went off into the kitchen to fetch a fruit cake she baked earlier while he had gone to the village of Tora to see the lawyer.

"Oh, Mary what a beautiful fruit cake you've made, just like the ones my mother made for us when it was my birthday, or my brothers' or sisters'," he said smiling.

"Well I need to make many more of them before I can become as good a cook as your mother was, with that big family of yours and if you will permit me, dear husband, to tell you, it won't be very long before I will follow in your mother's footsteps." She said with a twinkle in her eye.

"Mary? I questioned, "It's written all over your face you have something to tell me, what is it?

I was very eager to know what my wife was hiding from me. In fact I had noticed that in the last few days Mary had been very strange. More than once I noticed she had been feeling sick. But Mary wouldn't say anything. She just shrugged her shoulders and ran into the kitchen, laughing and saying, "Renato, you've had too much to drink."

She knew I wasn't silly of course, but she wasn't prepared to tell me anything until the deal for the farm was made and the purchase official. Majestic Heights in the valley would secure the future for our family.

I ran after your mother to the kitchen and took your mother by surprise, putting my hands upon her waist to make her turn round to me. Then I kissed her in a very passionate way and said, "Now, my dear Mary, it is time for you to reveal the secret that you are hiding from me," I said smiling.

"Well that was very nice," she said. "If my secret makes you behave in this manner I quite like it, but you need to wait until I can no longer hide it from you."

My heart started to jump for joy, because I understood what Mary was saying, but I didn't let the cat out of the bag!

I answered. "If that is the case I would be very happy to behave in this manner from now until the secret reveals itself." Your mother was very happy."

Chapter 12

"A few days later a smart carriage stopped at the last house in the little village of Cave. Two smart gentlemen knocked at Renato and Mary's door. Mary opened the door, and she was mystified to know what those two elegant gentlemen wanted from her husband.

She asked, "Sir, may I know your name?" "Certainly," he said. "I am Falciano and this is my assistant, Stevens."

"Oh, please come in." she said. "My husband would be very pleased to see you, but unfortunately he is not in at moment. He went to the house of the shoe maker. It's just a few minutes' walk away from here. I will send a message and he will be here in very short time."

Mary took them into the sitting room, and offered them a cup of coffee. While the percolator was making the coffee, Mary called on her neighbour, saying,

"Bernadette, I need your help now. You must go to Eduard the shoemaker, and tell Renato to come home at once, because he has two very important gentlemen waiting for him here now."

Then she rushed indoors, straight into the kitchen to have a look at the percolator. It was boiling way and releasing a very strong aroma of coffee. She prepared the tray with the best china cups from her display cabinet, special biscuits and a couple of small cakes she had baked early that day. Then she went into the sitting room where the gentlemen were chatting away by themselves.

Mary entered the room with the beautiful silver tray of coffee, biscuits and cake. Then, she put the tray on the small coffee table and said; "Gentlemen, as I said before, my husband won't be long now."

While she was speaking her husband came in through the door. "Good afternoon Gentleman, this is a very pleasant surprise." He stretched out his arm to shake their hands.

"Well, Mr Renato, we have met before. This is my

friend, Stevens, who is also my private secretary. I would like to take this opportunity to introduce him to you, Mr Renato. I need to go abroad for a long period of time and if you need any assistance, while I am away he will be here to help you."

"Now, I made a deal with the Duchess for the purchase of the Farm and I think it is a good deal but of course you must decide if this is the right contract for you. If you think you can afford it, I will be happy to finalise the deal. I will leave it with you for a day or two, so that you can make the final decision. We really must go now, but you should contact me or my secretary Stevens as soon as possible."

They shook hands before they left and Renato said, "Sir, I'm very grateful to you for helping me to achieve the dream of my life."

They smiled, and away they went in their smart carriage pulled by two white horses, towards the village of Tora.

I ran to your mother and our two boys and I said.

"My family, today we have had good news. I think we have achieved our dream. The lawyer made a good deal with the Duchess and looked for a figure that we can afford."

Mary jumped out of the chair where she'd been sitting.

"This is good news. At last we can now sell this house and make plans for the future. We will have a farm of own, and now I can tell all of you that our family will grow again. In four months' time we shall have another child, God willing."

I was very excited at the news even though I had already suspected what her big secret was.

"Mary," I said. "This the best news a wife can give to a husband today. At this special time I feel as if I can touch the sky. All our dreams seem to be coming true. We ran towards each another and danced round the kitchen."

"My dear wife," I continued, "Now is the time to sell our little house in the village and go to live on the farm.

We shall call it 'Majestic Waterfall' and we will invite many people from the village to help us to celebrate our dream. Now we are even more blessed, for we have our two boys and soon our new baby when she or he arrives."

Four months later our family was overjoyed when the new baby arrived. We thanked God that she was alright, and above all, a baby girl. Of course our two boys were disappointed. They had always hoped for another boy like themselves but I knew they would get over it.

"Now we will soon be able to move into our farm house," I said.

"Oh, Renato, you can't say that, until you have signed the contract," your mother reminded me.

"Yes Mary, you are right," I conceded, "But I can assure you, tomorrow morning I shall go to sign the contract and I promise you we shall have a great celebration, for our new baby, and our new home. A celebration the village will remember for many years to come. I was very happy and now I'm over the moon."

"Renato, one day at time." She warned me, "But now we will have a light supper, and tomorrow you shall arise early and go to sign the contract." After that we will begin to plan, to achieve what we have always hoped for," said Mary.

"Mary, I'm a very lucky man. I have married a beautiful wife and above all you have given me three lovely children. Plus you are also a very wise woman, which I thank God for." I told her with a big grin on my face.

"Go on with you. Now you will make me believe I'm something that I'm not, and you're embarrassing me," she said.

But underneath I know she was very happy, knowing her beloved husband appreciated her very much indeed.

"Mary", I protested, "I didn't intend to embarrass you. I meant what I said, and I will always love you. I think you are fantastic in every sense of the word." Then I took her into my arms and sealed my words with a very passionate kiss.

Mary went into the kitchen to prepare the supper and in an hour or so she called me and the children.

"Okay, Renato", she said. "Supper is ready, and we shall enjoy it with our children because tomorrow we will have a busy day."

"That's okay by me, but by the way what is for supper?" I asked her.

"Earlier, I prepared a chicken soup which I know you always like, then I went into our vegetable plot at the bottom of our garden. There was a beautiful lettuce and some lovely ripe tomatoes, and cucumber, and so I have also made a nice omelette. You and the children can have a glass of red wine, because they are old enough to drink together with you, in moderation, but I can't because I am breast feeding the baby. As this is a light supper I hope the baby and I will be able to have a good night."

"First thing the next morning, your mother got up from the bed and as usual after washing herself and looking after you, Angelina, she went into the kitchen to prepare breakfast the American way. Fried eggs and bacon, toast with marmalade and black coffee with plenty of sugar because I was always talking about that is how the Americans eat their first meal of the day."

I was going to the lawyer's office to sign the contract, so that we could make plans for our new life on the farm so not long after your mother left our bed, I also left the bed and immediately washed and shaved myself. I put on my best suit and was ready to go to the lawyer's office, but I wasn't giving up my breakfast for all the tea in China. I went into the kitchen to embrace your mother, and we all sat down together and enjoyed our breakfast. Your mother was smiling when she said, "Now I'm sure I married a smart old man."

"Mary", I said sternly. "I enjoyed your compliment, and I liked what you said about me being smart, but not so much of the 'old'. I can assure you I still feel younger than I look." I told her.

"Oh, dear me, darling, I was only teasing," she said. "You know how much I love you, and you also know you are still very young to me. We have many years to enjoy together and, God willing, with our family, one of which is only a few weeks old. But I know she will grow fast." she said, smiling.

"Mary I must go, otherwise I might not find him in. As you know he has already told me he will be going away for a long period of time, and while he is away his assistant will look after our business, but I'd rather like the lawyer himself to sign the contract."

"Oh dear me," your mother said, "It's very late. The coach must have left by now. There is a chance someone will be prepared to take you in his carriage to the village of Tora. Usually some people go there on business. Maybe one of them will give you a lift, but of course you might need to pay something."

"Well I will try, but if it is not possible, I shall walk, just like I have done before. I know it is a long way, but walking is good for the health." I said to your mother.

"Well Renato, see what you can do. I hope everything goes well, and that you come home in good time. I assure you I will prepare a good meal for your return."

I embraced your mother and said, "I will try my best, and I hope to be home as soon as I can."

I ran down the staircase and turned towards the village square, hoping to find somebody willing to give me a lift. When I arrived in the square I saw the postman collecting the mail bags to deliver to the station in Tora for transport to the district general post office.

"May I ask you a big favour?" I asked him. "I need to go to Tora but I missed the coach. Could I travel with you? I'm willing to pay, whatever the cost."

"Of course, you can come on board, and it won't cost you anything at all. After you have finished your business, come back to the station again. I may still be there, and if I am there you can come back with me to our village," said the postman.

He drove the carriage smiling away, seeming happy to have somebody with him.

I broke the silence, "I can't thank you enough for helping me today, and if at any time you need assistance with anything and you know I can help, I will be only too glad to, and would be honoured to be able to do so."

The driver smiled and said, "I heard you are buying a farm. When you open it and welcome your neighbours I would be glad to be among your guests."

"Indeed, you will be the very first one on my list when that happens," I assured him. After twenty minutes we arrived at the station of Tora and I walked towards the village. After ten minutes, I reached the lawyer's house. I knocked at the big oval door and, as before, the young girl opened the door, and said, "Good morning Sir; we have met before."

"Yes, Miss, I have been here before, but now I have an appointment with lawyer Falciano," I told her smiling.

"Please come in," she said, and took me into the waiting room. "Will you please make yourself comfortable." Then she left.

Not long after that the lawyer Falciano walked into the waiting room.

"Ah ....Mr Renato, you have decided then?" he said.

"Yes Sir, I'm very happy to know the farm will soon be mine, and I want to thank you for helping me to materialise my long cherished dream." I had tears in my eyes.

"Ha! Mr Renato. I have only done my job, and now I need your signature here. Tomorrow my assistant will go to the Duchess, and the job will be complete."

We shook hands and on the way out I thanked the young girl with a small tip.

"But Sir, I haven't done anything," she said. "I just opened the door to you, and nothing else."

I said goodbye and ran and skipped all the way to the station where the driver of the carriage was waiting for me. When I spotted him I waved my hands up in air in the excitement of seeing him there. "John, John," I yelled, "I have made it."

He said, "Renato, you have lost you head, what has happened to you?"

"Oh, John...I, thought you knew why I came here." I answered.

"Yes, yes I knew you came here to see the lawyer in order to purchase the farm, but I didn't understand that the deal was to be finalised to-day."

Chapter 13

"Well John," I said. "Now you know. I can tell you, that very soon we shall have a big party in the farmyard and you will be the first one to be invited." I had a big smile on my face.

"Well, well. I look forward to the opening of your farm. But for now we need to deliver this bundle to the General Post Office in Conca and then go back to the village to tell your wife the good news," said John smiling.

So we both climbed into the carriage and headed towards Conca. The road was very, very shady, but that didn't trouble me. I was very eager for the horse to go faster, but at the same time I felt sorry for him. Every minute that passed seemed like hours to me, because the only thing I had in my mind was to go back and tell my wife the good news.

At last we reached Conca Della Campania and delivered the mailbag to the general post office. Then in no time at all we arrived back at the village of Cave.

I said, "John, I don't know how to thank you for taking me to Tora Station, but I'm very grateful for what you have done for me today. I will see you at our family party when the time comes."

He said, "Thank you Renato. I look forward to that day."

We embraced one another and John climbed back into his carriage and returned to his family home. I was very moved by the fact that the contract was now signed and I had indeed achieved the dream of my life. When I reached home, I climbed the stairs two at a time and, with a lump in my throat, I found it difficult to call for Mary. So I waited until I was able to regain my breath and then I called your mother.

"Mary, Mary where are you?"

"I'm in kitchen, as always," she called back, "Trying to prepare a dinner for our family, and looking after our little daughter."

"We need more than that," I told her, breathless with emotion. "We need to celebrate, because the contract has been signed and now we own the farm. At last the farm belongs to us," I said, embracing your mother again and whispering in her ear. "I do love you."

"From now on, we will start a new life. At the start it will be very hard, but we will be able to cultivate our own farm, and we will feel privileged to be able to grow our own food. We will have the spring water, chickens for eggs, and cows for milk and maybe more animal to help us along."

I got ready to eat the dinner your mother had prepared and I said, "Mary, now we shall eat the meal you have prepared, with a good glass of wine, and we shall continue to plan the next stage because I'm more than ready to start work."

You mother said, "Yes Renato, we shall eat dinner. I have made fresh tagliatelle and bolognese sauce, for our dinner, with salad and cold roast chicken. Then there's a nice chocolate sponge for after, as you have said, all with a bottle of our wine to celebrate the good news."

After we had eaten our dinner and drunk our wine, I said, "Mary, the dinner was very, very good and I enjoyed it very much. I must say I was very hungry. I hadn't had anything to eat since the early breakfast this morning, and now it is two o'clock in the afternoon."

"We've had an exciting day, and I didn't realise it was as late as that." I said thoughtfully,then, "I think I will have a walk through the village this afternoon and begin to tell people we have bought the farm."

"Our children will be over the moon," I said. "They will have plenty of space to run about and learn how to look after the plants, as well as the joy of looking after more animals as we acquire them."

Then your mother said, "Renato, you have missed out the very essential thing of our life." She said, with an anxious expression on her face.

"Oh Mary, I don't understand, what you are you trying to say." I asked her.

"I want to remind you that the Bible says 'Man doesn't live by bread alone.' That means attending church and school. You don't want our children to be illiterate like most of the Italian men you met when you went to America, do you?"

"Don't worry Mary, we will make sure our children attend church regularly, and also to go to school. When they are old enough, they will have a choice of work on the farm or having a trade of their own. We will employ the people from our village to help us when we require them. Mary, you don't expect me to rely only upon our children to help us to run this farm, do you?"

Your mother had a good laugh and I saw relief on her face.

She said, "Of course not! I also want our children to be able to do what they want to do in their lives. I agree with what you have just said. I pray the Good Lord will bless our land, and our children with good health and good manners now and into future generations."

I laughed and I said to your mother, "I'm sure he will, Mary, our God is good. 'Ask and you shall receive; knock and the door shall be opened.' We will ask and we will knock, and if we do our best to look after our neighbourhood, then I'm sure everything will go according to His will."

"Your mother was very pleased with what I said."

Hours later there was a knock on our front door. Mary opened it and said, "Oh, Pasquale, I didn't see or hear any wind strong enough to blow you upon this staircase and knock on our door."

"There's no need for the wind to blow me to the top of your staircase," he said, "I came here to offer my congratulations to you and your husband on the purchase of the Duchess's farm."

"Oh, that is kind of you Pasquale, but tell me, how did you know about the purchase of the farm, because it only happened less than two or three hours ago?" said Renato.

"Well Sebastian, my friend, told me, but I wasn't at all surprised. If you remember, you had already mentioned to me your intention when we first met, soon after you came back from America." Pasquale said, smiling.

"Of course, Pasquale, and you also advised me to deal straight with the lawyer, because the agent of the Duchess was not to be trusted. We hope that you and John, and many more people from our village will come to the opening of our farm, to help us to celebrate the new adventure in our life, when we have settled down. And above all what is really important at the moment is the christening of our baby girl." Renato said with tears in his eyes.

"Yes, yes, of course we will come, and it is an honour for us to be invited to the celebration with your family on such a big occasion. I can tell you for sure, we admire you for the stamina you have shown."

Chapter 14

Renato put his hands over his head, and said,

"This is true enough. I don't think any other man would have cared to start work or buy a farm, as soon as he returned from America, but you see my friend, I always had an interest in farm work, and as soon as I returned from America I went for stroll in the country. I came to a path leading me through a beautiful valley under the foot of the mountain and there was a majestic waterfall crashing down to a big pond below. The fragrance of the many plants nearby, all in flower, made a wonderful scene. At that moment I decided that was where I would like to bring up my family, and give them the opportunity, when they are old enough, to decide whether they wanted to work at a trade, or cultivate the farm."

Pasquale looked at him and said, "Well, I have great admiration for your stamina and I wish the best luck to you both. Now it is time for me to go home, otherwise my wife will want to know what happened to me."

"Well, tell her that on your way here you met a couple of bandits and they tried to kidnap you, but you managed to escape." Said Renato, laughing.

"My wife doesn't have any sense of humour. If I said that to her there is a chance I would be rolled down the staircase. Then I might need to come back, and ask you to take me in as a lodger in your new home!" said Pasquale.

Then we all started laughing and I said, "Well, if that's the case you'd better run. We can't allow that. In our country there is no such thing as divorce yet. As we have already said, you can come and help us to celebrate, but make sure your wife comes with you!"

"Renato and Mary," said Pasquale. "I promise you both, if you need any help we are ready to do whatever you require."

Then they hugged each other, and he ran down the stairs and out, towards his own house.

"The next day, most of the people in the village knew about Renato's purchase of the Duchess's farm, and they also knew about our intention to invite most of the people of the village to help celebrate our new life on the farm and the birth of our baby girl."

"A few days later, the rumour began to go around the district that our house would be for sale. The people of the village knew and understood that we would require help to move from the village to the farm. Some of them decided to meet so that they would be able to organise the best way to help us."

Some of them came with carts pulled along by their horses, and others with mules or donkeys. We were overwhelmed at the help we received, and more than ever we were determined to invite all our relatives and friends, and all those who had made such a big effort to help us to move from the house to the farm of our dreams.

After we'd settled down we thought about asking advice from our relatives, because we knew we didn't have the facilities to entertain a large group of people. One of my brothers said,

"Not in a million years would we expect this big surprise. We are all very proud of you both. You don't need to worry because from this week we will do whatever it takes to make everything go smoothly."

Your mother and I couldn't hide the emotion we felt, knowing my brothers were being so helpful. Two weeks later my brothers came to see us again and they said, "Renato and Mary, we came here this evening to see when you are moving."

Chapter 15

'The celebration of the blessing of farms'.

"We told them that the middle of June would be fine. The days are long, and the weather is just right for this kind of entertainment." We hugged each other and then both of them left."

"The next evening the brothers went to the Workingmen's Club. They organised the people of the village to see who was prepared to give a helping hand towards what would be a beautiful day of happiness for most of the village. The middle of June was approaching. Many women went to the priest and the Mayor to ask how they could help. The priest asked, "Ladies, how many of you can cook?" They all answered with one voice, "We all do."

"Yes, yes", said the priest, "But what can you cook."

A few of them put up their hands and said, "We can make very good biscuits, and all sort of cakes and pastries."

Some of them said, "We can cook food like roast meat and vegetables and puddings."

Others said, "We can make bread and pizzas." And a few said, "We can prepare everything for a good a buffet for afternoon tea, for all the children and grow ups alike."

Now, they said, "We now need to organise who does what to ensure we will make enough food, so that everybody will have enough to eat for this special occasion."

"Well," said the priest with a smile, "I need say no more. You ladies are able to organise it between yourselves and I look forward to eating some of the special food you are going to prepare."

The priest shook the ladies' hands and went away.

The ladies looked at one another and one lady said, "We need to have a meeting between all of us very soon, so that we can decide together who does what."

In a short time they all agreed, and went home to their families.

At the same time the Mayor was looking around the district for a band to play for that special occasion. As far as everybody knew, this had never happened before and a celebration like this might not happen again in the future. After the Mayor had made many inquiries he managed to achieve what he was looking for, which was the right band for his requirements.

We were excited to see so much response all around us. We went looking round the farm to gather fruit and vegetables and were surprised at how much our farm had to offer.

I said to your mother, "Mary, I'm overwhelmed to see how much fruit and vegetables are ready to pick. This is much more than we expected. It's enough to supply most of the people in the village, plus our party!"

I rubbed my hands together with a satisfied smile on my face and then I started singing Neapolitan songs. Your mother said, "I expected to hear an American song, after all that is the country that helped you to achieve the dream of your life."

I answered, "You're right, Mary, but the fact is I didn't learn any American songs. I only learned rude words!"

Your mother was quick to scold me. She said "Oh, Renato. Shame on you, to learn only rude words, in a foreign country." And then she gave a deep sigh.

"I asked her, "What is matter with you now, Mary?"

"Well, Renato," she said, "I can't help feeling sorry for the young lambs. They are so little and so cute, jumping and skipping round the fields." There was an expression of sadness on her face.

I said to her, "Mary that is the worst part of being a farmer's wife, especially regarding the animals we care for in our farm. But there is one consolation, I can assure you. They don't know anything about their fate."

She looked pensive, "Renato, she said, I know we have a very large kitchen, but how can the women prepare and cook all the food we need for so many people?"

I told her, "Mary, some of them will prepare their speciality in their own homes. Some others will come here and use our kitchen, and if necessary, some of them could use our large room that has the big roasting oven for the meat, pastries, bread and pizzas and anything else that requires that type of oven. So you don't need to worry. Everything will go as planned."

Two weeks later we couldn't believe our eyes. Opening the window, we could see we were being invaded by men doing all sorts of jobs. Some of them were trying to make a place for the priest to be able to say Mass. Some others with carpentry skills were very busy making a special merry go round for the children. Large tables for groups of people, some for older people, and many long tables on which to spread out the banquet were put in place. We knew many women were busy cooking in their own homes. Others were in our kitchen preparing all kinds of food to make a spread that would be remembered for years to come by the people of the village."

The man in charge would explain to the children how to enjoy playing on the merry go round, and the others would play all kinds of games. There would be music and dancing for everybody else.

After a couple days of very hard work, the farm was ready for the big day. On Sunday, 6th of June, the priest announced to his congregation that the blessing of the farm would be on that day, at 11 o'clock in the morning.

The Priest and the Mayor climbed into their carriages and followed the band, and with a procession of people and children walking behind, they made their way from the village square towards our farm. We were all very excited, and dressed up in our Sunday best, when we heard the sound of music and the singing of hymns coming towards our farm. All our family ran out onto the terrace of the farm house, clapping as the procession got near.

After the Priest had celebrated Mass, and blessed the farm, he christened our baby girl, who we named,

Angelina. Then the family, the Priest and the Mayor, with their guests sat down at the long table that the carpenters had prepared for the occasion."

The starters were artichokes, salami, olives and cheese with garlic bread, some chicken and soup. One lady of the village made a special starter called 'Italian Platter'. It was mozzarella cheese, lean Parma ham (prosciutto), artichoke hearts and figs cut in quarters and arranged on big serving platters. Then there were mangos sliced into strips and arranged on a long plate.

For the main meal we had pasta with raga and plenty of pecorino cheese grated on top.

After that, roast lamb, roast chicken or saltimbocca (veal) with roast potatoes, broccoli, carrots and peas.

There was Tiramisu for the pudding or one of the other special puddings which the ladies had made.

After this huge feast the guests were served with espresso coffee and a liqueur of their choice poured into the coffee. It all began at three pm. The people came and the music started. There were people dancing on the lawn, the children playing on the merry go round and all the other entertainments prepared just for them.

"And now, my dear daughter, you know all about how we came to be here. Now I need go to bed because I have a busy day tomorrow."

Angelina said, "Thank you Dad, you have told me a long story and a lovely one, and I do hope I can write a good essay about your ambitions and achievements."

Chapter 16

The fear of War was now becoming a reality. The children didn't understand why so many families were upset to see their beloved fathers and young brothers begin to disappear.

Angelina loved her school and she was so much looking forward to writing the story which her beloved father had told her about the sacrifices he had made to achieve his ambition. To have gone to America, and been able to keep the promises he had made to his wife Mary. Then after his return with enough money to buy a farm and support his wife and children, to be able to grow enough food and generate enough money to provide his children with a good education was indeed an achievement. But then one afternoon, Angelina overheard her father talking with another farm owner who lived not very far from them.

Angelina's father said, "I'm very sorry to see those young boys being sent out to the borders of the Alps with heavy guns to fight the enemy. When you think that it wasn't that long ago they were our old allies. When I was in America, I had to make a choice of whether to stay there and join the American army or come back to Italy and take a chance with the Italian government." He sounded apprehensive.

The Italian newspapers had reported that Italy was allied with Germany and Austria-Hungary, in a triple alliance. And they had emphasised, that in theory, Italy should have joined the side of those nations when the war broke out in August 1914. Well Italy didn't!

On the 23rd of May 1915, the Italian Prime Minister Antonio Calendar issued a declaration to support new allies against the previous allies. In order to keep the goodwill of major countries and avoid neighbour conflict they said that the treaty they signed in secret was the Treaty of London. Britain had offered Italy a large territory in the Adriatic region, Tyrol, Dalmatia and Istria. Of course the offer was too tempting to refuse. (In other words they found a loophole.)

However, the newspapers said that Italy had little choice because of their location, a bigger standing army, and the fact that they were on a peninsula. As Austria and Hungary had no ports, Germans concentrated on them. But Italian speaking people near the northern frontier had always dreamt and hoped that it would be better for them if there was a war. It was true however, that the majority of Italian people and the majority of their parliament didn't want anything to do with the war.

The Messenger paper reported as follow:-

'Many socialists have supported the government's stand in keeping Italy out the war. Nationalists are horrified. To start with Mussolini was against the war. In July 1914, the Italian people marched through the streets of Rome and the squares of many cities, waving their flags and shouting. 'Down with the war! Down with the arms and up with humanity! ' Then Mussolini changed his mind, and he began to say that the war would be nothing more than a great drain. And, "We don't want to be spectators but fighters."

The socialist party kicked Mussolini out and many young socialists agreed with him, leaving the party and following him.

On the 26th April 1915, it was reported that Italy had entered into the war. The government wanted go to war because, as it was said before, the secret Treaty made in London, offered Italy a large section of territory in the Adriatic. Naturally such an offer to Italy was difficult for them to refuse. Italy understood that Britain, France and Russia wanted Italy on their side so that it would be easy to open up the south Western Front .The new Allies wanted to divide the Central Powers so that the western and the eastern fronts would be weakened. It is understood that it was a plan that Italy had to play a part in, and it required military backing, but that was never forthcoming.

The Italian troops made little advance inside Austria. In October 1917 the Italian army had to fight the whole Austrian Army and about 7 divisions of the German army .The Italian Army lost about 300,000 men and Italy didn't get what the treaty in London had promised.

The war was lost and the psychological impact was shame and humiliation. The Italians didn't get what the Allies had promised, and that created a lot of resentment.

Chapter 17

The armistice unfortunately, didn't stop the pandemic of influenza or the suffering of soldiers who were left injured and permanently disabled. If that wasn't enough, the Spanish Fever killed about 70 million people all round the world. The outbreak of the Spanish Influenza started in the Middle East, and then rapidly reached the Western Front. Not long after, the epidemic took on a milder form. But from about the third summer the patients with the influenza reported very harsh symptoms, which led to bronchial pneumonia, septicaemia and many more complications. An untold number of people died of their symptoms.

The Red Cross played a vital role. In Italy with the help of the Red Cross, the nuns and local women offered remedies with homemade herbs, without much success.

The Italian people started to emigrate more than ever, to America. From 1918 to 1920 two million Italians emigrated to America thinking that by doing so, they would escape the epidemic, but what they didn't understand was, that the influenza had no mercy, no borders, and no boundaries.

In no time at all the United States of America was invaded by immigrants from all parts of the world, including Italy. Because the pandemic touched both rich and poor, no part of the world escaped it, and there wasn't anybody to blame.

The news reported that some people were so frightened about contracting the Spanish Influenza, that they would rather poison themselves than wait for the influenza to attack them. True enough some of them decided to take their own life. The virus became more and more destructive and it was mostly the young and very old people who died. It became impossible to have any sort of religious service before the burial. Church bells stopped ringing. Many of the young people who managed to return from the war were paralysed, and of those who managed to survive many of them lost their hair.

The aristocrats found difficulty in running their palaces, villas and farms because most of the young people had perished.

The ones who survived carried on doing the work that was needed until the new generation was old enough to replace the ones who'd died. The peasants who survived the 'flu epidemic, had no choice, but to work on their own small plot of land. Others worked for people who needed their labour on a daily basis. Many more continued to emigrate to America and many other parts of the world.

Some of the peasants managed to rent farms and share the fruits of their labour. In the village there were three shoemakers who had been disabled in the war. They had no legs of their own but had a pair of wooden ones. There were two carpenters, and one blacksmith. There were only two parish churches and only one priest. There were two doctors for the 6 villages.

Down in the valley, plants and green grass were growing for the animals on the farm to eat. Even the war couldn't spoil the fragrance or the beauty of the majestic waterfall. However, life for the peasants was very primitive. The houses had no running water or lighting and no facilities for their personal hygiene. The only means of keeping themselves clean was a bowl of water for washing their face, and for their bath an old tin of copper.

On winter evenings most grandmothers would sit round the fireplace and tell stories of the fairies and gremlins of long ago who were thought to have lived under the floor boards in the old houses and most of the time played tricks around the house. The old people believed in a lot of superstitions. If you saw a broom left of the front door step, it was firmly believed that it had been left by a witch and that witches could come and visit throughout the night while people were sleeping in their beds and harm their children. However, before they could enter the house they needed to count all the bristles on their brooms.

Even these days you can still see people with a gold chain and pendant in the form of a horn hanging round their necks to prevent the witches putting an evil spell on them.

There was one old house and the old lady who lived there was telling everyone that about eleven o'clock at night she heard a lengthy lament which sounded human.

There is a true story, that many years ago, the castle was occupied by Feudal Lords who had enormous power over the population of the whole district and even further afield. They would travel on horseback or in a carriage pulled by white horses. When they travelled through the villages the people needed to bow as if to royalty.

When a young couple got married, the bride was expected to sleep with one of the feudal lords first. That was their law over the people. But one day a bride refused to comply. The Lord sent his guards to capture the bride and take her to the castle. He then gave orders to let all the people of the district know that if any other bride refused to obey their law, which they saw as their right, they would be punished also. A platform was built in the village square on which the bride was placed. Then an order was issued to the guards to stone the bride to death in front of the multitude of people to serve as an example to any others who defied the law.

For a long time afterwards the villagers said they kept seeing the figure of a young lady walking round the square, who then disappeared.

Chapter 18

Now the war and the Spanish fever were things of the past, the deep recession and poverty continued to affect more and more people. With a big struggle, however, many managed to survive. The Italian people, and most of the rest of the world continued running their businesses or cultivating their farms and, with great difficulty, life gradually returned to normal.

One morning, Renato looked at his wife and said,

"Mary have you noticed that Angelina and Beatrice have developed into two young ladies. Wouldn't it be nice if, one day they could each meet a young man with the same ambitions as us?"

"What do you mean Renato?" Mary asked her husband.

"I mean what I said, Mary," Renato answered.

Mary looked at her husband and said, "Well, yes. Angelina and Beatrice are two young girls and in our village there is nothing to entertain them yet, but there is a rumour of a young man just like Pasquale's sons, entertaining young people with his music, just like they used to do. I hear there is another young man who is very musical and I've been told is very active, very talented and also very charming."

"Renato raised his eyebrows and said,

"Mary, don't be silly now. I wasn't thinking for one minute about them meeting young men. Our girls go to the village on Sunday because the priest celebrates the S. Mass and in the evening the Gospel Services."

Mary said. "Maybe that is the situation now, but I wouldn't be at all surprised if our girls, like many girls, don't get infatuated with this young man, or any other."

One Sunday afternoon, Mary noticed the girls whispering and giggling between themselves. She thought their behaviour was very unusual.

"Come girls, what are you whispering about?" she asked them.

The girls looked at one another and said, "There is a rumour in church that the priest may announce something about a trip to Rome. If anyone is interested they need to put their name on the list."

"Goodness me, that would cost some money" said Mary.

"But mum, we never go anywhere. If it happens it would be very nice for us to go and visit Rome. Anyway, it's just a rumour! " said Angelina. Then together, the two girls walked out of the house.

Beatrice faced Angelina and said, "Angelina, I've never heard that rumour."

"Don't be silly, Beatrice. Mum wanted to know what we were whispering about." Angelina said nervously. "Look, I heard my father telling my mother about his ambition for both of us to marry a farmer."

Beatrice lifted both her hands up in air, and with a loud voice said, "You must be joking, Angelina." "Your father is my uncle, and he can't make me do what he wants. Besides, marriage isn't like that. You need to fall in love with a man before you get married to him."

Angelina laughed. "Yes and believe me, I will never marry a farmer. I'm like you. I want to choose my man, and it must be someone better than a farmer."

Beatrice laughed. "Do you realise that after the First World

War, and the Spanish influenza, there is not much to choose from."

Angelina thought for a moment, then she said, "Well then, we will just have to remain single."

Two weeks later, the priest spoke to the congregation about his concern that the young and older generations didn't have anywhere to socialise in the village."

"It would be good for them, he said, "If the church could build a club for the senior people where they would be able to meet and listen to radio news, and also where the young people could get together and play games."

The girls were devastated.

Angelina said. "Not long ago the priest said in church that he was hoping to arrange a trip to Rome for the young people, and now he says he wants to build a club. I expect my parents must be very happy because now they don't need to give us money for the trip!"

Four months later the club was up and running. Every Monday to Friday from 12 noon until 8 pm the senior generation met and listened to the radio news and maybe had games of cards. Saturday afternoon was just for the young people, and they were able to play music and dance.

Beatrice said, "What the priest has forgotten is that the men work all day in the fields or in their shops. I don't think they will have much time to spend in the club."

Angelina laughed. "Maybe that's better for us, maybe better for all the youngsters, as well."

The girls wasted no time in asking their parents' permission to go to the church club. Beatrice and Angelina were very excited, dressing up for the occasion, and then going off to the new club in the village.

When they got there the music had already started. There were about a dozen girls and boys. There were tables and chairs set out and on a table there were some fruit juices, sandwiches and homemade cakes for them to eat during the evening, that had been prepared by some of the parents. Angelina and Beatrice sat near the table admiring the home made cakes.

Angelina tapped Beatrice on the shoulder and said, "Look at that young man with the guitar."

Beatrice looked, and said, "What about him?"

Angelina laughed and said, "I like him."

"Goodness me," exclaimed Beatrice. "We've just arrived here and you're already telling me you like someone. You don't know who he is or what his name is, or anything about him and you tell me you fancy him?"

Angelina said, "Well, I didn't say I fancy him. I like his music and his smile and I wouldn't mind talking to him, to see what he's really like."

"Angelina, for the time being, let us just enjoy the

music. We have plenty of time to get to know this young man, if your father and mother let us continue to come."

Angelina stamped her foot and said, "Do you mean my parents may not let us come here again?"

"Angelina, behave yourself." said Beatrice, "Otherwise your parents may not let us come here."

Angelina put her head down and didn't say any more. The music become loud and fast, and the young man with the guitar was singing some very comic songs. Some passers-by couldn't help hearing what was going on and some of them joined the young people.

Chapter 19

The music became louder and louder into the evening. Angelina said to Beatrice, "We should go home as you said. If it gets too late, my parents really won't let us come any more, and I don't care what you say, I like that young man and want to get to know him."

Beatrice looked at her and said, "Yes Angelina, you have surprised me. The first time you saw that young man, it seems to me you had already fallen in love with him."

"I didn't say I loved him," said, Angelina. "I would just like to know all about him."

Beatrice lifted her eyes upwards. "That is what I just said. You are already in love with him."

"Hoof! Let's go home," responded Angelina. "And I do hope you aren't going to mention anything to my parents, otherwise we can forget our Saturday evening out."

"Oh Angelina," "I'm not as silly as you think, after all I like coming to the church joust just as much as you do and you never know, one day we might both meet the man of our dreams here."

"Ok, we'll shake hands on that." Angelina said.

They laughed and skipped all the way home. When they reached home they ran up the stairs two by two laughing and giggling as always. Angelina's parents and her brothers were all waiting to hear all about the new church club. As they went in through the door they both said together in chorus, "We've had a wonderful evening. The music was nice, and there were a lot of sandwiches and cakes, made by the parents of the young people, or maybe by the members of the church club, and they were exceptionally good."

The family burst out laughing and the father said, "Alright young girls, you've had your fun, but now it is time to go to bed, because tomorrow we have many people from the villages coming here to help us reap the harvest of wheat, so you both need to help your mother with the cooking."

The girls looked at one another and Angelina said, "Yes we will do our best, father." They went into their room and began to chat with each other.

Beatrice said, "Angelina, what was it you found so attractive about that young man with his guitar?"

Angelina was thoughtful and had a dreamy look in her eyes.

"Beatrice, the minute I set my eyes upon him and saw his green eyes and his thick brown hair, and heard his voice, my heart began to pound enough to take my breath away."

Beatrice, more intrigued than ever, said, "Oh Angelina, I don't understand. What do you mean?"

"Oh, Beatrice, I mean the first instant I saw him my heart started beating a hundred a minute. Now we'd better go to sleep, otherwise we won't manage to help our mother in the kitchen tomorrow, and then you know what will happen to us if we don't obey."

Beatrice nodded. "If we don't obey, for a start your mother will be very angry and might send me back to my parents, and believe me, without any doubt, we will never be able to go out and enjoy ourselves together again."

"You're right Beatrice, we'd better do as we were told otherwise my father will be furious with us and as you say, that will be the end of our evenings out and any chance for us to meet the men of our dreams."

"So, let's go to sleep now," said Beatrice. "And maybe we can manage to get up before anybody else and go to the kitchen garden to gather all sorts of vegetables for auntie tomorrow."

Chapter 20

The next morning Angelina touched Beatrice.

"Wake up Beatrice," she said. "We must get up now because today is a special day for us. We need to go to the vegetable garden to gather as many vegetables as we can for my mother. She has to cook for the people coming to help father with threshing the wheat."

"Alright, alright we shall, but let's wash ourselves first." Beatrice said in a bored voice.

"Well, we must have a very quick wash, otherwise as the sun rises it will be too hot for us to pick all the vegetables my mother needs to prepare the meal for ten people. It isn't easy to be near the oven and the stove on such a hot day. Besides, we need to help her to prepare the vegetables," said Angelina, with a pensive look on her face.

"Yes, yes we will do what it takes to be sure that auntie has everything she needs, and we'll do more than just prepare the vegetables. We'll help to prepare the meal for the people coming to help your father as well."

While Beatrice was talking, she was going down the steps towards the garden shed, to pick up the tools needed to dig and pick the vegetables and whatever else they needed for that day.

The vegetable garden was about five minutes away from the house. Angelina and Beatrice took two big baskets with them to take home all the vegetable Mary would need.

They took home red peppers, yellow peppers, onions, many large courgettes, garlic, basil, tomatoes, parsley and all sorts of different vegetables that could be used in the kitchen. They returned to the farm and Mary was overjoyed to see the girls with the baskets full of vegetables.

"Now girls, I need your help." Mary said.

"Yes mother," said Angelina. "Tell us what you want

us to do, and we will do our very best."

Mary said, "Well, as you know, early this morning many people will come here to help us to thresh the wheat, and we need to prepare a big dinner for them. We need to make a very colourful and tasty marinated Mediterranean vegetable tart, served with fresh bread or tomato toasts."

This is the recipe

(1) Three onions
(2) 6 red (bell) Peppers
(3) 6 yellow (bell) peppers
(4) Large courgettes
(5) 6 Garlic cloves
(6) 3 tbsp. Balsamic vinegar
(7) 159g of anchovy
(8) 100g black olives, halved and pitted
(9) 3 tbsp chopped fresh basil, salt and pepper

Tomato Toast.

(1) Small stick of French bread.
(2) 3 garlic cloves, crushed
(3) 4 tomatoes, peeled and chopped
(4) 3 tbsp. of olive oil

Cut three onions into wedges, core and deseed 6 yellow (bell) (peppers,) and 6 red (bell) peppers, core and cut in into thick slices. Also 6 large sliced courgettes, 4 garlic cloves, chopped, and for me, a big bunch of fresh basil.

(1) Put 6 tbsp. olive oil in a large, heavy based frying pan.

(2) Add the onions, bell peppers, courgettes and garlic and fry gently for about 40 minutes, stirring occasionally. Add 3 tbsp. of balsamic vinegar, 150g of chopped anchovy, 100g of black olives, halved and pitted, salt and pepper. Spoon onto long plates and sprinkle with chopped basil.

Now girls, while I prepare the main meal, you will prepare the tomato toasts. You will need a small stick of French bread, two or three crushed garlic cloves, tomatoes, peeled and chopped and about 6 tbsp. olive oil.

The TomatoToast.

Cut the French bread diagonally into 1cm, or inch slices.
Mix the tomato, garlic oil and seasoning over each slice of bread together and spread thinly
Place the bread on a baking tray drizzled with the olive oil and bake in a preheated oven at 220C or 425*F Gas7 for 5- 10 minutes. Serve the tomato toast with the Bell Pepper Salad.

Mother said, "Now you have prepared the starters, I need to make Conchiglie Pasta Carbonara for the second course, but for that I must prepare the classic sauce for Pasta Carbonara to eat after the starter and this is the recipe:-

(1) 3 tbsp. olive oil
(2) 120g butter
(3) 300g of Pancetta
(4) 4 fresh eggs beaten
(5) 6 tbsp. milk
(6) 3 tbsp. thyme
(7) 3 kilo of fresh or dried conchiglie rigati
(8) 150g of parmesan cheese grated
(8) Salt and pepper

Lightly cooked eggs and pancetta are combined with cheeses to make the rich, classic sauce.
Mary said," Before I cook the Conchiglie Allay Carbonara, I need to make the pan cooked chicken, so that I can serve it just as the pasta is finished. And this is the recipe:-

(1) 12 breasts of chicken, part boned
(2) 100g butter
(3) Tbsp. olive oil
(4) Red onions
(5) 6 tbsp. lemon juice
(6) 450 ml dry white wine
(7) 450 ml chicken stock
(8) 6 tbsp. plain (all – purpose) flour
(9) 4 cans artichoke halves, drained and halved
(2) Salt and pepper
(3) Chopped fresh parsley

To cook the chicken, Mary oiled a large frying pan and took the 12 chicken breasts, seasoned with salt and pepper and added the chicken, frying it for twenty minutes on each side until lightly golden. Then she removed it from the pan using a slotted spoon. Next, she tossed the onion in the lemon juice and added it to the pan, stirring for ten or twenty minutes until just beginning to soften. Returning the chicken to the pan, she poured in the wine and brought it to the boil, then covered the pan and simmered gently for one hour and twenty minutes.

Removing the chicken from the pan, she reserved the cooking juice and kept it warm. Then she brought the juice to the boil and boiled it very rapidly for twenty minutes, blending the butter with the flour to form a paste. She reduced the juice to a simmer, spooned the paste into the frying pan, stirring until it thickened. Angelina's mother, Mary then adjusted the seasoning to her taste, stirred in the artichoke hearts and cooked for ten minutes. Finally she poured the mixture over the chicken and garnished with chopped parsley, adding roast potatoes and broccoli.

"Dear girls, now you can go and set the table for the guests, while I make the dessert."

"Yes, mother we will" Angelina said, and Beatrice smiled and said, "Auntie, we will set the table and make sure we are very social with the guests, the way you like."

Mary returned her smile, and said "I'm sure you will do

your best, and Rena too, will be very proud of you both."

Maria was very pleased to see both girls take such pleasure in being able to help her in every possible way.

Dessert Peaches with Mascarpone

    (1) 1300g of Mascarpone Cheese
    (2) 120g pecan or walnuts chopped
    (3) 1 tsp sunflower oil
    (4) 6 tbsp. maple syrup

Mary took twelve peaches, cut them in half and put the pecans and some walnuts together in small bowl until well mixed. Then she left them to chill in the refrigerator until she needed them.

She brushed the peaches with a little oil and placed them on a rack set over medium hot coals, and grilled them for 5-to ten minutes turning once, until hot. Then she transferred them to a serving dish and topped them with the mascarpone mixture. Next, she drizzled in the maple syrup over the peaches and mascarpone filling and waited until the time came to serve them.

After ten hours, when their guests had almost finished threshing the wheat, they were ready for a well-deserved dinner. As they came in one at time, they went in to the wash room to give themselves a good wash. And one by one they all went in to wait for dinner to be served.

Before dinner, Mary came in with a tray of glasses and a bottle of Sherry.

"Ladies and Gentlemen, thank you for coming here today and working so hard to help us with the threshing of the wheat. This was a job we couldn't ever have managed without your help. Please drink a glass of sherry and dinner will be served very soon, thank you."

Mary went back into the kitchen, while her husband said,

"Come in everybody and let's sit at the table. As my wife said, dinner will be served very soon."

Renato made sure that Angelina sat next to John where there was an empty chair. The next chair was for Jimmy but next to him there was another empty chair. When everybody was accommodated, Angelina and Beatrice entered the dining room and put plates in front of each person sitting at table including the empty chairs.

Back in the kitchen the mother said, "Now girls, you serve the starter while I cook the Pasta Carbonara. Serve the Mediterranean Vegetables on two long platters including the empty places, and then you both are to sit and eat with the guests and be sociable with them."

The girls gave Mary a curious look, then, shrugged their shoulders and off they went into the dining room to do as she had said, even though they were not impressed with what she had told them they should do. 'Be sociable' she'd said, 'and serve wine to everyone round the table'.

While the guests were eating, Mary was cooking and preparing the Pasta Carbonara. After a while the starter was finished and Mary was ready with the second course.

The girls cleared away the plates from the starter and brought in clean ones, before Mary brought in two big platters, one at a time, with the Pasta Carbonara. Then she sat at the table and thanked the family and the people who had done so much for them that day, and also on many previous occasions. Everybody stood up and clapped their hands at her speech in appreciation of the help they'd given to her family any time they needed it. They all enjoyed the Pasta Carbonara very much.

Angelina and Beatrice got up from the table, removed the plates and replaced them with clean ones. Mary went into the kitchen and came back with an enormous long serving platter containing the pan cooked chicken with broccoli and roasted potatoes and peas.

Angelina and Beatrice realised both parents were keeping an eye on them both, to see if they made an effort to talk to the guest next to them, and more than that, one of them, John, was the son of the farmer who lived not very far from them. Jimmy, sitting next to Beatrice, was a friend of John's.

Yes, they did talk to them, and that pleased both parents very much. After they finished the pan cooked chicken with the roast potatoes and the broccoli and peas, it was time to serve the dessert of peaches and mascarpone.

Mary made to move and both girls stood up. Angelina said, "Mother, you now need to sit and not move, because it is our turn to serve the dessert."

Mary looked at them and said, "Yes, my dears." Angelina followed Beatrice into the kitchen and said to her, "I think we both realise what my parents have done today."

Beatrice said, "I'm like you. I also realise that it was a set-up, but we need to go on playing the part of being very good and also very sociable towards our guests. We will talk tonight, but for now let's get on with serving the dessert."

The girls, both came in with a platter each full with a lovely dessert of peaches and mascarpone. One served one side and the table and the other, the opposite side.

The dinner was a success all round.

Then Mary said, "Now ladies and gentlemen, we will all go into our sitting room for a chat and to relax." She then went into the kitchen to make the coffee for the girls to serve all round the guests.

Angelina was aware that John kept following her with his eyes. Her mother was meanwhile preparing the coffee and when it was ready she called the girls and said, "Angelina and Beatrice the coffee is read to be served in the sitting room." They called back, "Yes mother, we will do our best."

After a long chat, the guests were ready to say goodbye to their hosts. But John and Jimmy had no intention of leaving before asking the girls when they would be able to meet them again.

Angelina and her cousin looked at one another knowingly and said with one voice, "You are our family friend, and there will be many occasions like today, and we sincerely hope that it won't be very long before our father needs your help again. Without any doubt, we shall meet here or in the village like we do most Sundays.''

John and Jimmy were disappointed at not be able to achieve their hopes while they were working in fields threshing the wheat.

After they went, Angelina said to Beatrice, "That was a set up by my parents, and I will refuse, more than ever, to accept my parents' plans for me to become a farmer's wife, just like mother.''

''Yes, but let's talk about that when we go in our room later on,'' Beatrice said with a smile."

After they finished helping Mary, they went in their bedroom, and Angelina was eager to know what Beatrice thought of the setup by her parents.

Beatrice said, "I'm with you all the way. Your parents can't expect you to marry who they think is the right man for you. If that is what you say, nobody should expect either of us to marry a man they chose. Marriage isn't like that. We will only marry the man we fall in love with whether they like it or not.''

Chapter 21

A week later, after Mass, the priest announced to his parishioners that he would like to arrange a pilgrimage for the young people, to the excavations of Pompeii, and to visit the cathedral. If any young people were interested they needed to sign the register and pay a twenty lire deposit to cover the expense of the transport.

The girls were very excited as they had never left their village before, and for them to go and visit the excavations of Pompeii and the Cathedral would be a fantastic experience.

The Cathedral was built many hundreds of years after the eruption of Vesuvius and nothing was known about what lay beneath the land around Vesuvius. When a few peasants started to cultivate the ground for farming and started to dig, they began to find antique vases and other more interesting artefacts. They informed the authorities but not before they had taken possession of many treasures to make their fortune. When the authorities came, more and more treasure was found, until the city of Pompeii was discovered, lying under the ash from the eruption of Vesuvius .

When Angelina told her mother about the pilgrimage, she was not amused, knowing that Renato was more concerned for the vineyard, now that the harvest of the grapes was ready to take in. It would be far better if the young people would come to help him gather the grapes, instead of wasting time to go on a pilgrimage, which according to him was a waste of precious time.

"Your father would be more interested if I told him the priest had told his parishioners that there is work for young people on his farm," she told Angelina.

Mary knew that according to him they would have a lot of fun, and for some, their family would appreciate a little help.

The girls were disappointed and looked downhearted at

one another. "Oh mother!" Angelina exclaimed. "How can you expect young people to pick grapes rather than going on a pilgrimage?"

The mother then gave them an evil look.

"I would like to know how the priest can think about a pilgrimage when he knows jolly well that the war and the Spanish influenza killed millions and millions of people, and therefore, there are not now enough peasants to cultivate the land." She said.

"That's the reason we're in such a bad recession. People in the city are dying from starvation because not enough food is being produced, and the little there is costs a lot of money to buy."

The girls were now getting very agitated. "Okay then mother", said Angelina, "Tell us how is it that by renouncing the pilgrimage, we would help the recession?"

The mother gave an impatient sigh.

"I already told you, there are not enough people to work. Most of the old ones are invalids because of the war and the new generation is not old enough to train or follow any kind of profession, but they are old enough to cut grapes, with special scissors and supervision."

"Young people need to realize," she went on, "That the sooner they learn to work, the better it will be for them, and our country, so that we able to come out of the recession."

"So, you go and tell the priest that it will be far better for the young people to pick the grapes than going on a pilgrimage. Tell him that it will be much more fun, and it will help everybody. We would be able to pay them, not with money but with oil, flour and whatever we have on our farm. If some of them need money we will do whatever we can to give them what they have earned."

Angelina and Beatrice realised now that they had no chance of going to Pompeii. It was better if they went back to the priest and told him what their mother had explained them.

A week later the priest announced in church that the

pilgrimage was cancelled. People couldn't understand why the pilgrimage for the young people wasn't going to happen. They came out from the church whispering among themselves. Some of them said they thought the priest was going out of his mind while others said they knew their priest had always been a friend of Renato and Mary, but cancelling the pilgrimage made no sense.

However some of the villagers were saying that the priest thought it was far better for young people to go and help in the vineyard and earn some money to help their family. They knew that many parents hadn't the money to feed their family so how could they have money to give to the youngsters for the pilgrimage. Maybe that was his reason for cancelling it.

Chapter 22

A week later the priest announced that if any young people and their parents would like to be involved in gathering the grapes on Renato and Mary's farm, they should meet in front of the church on the morning of 28th October.

The priest was amazed to see so many people, young and old come to the front of the church and wait for him to organize the assembly. He chose a young boy to walk beside him carrying the flag of the church with the picture of Jesus on it, and they were accompanied by two young men, one with a guitar and the other with a trumpet. Many more joined in, with other musical instruments.

The joy of the family was indescribable when they saw so many young people coming towards their vineyard, and singing rousing hymns.

There was a lot of food and a lot fun for all of them. Among them, Renato noticed John and Jimmy and that pleased him immensely. Angelina didn't care for John or Jimmy. Her heart started to race very fast and her face became red like a ripe tomato.

Beatrice looked at her cousin and said, "Angelina, may I know whatever is the matter with you to-day?"

Angelina was trembling all over as she said, "Beatrice can you see who is here today?"

Beatrice was puzzled. She said, "I know that John and Jimmy are here and I'm sure your father has arranged that as well."

Angelina had a determined look on her face, as she said, "It won't worry me at all what my father says, or does, because I have realised that among those people there is the young man who has affected my heart so strongly that I feel quite unwell, but at the same time very excited."

Beatrice was shocked. "Goodness me, who is it? Who is it? Tell me, I'm getting worried about you."

Angelina was quite breathless as she said "It's not my

mind you need to worry about, but my heart. I'm not able to control it. Every time I see that young man with his guitar, I want to rush over and tell him how much I like him, but as you know, I haven't the courage to approach him."

Beatrice frowned. Oh no, don't tell me, it's the young man we met in the church club. Is he the one you're talking about? I thought you'd forgotten all about him."

Beatrice had a look of apprehension on her face.

"Not for a moment can I get him out of my mind. I keep seeing his black hair and his hazelnut eyes, and hearing his music. I think you're right, Beatrice. I'm madly in love with him," Angelina said.

"Well I have a secret to tell you as well. I'm also in love with a young man." Beatrice said.

Angelina was flabbergasted.

"How can you be when we've always been together? I've never noticed anyone to suggest that he was the man of your dreams," said Angelina.

Beatrice gave a sigh and said, "It's very silly of me I know, but do you remember our last day of school? The teacher said that it would be nice for us to have a school reunion, where we could talk about the progress we've all made and what we would like to achieve in our future. Can you remember the young man who was sitting next to me? His name is Giuseppe. He told me he would like to have a chance to be an apprentice to a local carpenter, and the opportunity to meet his daughter, Maria. When he said that word, Maria, I felt a knife go right through my heart. Since that time I haven't seen him anymore. Nevertheless I can't forget him and my dream is to be able to meet him again and tell him of my feelings towards him. Anyway he is after Maria, the daughter of the carpenter. Maybe he will have a good laugh to himself if he gets to know about my feelings for him. He will think to himself, what a silly girl she is."

Angelina listened quietly and then said, "So, that makes two of us. We're both in love with men who haven't any idea about us, or us about them. Now it is up to us to find out all about Giuseppe and Domenic, whether we really like them or if it's just another fantasy of ours."

"Now we are here, in my father's vineyard, it seems to me that my young man is just like he was that Saturday evening in the church club, having a great time. Now I need to get to know him before I make a fool of myself. Only then can I be serious. It's up to us to find out if either of them they are already with some other girls or not."

Beatrice laughed, "And how do we do that?"

Angelina faced her cousin and said, "Well, we already have Domenic here, this is my chance to go to him and chat him up, then I shall have an Idea of what kind man he really is."

Beatrice was amused and said, "We will do our very best, but it isn't very easy. I need to investigate if Giuseppe really has achieved his dream to meet Maria, the carpenter's daughter?"

Angelina smiled at her cousin and said, ''Well, you already heard that Giuseppe didn't get the apprenticeship he really wanted, because Maria's father moved away to Rome with his family. He had an opportunity for a better job to make things better for him and his family. Now I have heard that Giuseppe is helping his father in his shoe shop."

Angelina had a determined look on her face. "So, I will go round to the vineyard and try to get Domenic's attention, talk to him about his music in a way that I might have a chance to befriend him."

Beatrice said, "Well you have a lot of confidence in yourself. But the important thing, at the end of day, is to achieve the purpose of finding out about our young men."

Angelina said, "Yes, I know I'm impulsive, but I will do my utmost to make sure that I'm not taken in."

So Angelina took the basket and big scissors and went close to where Dominic was laughing and talking with the other young men as he cut the grapes. He was telling the other men all about the concert, saying how much he was looking forward to the big concert next Saturday evening.

Angelina took a deep breath and approached him. "Oh yes, where is that, may I ask?"

Domenic lifted his head up and said, "At the church club, of course, but I think we have met before."

"Oh, yes, my cousin and I were there the first night the club opened, and we really enjoyed the music. If my father permits it, we will go again." she said, giving him her best smile.

"Why would your father not give permission, may I ask?" He seemed surprised.

"Oh well, my father is an old man, and he doesn't understand the young generation, but we will do whatever it takes to go to the club. We both really enjoy your music. You and your friends are so entertaining and we don't want to miss the concert."

Then Domenic asked," By the way, what's your name?"

"My name is Angelina, and my cousin's name is Beatrice." She answered coyly.

Domenic thought for a minute, then he said, "Oh, wait a minute, isn't Beatrice a friend of Giuseppe, the son of the shoemaker?"

Angelina was taken aback when Domenic mentioned the name of Giuseppe, "Do you mean that you and Giuseppe already know Beatrice?" She asked.

Domenic said, "My father took me to the shoe shop, and I met Giuseppe. He was telling me all about how this district became very poor after the war and the Spanish Influenza. Everyone had to work very hard to survive. The children had very little schooling, but the little they had was very good, in fact he said they achieved quite good marks. He was telling me about when he met two young girls, one of them named Beatrice and her cousin named Angelina and he said they were very clever."

Angelina was surprised at what she was hearing. The way the young man talked must mean he was new to the district.

She took the opportunity and looked straight at him, she said, "It may surprise you, but I'm Angelina and my cousin is Beatrice, and the vineyard belongs to my father."

He seemed speechless for a moment. Then he said, "Well, well, you and your cousin must be very rich."

"We're certainly not," she retorted, "We have our own farm, but we haven't much labour to help us cultivate it as we need to. That's the reason the priest asked the people of the village to come and help us. When my father can't pay for the labour with money he will pay with the farm goods that we produce. But, it seems to me you are not of this district."

"I'm certainly not. I'm here with my family, because my father is a merchant. He buys forests of wood, and employs a lot of men to help him cut the trees. With the branches he makes charcoal."

"Then tell me, which part of Italy do you come from?" Angelina asked Domenic.

He replied, "I come from Avellino, near Naples."

Angelina was more curious than ever. "So, how did you and your family end up in this part of the world?"

He started to turn away from her, saying, "That's a long story, and I need to get on to help your father gather the grapes, otherwise I won't be doing what I came here for. Then your father won't be very pleased with me, but we can always meet again and I will be able to tell you the reason why we left our district."

Then he put his head down and continued to cut bunches of grapes.

Angelina said firmly, "We shall meet again at the church club."

He nodded his head and said, "I would like that."

Angelina's father had almost succeeded in his dream of being able to gather all the grapes of his vineyard in one day, with the help of the young people of the village. He stood up and he rubbed his hands together then grabbed a big round copper plate and with a wooden hammer to beat on it and the attention of young and old. The he said in a

95

loud voice.

"My dearest friends, young and old, it is impossible for me to say how grateful I am to all of you, and I haven't forgotten the help of our priest in cancelling the pilgrimage to Rome for my benefit."

"Now, I do want to tell you all, that you are always welcome back here on my farm, if you need help of any sort and you know I can help. I will always do whatever possible I can to help. As I said before, you have done me a great favour and I will pay you all, the money you have earned today."

All the people clapped their hands, and one by one collected ten lire and went back to the farm for the refreshment prepared for them all.

The young people took the opportunity to show off their talent with their music and songs, by inviting everybody to join with them singing and dancing until late into the night.

Chapter 23

Angelina and Beatrice were developing into pretty young ladies and Angelina's father became very anxious about the future of his daughter and niece. The only thing he wanted for his precious daughter, and for his niece as well, was for them to become farmer's wives.

The girls realised that Joh, and Jimmy were often invited to the farm for Sunday lunch. That began to bother the girls very much. One Sunday afternoon they thought it was time to tackle the problem with their parents, once and for all.

They waited until their guests went home then Angelina and Beatrice went into the sitting room where Angelina's parents were relaxing and apparently having some sort of discussion.

Angelina took a deep breath and started, "Mum and Dad, what is going on?"

Mary answered cautiously. "Our dearest girls, we only want what's best for both of you."

Angelina gave her parents a suspicious look, and said, "What do you mean by, the best for us?"

Renato answered. "Well, you see I went all the way to America, worked hard and saved to provide security for my family. When I came back I was able to buy a farm so that none of you would ever need to worry about anything. Our farm produces enough food for us and for many generations to come."

Both girls looked a little uncertain for a moment. Then Angelina came to her senses and remembered what she had come to say.

"But mother, father, neither of us intend marrying a farmer or anyone else until we meet the man of our dreams, who is the right one for us. Surely you can understand that you can't choose a man for us. A marriage is not a piece of cake to eat and that's it. We need to fall in love like you have both done. So that is what we wanted to say.''

Having said their piece they both escaped into their bedroom. They hugged themselves and were satisfied with their show of bravery in confronting their parents. With one voice they shouted, "We've done it, we've told them. Surely they must understand now that we will not be told by them who our future husbands will be."

When they had both calmed down, Angelina said,

"It's going to be Christmas next month so we shall need to be good and impress my parents, because we'll need new dresses and overcoats. We have to make sure no one else will be better dressed than us if we want to impress young men like Domenic and Giuseppe. Beatrice, do you think that we will be more glamorous than any of the other girls?"

Beatrice was not convinced about that and she said, "Angelina, I'm not so sure about that. How can we ask for new overcoats and beautiful dresses, when we have behaved so badly? We haven't been very polite towards your mother and father, and now I personally don't know how we are going to find the courage to go and ask them for all that?''

Angelina answered, "I do understand. We've been very rebellious. We didn't really mean to be unruly but we had no choice did we? We couldn't let them make us marry somebody just because they thought that person would be the right ones for us."

Beatrice shook her head and said, "I know, but now it's very difficult to make them love us again. Can we regain their confidence and expect them to feel about us like they did before this incident?''

Angelina gave a deep sigh, and then said, "Well for a start, we must try being more active round the house and in the fields where they need us."

"But we already do that," Beatrice pointed out, and she spread out her hands in a gesture of uselessness.

"Oh, don't worry Beatrice, Christmas is not here yet. In a week or two we can begin to mention to them how important it is for us. After all it is winter time and it is very cold. They have no other choice but to do their best. After all I'm still their daughter and you their niece."

"Besides," she continued, "I know my mother would never permit us to be inferior to the rest of the village girls, no matter what we've said or done. And, I can tell you something else, my father in his mind, believes we are gentry. The most well off in the villages around us, but that is not true at all. If you ask me, he is a very silly and deceived man, because we are surrounded by very rich people like the Duke and Duchess. We just own a farm where we need to work very hard day and night to cultivate the ground to make it fruitful, and he thinks he is very well off. In his mind he is better because he has no need to work for anyone else to feed his family. For that reason, he thinks he is above everybody else, and that is ridiculous. I tell you this, Beatrice. His pride won't let us be dressed like any other girl in the village because he thinks we need to be more sophisticated."

"So don't worry, my dear cousin. He will make sure mother buys the best of clothes, so that we can show off in front of all the others in the village on Christmas day."

Beatrice looked doubtful. "I don't think it's as simple as that."

A few days later Angelina's mother called her daughter and niece into the kitchen and said,

"Angelina and Beatrice, on Sunday we have guests for dinner. I want you, Angelina, to make egg pasta like you always have done, because I know you can make it much better than me. You, Beatrice, need to have a good clean all over the house and I notice in the garden there are some beautiful yellow and red roses that would make our living room just beautiful."

Beatrice nodded her head and went out.

Then Angelina said, "Mum, what shape pasta do I need to make?"

Her mother looked puzzled. "Do you mean the shape of the egg pasta?"

"Is the egg pasta for noodles or lasagne?" asked Angelina.

"For noodles of course, and you can also make a good sauce with tomatoes and minced meat. Nobody can make that better than you, my dear daughter."

Angelina looked her mother in the eye and said "Mum, who are the guests who are coming here tomorrow for dinner."

"Oh dear me," said her mother, all flustered, "I thought you already knew that. It's John, Jimmy and their parents."

Angelina suspecting as much was nevertheless shocked. She rushed out, pulling the door shut, behind her, and running into the garden where Beatrice was cutting the roses for the living room.

"Beatrice, I can't believe it, did you know who is coming for dinner tomorrow?"

Beatrice said, "Well, I had an idea?"

"Tell me more about your idea that I didn't know anything about," Angelina said, crossly. "Who are these people?"

Beatrice was hesitant, troubled by the look on her cousin's face.

Very slowly she said, "Well, yesterday I overheard your parents talking and they were very excited by the fact that John and Jimmy's parents had accepted their invitation."

"Oh Beatrice, you must be joking", groaned Angelina.

"No I'm not joking, but remember, I thought that your parents would not buy us the special coats and dresses for Christmas? Well, I also overheard that they will, if we will only be good girls and make a good impression on John and Jimmy's parents tomorrow."

Chapter 24

Angelina was beginning to get very anxious.

"Well as I understand it, if we behave ourselves and make a good impression on them, eventually they will speak to the dressmaker who lives in the cottage near the monastery, because although she may charge more than anybody else, she is one of the best ", said Beatrice.

"Oh yes," said Angelina, "It must be the dressmaker who lives in the small cottage not very far from the monastery where little John went to play with Peter, the old ladies' grandson."

"Yes," said Beatrice, "I think so, but do we need to make a good impression?"

"Oh, now I know, my mother and father want us to impress John and Jimmy's parents, with the hope that one day they will defeat us, and we will marry the men they always wanted for us."

Beatrice said, "Well then, we must play their game if we want to have best dresses and overcoats for this Christmas so we will do just that! As we said before, we will not let them choose a man for us, we shall marry who we want, and not who they think is best for us."

Angelina went back into the house, and she asked her mother, "Mum, what is the menu for tomorrow?"

Mary said, "Well, I think we'll start with Eggplant Rolls, and I will tell you what to do. Next we will have Noodles À La Bolognese and for dessert we'll have Italian Bread Pudding, but I will help you and here are all the recipes you need.

(1) Two big aubergines sliced liberally with salt and left for 8 to 10 minutes to extract the bitter juice. Turn the slices over and repeat. Rinse well with cold water and drain on napkins.

(2) Heat the olive oil in a large frying pan and add the

garlic, frying the aubergine slices lightly on both sides, a few at a time. Then drain them on the napkins.

(3) Spread grated Mozzarella and torn pieces of basil leaves on top of one side of the aubergines slices. Then season with a little salt and pepper. Roll up the slices. And secure with wooden cocktail sticks.

(4) Arrange the aubergine rolls in a greased ovenproof baking dish, and place in a preheated oven, 180°C or Mark 4 and bake for 8 to 10 minutes.

(5) Transfer the aubergine rolls to a warmed serving plate, scatter with fresh basil and then serve at once.

Now dear daughter, we come to the main course. And remember that there will be 8 of us. This is what we need to make the Noodles À La Bolognese.

2 tbsp olive oil
2 onions
2 garlic cloves
2 carrots
2 sticks of celery
100g of pancetta
1kg lean minced beef
800g tomato passata
4 tsp dried oregano
2 cups red wine
Salt and pepper
1400g noodles

(1) Heat the oil, add the onions finely chopped and cook for 5 minutes.

(2) Add the garlic, carrot, celery and pancetta for 5-8 minutes or until just beginning to brown.

(3) Add the beef, and cook over a high heat for another 6 minutes until the minced beef is brown.

(4) Stir in the tomato passata, oregano and the red wine, and bring to the boil.

(5) Reduce the heat and leave to simmer for about one hour

(6) Cook the noodles in a big pan of boiling water for about four minutes until ready.

(7) Transfer them to a serving plate and pour over the

Bolognese sauce. Toss to mix well, and serve hot.

Now, the Italian Bread Pudding

(1) 4 small eating apples, peeled, cored and sliced into rings.
(2) 150g granulated sugar
(3) 4 tbsp white wine
(4) 600g white bread sliced with the crusts.
(5) 5 tbsp single cream, 4 eggs beaten and rind of 2 oranges cut into   matchsticks.

(6) Now, line a 2 to 4 pint deep ovenproof dish with the bread and sprinkle half the sugar over the apple.

(7) Pour the wine over the apples and add the bread slices, pushing them down with your hands to flatten them slightly.

(8) Mix the cream with the eggs, remaining sugar and the orange rind, then and pour the mixture over the bread. Leave to soak for about 50 minutes or more.

(9) Bake the pudding in a preheated oven at 180°C or

mark 4 for about 40 minutes or more until golden and set. Serve warm.

Angelina was astonished. "Thank you mum, I will do my best, but as you said, you need to be with me, if not it will be embarrassing in front of our guests tomorrow."

Her mother burst out laughing.

"Of course I will be with you, every step of the way, until the menu is completely finished, and then I will sit at the table with our guests, while you and Beatrice serve. I can tell them that Angelina and Beatrice have worked very hard to make sure we enjoy our time together, and give me the chance to sit with you and enjoy your company."

Angelina was surprised and asked, "Mother how can that be, when Beatrice doesn't know anything about this menu?"

Mary looked at her daughter and said, "Angelina, Beatrice doesn't know about the menu yet, but she knows that I've already asked you to make the egg pasta today, because tomorrow is an important day for us, and for that reason I asked her to have a good clean all over the house. For this the reason you will find her in the garden cutting the roses for the sitting room. I realised only a few minutes ago that you were looking for her, and indeed you did find her there in the garden. I'm surprised that you went to talk to her, and yet she didn't tell you anything about why she was cutting the roses."

Angelina shrugged her shoulders and went out of the room. She waited for the right time to tell Beatrice what her mother had told her.

Beatrice said, "I see Auntie and Uncle have planned everything well. Now we need to carry on with their game if we want to get the things for ourselves"

They both burst out laughing and went back into their bedroom.

The next morning Renato made sure the carriage was clean and the horses were ready to take the ladies to morning Mass in the village church. They knew they needed to be back in time to start cooking.

Angelina whispered to her cousin, "I do hope the priest doesn't preach for too long today. Sometimes when he starts he forgets to finish, but if that happens we'll need to come out before Mass is finished."

Beatrice looked at her cousin and said, "That will be very difficult. It would be embarrassing for us, and besides, your uncle and aunt definitely wouldn't permit that."

Angelina said, "All right, but then we need to explain to our parents that we might not be able to attend the morning Mass, but we will try to go the evening one."

Beatrice waved her hand and said, "Well you'd better explain it to your parents and see what they suggest."

Angelina, called her mother and father and said, "Mum and Dad, because of the situation we are in today, do you think we'd better stay behind, and prepare everything, so that when you both come back from church everything will be ready to cook?"

Renato and Mary looked at one another and said, "Okay, but you must promise you will wait for us, before you start cooking, and if the dinner is a bit late that won't matter. It's important that it's a success."

So her mother and father, with their two older sons, climbed onto their carriage, and Renato took the reins, commanding the horses to go towards the village.

Angelina took her cousin's hand and they danced round the kitchen and started singing with very loud voices, shouting, "We now have the chance to show what good cooks we are."

Beatrice stopped suddenly and said, "Angelina, that doesn't amuse me at all. Didn't we promise auntie we wouldn't do anything until they return from church?"

Angelina looked a bit annoyed, "Yes, I know, but we can start to prepare the aubergines for the starter, and maybe make the Bolognese sauce. Remember, I already made the egg pasta by myself yesterday."

Beatrice said, "Well if you don't mind seeing auntie

very upset, especially if what we prepare is not to her satisfaction, and by doing that the meal is spoiled, then it is your fault only. I will not take any responsibility for what you try to do with the aubergines, and don't mention the Bolognese sauce.''

"Okay, okay,'' Angelina said. "You have made your point, but nevertheless, I will still try and you've still got to help me.'' Angelina finished by stamping her feet on floor.

Beatrice said "So, now we'll start, and we'll follow the recipes very carefully as written.''

"First, we'll slice the aubergine thinly and sprinkle with a little salt for 10 to 15 minutes. Then we'll rinse well with cold water and drain on paper towels. Then we'll leave on the side of the work top," said Angelina.''

"Now we can start on the Bolognese sauce," she said.

"We need to peel, cut and chop two onions, put two tablespoons of olive oil in the frying pan, and cook for three minutes. Then we add the garlic, beef, carrots, celery and pancetta which has already been chopped and prepared. Now we cook for 4 minutes or until we think it is done.''

"Next," she continued, "We add the beef and cook over a high heat for about 3 to 4 minutes then stir in the tomatoes, oregano, and red wine and we wait for it to start boiling. Then we reduce the heat and leave to simmer for about 45 minutes, because we know that my mother likes it a bit more concentrated. I think we also need to add some tomato puree.''

"And I think by now my parents will be starting to make their way home," she finished.

Beatrice said, "I think they will have a shock when they see all that we have done. I only hope auntie won't be mad at us.''

Angelina answered, "Well if she is, maybe it's a good thing. In that way my mother will be so embarrassed for the mess we have made, that she and father won't be so keen to encourage John and Jimmy to ask us to go out with them again.''

Beatrice looked at her, and said, "Oh Angelina, they're not that naïve. Aunt and uncle know jolly well we are young and we have got a lot to learn before they can say what kind of people we will marry?''

While they were talking, they heard Renato command the horse to stop. Angelina and Beatrice held their breath as Mary walked through the door said, ''I can smell the aroma of a very special sauce. Angelina and Beatrice, what is it?''

Angelina spoke for them both when she said in a shaky voice. "Well, we wanted to surprise you. While you were in church we have partly prepared the aubergines and we made the Bolognese sauce, and now you have arrived, we can continue the menu under your guidance.''

Mary was surprised to see the aubergines well prepared and when she tested the Bolognese sauce she was astonished and thought both the sauce, and the aubergines were done better than she ever could have done.

"Well done girls. I must say I'm astonished. Therefore I shall ask you to continue with the menu by yourselves and I will make sure the house is ready to receive our guests.''

The girls were over the moon and they continued to prepare the menu as described.

At one o'clock their guests arrived, just as Angelina and Beatrice imagined. As their carriage stopped in front of the farm, Angelina's parents were there to welcome them. While they embraced one another, John and Jimmy's eyes were looking round to see if the girls were anywhere to be seen. Then seeing the girls at the top of the staircase they rejoiced and waved to them. Then they composed themselves and walked up the staircase behind their parents. When they all reached the top of the staircase they embraced one another and the guests were asked to enter the sitting room.

When they had all sat down, Renato opened a bottle of sherry, and said, "My dearest friends, this morning, our dear daughter with her cousin Beatrice asked our permission to remain behind because they wished to go to the evening Mass. When we came home from the church my dear wife discovered the two young girls wanted to prove to us that they could surprise us.''

"One thing we know for sure, is that this is the first time, so please let us sit at the table, and we will see what has come out of their labours."

With one voice the guests responded by saying whatever came out in the menu they were sure they would enjoy it and thanked the young ladies for making such a big effort. Then they wished them all the best for their future in the kitchen.

The girls blushed and thanked them for their understanding. Then they went into the kitchen to bring out the starter that was perfectly arranged in long plates accompanied with salami, black pitted olives stuffed with anchovies, mozzarella, small tomatoes and cucumber scattered with small pieces of basil.

The guests waited for the girls to sit down in the same places as last time. Angelina was next to John and Beatrice next to Jimmy.

Before the starter commenced, Renato as usual, said the Grace, giving thanks to God for the food they were about to receive, and the guests answered, 'Amen'.

After the starter was finished the guests got up from their chairs and clapped their hands to say 'bravo'. The girls stood up and thanked the guests for their appreciation at the effort they had made. Then the girls took the plates away from the table to replace them with clean ones for the main course. They came back with very large porcelain dishes filled with Noodles À La Bolognese and a big bowl of grated Parmesan cheese. Then they asked the guests to serve themselves.

After a while the main meal was finished and again the guests repeated their compliments, which the girls appreciated.

Again the plates from the main meal were removed from the table and replaced with clean ones for the dessert.

The girls came in from the kitchen with two more big porcelain dishes with an Italian Bread and Butter Pudding.

The guests were amazed and couldn't understand how these two young girls could produce such a delicious meal.

Angelina said, "It wasn't difficult really. We followed our grandmother's Italian Cookery book which is always kept in the library at the side of our French window."

The guests all stood up including Angelina's parents and their brothers and John's father made a speech.

"Angelina and Beatrice, between you, you have made the best dinner we have had for a long, long time."

The girls stood and bowed to their guests. Then speaking for both of them Angelina said,

''Thank you for your appreciation of the effort we have made. It was an honour and a privilege for us to serve you all, and we hope there will be many more occasions to repeat it."

The guests and hosts embraced one another and left.

Chapter 25

Back in their room, Angelina and Beatrice jumped with joy to know once again, they had achieved their purpose of making peace with the parents. The coats and beautiful dresses they wanted for Christmas were now much more secure, and in their minds they would be able to go to the church club and show off to the other boys and girls. More than that of course, they hoped to impress Domenic and Giuseppe.

After a few days Angelina said to her cousin, "Is it time to remind my parents about keeping their promise?"

Beatrice was dismayed to hear her cousin talk in that manner.

"Angelina, what do you mean, they need to keep their promise?"

"Oh Beatrice, you have already forgotten all about the dinner we made last Sunday to impress our guests and trying to make peace with my parents. After all, we did upset them when we rebelled against them, even if we had every right to do so but there is still a chance they will refuse to buy the coats and dresses which we desperately need for this Christmas, if we want to impress the young men we both like."

Beatrice was lost for words. "Okay, Angelina. Now I understand what you mean. If that's the case, our behaviour must improve. If there is a chance to make your aunt and uncle believe that it is right to marry a farmer so be it, then time will tell. For the time being we must play the game, do you understand, Angelina?"

"Yes of course I understand." Angelina replied.

Two days later, Angelina went to her mother and said, "Mum, Christmas is getter nearer and Beatrice and I would like it, if you and Dad could buy the material for our Christmas dresses. We have to make sure that the dressmaker can to do it in time for Christmas."

Mary looked at her daughter keenly and said,

"Yes dear, tomorrow you and Beatrice will come with me and your father to the shops to choose the material and the colours you both like."

Angelina was over the moon and ran to find her cousin who was in the salami room helping her uncle conserve pork meat, like Parma ham and many other products the Italian farms produced at that time.

She pushed the door open and shouted at the top of her voice. "Beatrice come out, I need to speak to you now."

Renato said, "Angelina, can't you see we are very busy. Instead of shouting, come in and help us."

"No Father, I need to go upstairs and help mother. I only need a few minutes to tell Beatrice some good news. Then I will leave you in peace."

Her father was very annoyed with his young daughter but he knew her well, and there was no point in getting upset.

"But for now, go upstairs and help your mother. There will be time later on when you can have a chat with each other."

He pushed her out of the door and closed it with the key.

"Now then Beatrice", he said, "We have a job to finish, and this is a job that can't be delayed. When we have finished then you can go and see your cousin and you will have plenty of time to chat with one another, but for now you need to be here until we have finished."

"Yes uncle," she said, and got on preparing the meat for the salami.

When Beatrice came out of the salami room she went straight upstairs to look for Angelina in the sitting room. Angelina's face lit up when she saw her. She ran towards her cousin, and embraced her saying,

"My mother told me that tomorrow we will go to town to buy the material we need for the new dresses and coats."

"Marvellous," said Beatrice. "I think at last we have achieved what we want from your parents, and now we only have to wait for Christmas to impress Domenic and Giuseppe."

Angelina couldn't stop laughing,

"Beatrice, it's just as I told you before. That if we played the game very carefully it would be a success, and we have done it."

"How right you are Angelina, later on when we go to our bedroom we will be able talk about the colour and the material we need to choose for the coats and dresses. For now though, we must behave ourselves until we have achieved what we want."

Angelina laughed and ran into her bedroom, waiting for Beatrice to return to discuss the colour and the material they must choose before going shopping with her mother.

In fact soon after that Beatrice entered the bedroom with a relieved look on her face and said,

"Oh Angelina, thank God today is over I thought the work in the salami room with uncle would never end. He kept on and on until there was no more pork meat left. He had no intention of stopping before that. He was prepared to work all night if necessary without any rest."

"Well, never mind, the important thing is you're here now, and we can discuss tomorrow." said Angelina.

Beatrice looked excited. "Oh! Do you think tomorrow will be the day auntie takes us to Cassino to buy the material for our new clothes?'' she asked.

"Yes, yes that is what I understood,'' Angelina replied.

"Oh well, that will be very nice after the hard work I've done with uncle today. I will appreciate a day of rest very much," Beatrice said.

The next morning Angelina became very excited as she watched her father preparing to attach the horses to the carriage. That meant that her mother was in her bedroom preparing herself to go to town with her and Beatrice to buy the material for their dresses.

So shouting loudly, she called Beatrice. "Beatrice get up immediately, father is already preparing the carriage for us, so that mother can take us to the shops."

In no time at all, the girls were ready and waiting for Mary and Renato to take them to town for shopping. It was a beautiful day and the family enjoyed every moment and purchased the material the girls had chosen.

The next day Mary said. "Today, I will ask the dressmaker to come to the farm, and measure both of you and then you can choose the style you want."

She had a big smile on her face. The girls jumped up and down for joy, happy with their success in getting the parents to buy them what they wanted.

Two days later the dressmaker came and asked the girls which one liked the blue material, and which other the light cream one with the overcoat to match.

Well Angelina chose the blue one to match with the coat, and Beatrice chose the light cream one, again with the overcoat to match. After only a few days the dresses and coats were completed. The girls were overjoyed with the dressmaker's work in making such a professional job and achieving such perfection with the material the mother had bought for them. Now they just needed the right shoes and handbag to go with the outfit but they knew without any doubt the parents would buy the girls just what they wanted.

Two weeks before Christmas the priest announced to the Sunday morning Mass, the beginning of the evening services to be celebrated every evening until Christmas Day. That pleased the girls immensely because that would be a good excuse for them to know exactly which day of the week Domenic and Giuseppe would be playing music in the church club.

So as never before, Angelina and Beatrice attended all the evening services and devotions by the priest of the parish until Christmas Eve, and after that it would be the Midnight Mass. They took every opportunity to find out exactly when the young men would be playing music during the Christmas holiday. One of the young men knew Domenic and Giuseppe and told the girls, that they played there every Saturday night, from eight to eleven o'clock in the evening.

The girls were very happy to hear that, but they had a problem. How could Angelina tell her father that they would like to attend the music concert at the church club at that time of the evening?

On the way home Angelina said to Beatrice, "I know my father and mother won't ever permit us to be out until that hour of night by ourselves.

Beatrice said, "I know. What if we suggest that your younger brother comes with us? I'm sure he also likes music. Maybe he would enjoy it and in that way I'm quite sure that auntie and uncle would agree to us going, with him there with us."

Angelina looked doubtful. "Do you really think my younger brother would come with us?"

"Why not," said Beatrice. "After all he is a young man himself, and I'm sure he is like every other young man and likes to have fun. Especially if he knew that there would be someone there that can play the guitar. Anyway we can just ask him, and we will see what he says."

"Beatrice, this is a good idea. "We can try, but we need to choose the right time to approach him if we want to be successful."

Two days later while her cousin Simon was milking the cow, Beatrice went over to him and said,

"Simon, next week it will be Christmas Eve, and as you know we all go to the evening service, and then we go to the church club to enjoy ourselves and wait for Midnight Mass. Angelina and I would be very pleased if you could come along with us. There are some young men who play lovely music and there is a special one who plays the guitar which I think you would enjoy. Being Christmas Eve, there will be a big buffet and plenty of food and wine."

Simon looked at Beatrice, then smiling, he said, "I know cousin dear, that you have asked me to come out with you two because my father and mother wouldn't let Angelina and you go by yourselves. You need me. I will think about it, and let you know.''

Beatrice was a bit disappointed, "Simon, please come. Angelina will be broken hearted if you don't. As you've already said, we have no chance of going on our own. Please say 'yes' if you really love us.''

Simon held up his hand in surrender. "Okay. I will come with both of you but I need to ask Mum and Dad and I will let you know what they say."

Beatrice gave him her best smile and then said, ''Oh thank you, thank you, Angelina will be over the moon when I will tell her there's a chance. I will go now and tell her that you will come with us to the evening service, and to the church club.''

Angelina was very happy to know there was a good chance that Simon would accompany them to the evening service. A few days passed before Simon found Beatrice and reported that his Mum and Dad had said that he could accompany them both to the Christmas service and the midnight mass.

Beatrice clapped her hands in delight, "Thank you so much Simon, I'm sure you will enjoy it too."

Beatrice was so pleased because Simon had said 'yes'. Both girls were immensely happy and Angelina had jumped for joy when Beatrice told her the good news. Now they knew without any doubt that they would be able to see Domenic and Giuseppe if they were going to be there that Christmas Eve.

Chapter 26

When Angelina and Beatrice heard the church bells ringing they began to get very excited. They were loud, and noisy enough to attract the parents' attention.

Mary went into their bedroom and said, "What on earth has happened to you two? Please explain what this noise is all about.''

They were both jumping up and down with excitement and had difficulty explaining their crazy behaviour.

Mary cried, "Stop! Take a deep breath and tell me what is going on with you two."

Angelina and Beatrice said with one voice, "Mum didn't you hear the Church bells ringing?"

She gave them a funny look and said, "Of course we heard, but it isn't the first time, is it?''

The girls dropped their heads down and said, "But mum, we are so happy because at last we can wear the lovely outfits you and Dad bought us for Christmas. Better still, we are so happy because Simon will be able to accompany us to the Church club. Then we will go to Midnight Mass. But Mum, will you help us to do our hair?"

For the parents it was a great relief to know that their son, Simon would accompany Angelina and their niece to the evening service, and after that they would go to the church club together whilst waiting for the Midnight Mass.

Mary said, "Yes of course I will help you both to do your hair, and your father and I are looking forward to seeing you wearing your new outfits."

"Yes, mum, of course." said Angelina. "You will both be amazed at how well the dressmaker managed to make the dresses and coats just as we wanted, and we promise both of you that we will behave ourselves."

Mary kissed them and said, "We are very proud of you both, and we are very happy to know Simon will stay with you until the midnight Mass is over and you will get home safely."

Angelina and Beatrice rejoiced in knowing that their parents were re-assured because Simon was accompanying them. What the girls didn't know was that Simon had also invited John and Jimmy to meet them in the church club after the evening service.

The church was almost full when they arrived and it was very difficult to find a seat, so they had no choice but to stand outside the door and when the congregation started singing:

"Tu scendi dalle Stelle......
O Re del cielo..........
Che vieni in una grotta al freddo al gelo......
O Bambino, mio Divino
Io ti vedo qui a tremare.....
Paroletta del mio petto.......
Quando a Questa poverta'......
Mancano panni e fuoco al mi Signore....
   You came down from the skies
   O King of heaven
   And were in a cave......
   In cold and ice
   In such divine poverty
   O my baby divine
  We see you here tremble
   O Blessed God
   How much did it cost you
   To love us …..

The congregation continued singing Christmas carols, but the girls were frozen, and had no choice but to seek shelter in the houses nearby, and wait there until the service finished and the church club would be opened. At the end of the service, the congregation began to go home, and the girls went to the back of the church to see if it would be open for the rest of the evening.

They were surprised to see many women of all ages

coming out of the club, some of them with empty containers, and some other women going in with big containers full of all sorts of sandwiches and small cakes, and many bottles of fruit juice. Then they realised that one of the women was Mary, Angelina's mother. That was a surprise. They never thought for one minute that their mother would do such a thing for them and for the other young people on that Christmas night .

They caught her attention, and Angelina said, "Oh, how kind of you to do this for us, mother.''

The answer was. "Well girls, you didn't expect that all those ladies would do something for their children and I would just do nothing?''

Angelina replied, "Yes mother, we thought you were far too busy with all the preparations for tomorrow, since we know Grandfather and Grandmother, with all the aunts, uncles and cousins will be at our home for dinner. Mother, will you tell us why every Christmas you always invite our grandparents with all their family?''

Her mother seemed a bit annoyed, "I'll tell you why, because there is a saying. 'Christmas with your own, and Easter with whom you like'. And now children, I need to go, because your father is waiting for me, but I want you to promise, Simon, that you will look after the girls, and make sure they come straight home after the Midnight Mass, and not one minute later.''

"Of course Mum," Simon replied.

Angelina and Beatrice went into the church club, and they noticed that Simon was looking round. The girls were worried as to why Simon he was doing this. Who was he looking for?

Then they noticed John and Jimmy coming through the door of the club. It seemed to the girls that Simon immediately relaxed as he walked over to them.

"Oh John and Jimmy, for a minute I thought you weren't coming tonight."

"Oh yes", they assured him. "We wouldn't miss this occasion for all the tea in China."

Soon after, the girls noticed Domenic and Giuseppe and a few other young men, and also several young girls, walk through the door of the club. They began mixing with one another and in no time the club came to life with very loud music. They all started dancing to the beat of Cha-Cha, then the Waltz, and then the Mambo-Mambo Italiano.

When the interval came and the music stopped, the young people all started to chat to one another and help themselves to the buffet. There was an appetising spread comprising of all kinds of sandwiches, a variety of pasties, and small cakes prepared by the young peoples' parents and friends of the church club.

Domenic and Giuseppe put their guitars in the corner of the room with other the musical instruments and then mingled with everybody and they all greeted one another, wishing them a Merry Christmas and Happy New Year. Domenic tapped Giuseppe's shoulder and said to his friend, "Do you see what I see, Giuseppe?"

Giuseppe gave Domenic a curious look, and said, "Yes, I see a lot of young people here this Christmas night, and I also see two young and very pretty girls, one with a blue dress and coat and the other with a cream dress and coat. And I'm sure you know one of them?"

Domenic answered, "Yes, I know both of them. One is Angelina the farmer's daughter, and the other one is her cousin Beatrice. I met them when the priest arranged for the people to go and help gather the grapes in her father's vineyard and Angelina tried her very best to chat me up."

Giuseppe laughed, "Oh yes, I also think I know Beatrice. If I remember right, I met her on the last day of our school. There were three or four girls and Beatrice was one of them. I'm very surprised that Beatrice is Angelina's cousin."

"Oh! Well hopefully we shall soon have an opportunity to chat them up," said Domenic.

Giuseppe made a 'no' gesture with his hands. Then he said, "No Domenic, this evening is not appropriate, because Angelina's brother, Simon is here with his two male friends. If we try to chat up the girls it could cause an argument, especially as it is Christmas Eve. You know as well as I do, there are many young people about, and some of them are already drunk and that could create some uneasiness between us. I'm quite sure there will be other occasions to make friends with them.''

Domenic said, "All right, we will just introduce ourselves and try to have a friendly conversation with the brother and his friends, and after that we will return to our music.''

Giuseppe was unsure. "Domenic, you have to convince me. Promise me you will keep your word. After a small conversation with them, we will return to our music and that means for the rest of the evening.''

Domenic looked at him and said, "I promise you we will play the music for the rest of the evening, until Midnight Mass.''

So Giuseppe and Domenic, having both agreed on their action, waited for the opportunity to approach Angelina and Beatrice, at a more convenient time.

When the opportunity arose, Domenic and Giuseppe walked over towards Simon and their friends and said, "Oh, look who's here.''

Simon frowned, and asked, "Do we know you?"

Domenic replied. "Yes, of course, we met you all when our priest organized the gathering of the grapes in your father's vineyard. It was a joyful day for all of us. We hoped to meet you all again, but for now we need to go back to play our music. We wish you all a Merry Christmas and a Happy New Year, and also all your families.''

There were mutterings in reply of, "the same to you and your families."

Then Dominic and Giuseppe, and three other young men, went back to their music and began playing the Neapolitan Tarantella. The young people and some not so young kept dancing until the service began at midnight.

After the service many people stayed to watch the

fireworks, but Simon said,

"Angelina and Beatrice, we need to go home now because mother needs to go to bed. In the morning our grandparents and their family will come to us for dinner, so mother needs to get up early, and she needs both of you to help her, so come on."

Angelina and Beatrice were disappointed and sad. They had been dreaming of having a chat with Domenic and Giuseppe for a long time but instead the evening had ended with a smile, a handshake and good night.

The next day was Christmas Day and Mary with her daughter and niece, were very busy cooking Christmas dinner for them and their guests so it was the father who took every opportunity to inquire about the music and the people who were at the church club that Christmas Eve.

His son, Simon said, "Dad I can only say it was a pleasant evening. There were all sorts of people, young and middle aged, but what impressed me most were the few young men playing music. One stood out from the others. He started by playing the guitar, then he played the accordion, and after that, the small hand organ, the one you put in your mouth, like Pasquale's sons did to keep the village alive with their music."

"Of course, most of the time they used to create a lot of bother for their parents because the young girls kept going to them to complain about their sons. Also they complain to Pasquale and his wife about their sons declaring love to most of them. The boys were only messing about. In reality their 'love' for the young girls was just a pastime for that evening."

"It seems to me that Domenic is a very nice young man, and also very talented, and above all he doesn't bother anybody. He just plays his music and that's all."

Renato looked at his son and said, "I believe I met this young man when all the people of the village came to help us gather the grapes in the vineyard."

"Yes father, he was there."

Renato said, "We should find out which district he

comes from, because he doesn't have our accent."

Simon said, "I don't think that would be a problem, in time we will know where he comes from."

Chapter 27

Some days later Simon noticed that his sister was very melancholy and he was concerned about her. He asked, "Angelina, what is wrong with you?"

Angelina answered, "Why do you ask me that?" Looking into her face, he said, "Because I see there is something I don't understand. Tell me are you in love with someone?"

Angelina blushed. "Certainly not, and if I was, it wouldn't be with anyone our parents would accept."

Simon was mystified and now he knew there was something buzzing in her mind, but what could it be? He scratched his head and said, "How do you know our parents wouldn't like it if they don't know who it is?"

She answered, "I know that our parents want me and Beatrice to get married to farmers, but that we will not permit them to choose our future for us. We will both only marry the man we fall in love with and nobody else."

Simon laughed, but he was thinking to himself that he could see that Angelina and Beatrice were going to create a few problems for his parents. However, he needed find out if it was only a teenage fantasy that was going around in her little brain. Time would tell, he knew, but if there was someone, he thought he should find out who it was. For the time being though, he was going to keep quiet."

After a few days he saw Angelina and Beatrice whispering to each other. He wanted to know what was going on and what the whispering was all about. Simon's curiosity grew stronger but he knew the best thing was to keep quiet, until something transpired. A few days later, he went into the village and he found out that there were some carnival festivities going on. Domenic was there, playing his guitar and singing Italian songs and people were clapping their hands. He seemed very excited to see so many young people clapping and dancing to the beat of his music.

Simon ran back home to tell his parents and old brother. "Did you know there is a carnival in the village? It would be nice if we could go, and take a cake. Angelina and Beatrice could come with us." Renato and Mary agreed. "It will nice to have an evening by ourselves," said Mary and know that you will all be there together enjoying the music.''

Angelina and her cousin were in the garden, having a chat with their neighbour, when her older brother Roberto came out of the house and ran towards them.

He said, "Come on you two. Simon and I are going to the village for the carnival, and you can both come with us.''

Angelina was over the moon, because her brothers had invited them to the village feast. Her first thought was whether Domenic and Giuseppe would be there. She pulled her cousin by the hand and said, "Come on Beatrice, we can't miss this opportunity.''

Beatrice couldn't understand what had come over her cousin. Her impulsive behaviour was at times unbearable. She resisted Angelina's tug on her hand and said, "What can't we miss and what are you talking about?"

Angelina had a determined look on her face. "We need to go upstairs and put on our best dresses because my brothers, Roberto and Simon, are taking us to the carnival which is on now in our village. We must do it quickly so that we might have a chance to see Domenic and Giuseppe.''

They ran upstairs into their bedroom, and changed as fast as they could then went into the sitting room to find Mary and Renato.

"Mum and Dad," said Angelina, "Thank you for letting us go with my brothers to see the carnival in the village.''

Mary and Renato smiled, "We are happy that your brothers are coming with you, now go and enjoy yourselves.''

They ran downstairs where the boys were waiting for them. After twenty minutes of walking they reached the village and Domenic with another four boys were already playing village songs. What Angelina and her cousin noticed was that there were many young girls and boys singing and dancing, and at the end of the songs, they heard one of the girls say to another, "Domenic was singing for me." Then another girl said, "No he was singing for me." While another girl said, "No, he wrote that song for me."

Angelina was mystified. She and Beatrice were wondering how that could be.

"That's the song my father always sang for us when we were little girls," she said to Beatrice, "So how can any of them say that that song was written for them?"

Beatrice approached one of the girls and said, "How can you say that song was written for you when we remember as little girls, our father always sang it to us?"

The girls moved away and mingled with the crowd, disappearing for the rest of the evening. That pleased Angelina and her cousin, and they tried their very best to have a chat with Domenic, Giuseppe and the rest of the boys playing the music with them.

However, Roberto and Simon soon realised that Angelina and her cousin were whispering to one another all the time and they wanted to know what it was all about. Was it necessary for them to find out what the whispering was all about? Did the girls have a secret? Or was it just girlish silliness? The brothers decided to keep an eye on them all the time, and they soon realised that they had become infatuated with the two young men, Domenic and Giuseppe. At the same time they could see that the young men didn't take any notice of Angelina and Beatrice, but treated them like all the other girls when they tried to speak to them.

The brothers then understood that they were just two young girls enjoying their fantasy and that wouldn't last long.

When the show was finished they all returned to the farm, the brothers worrying less about their young sister and their cousin.

As the days went by, Angelina's parents began to realise their daughter's mood was changing, more and more, and they couldn't understand the reason for it.

Renato said to his wife, "Mary, I need to know why our daughter is behaving so strangely." She agreed, so he called his son Simon and said, "We need to know. What is the matter with your sister? Your mother and I are very worried about her strange behaviour."

Simon said, "Father, why must I ask Angelina. You are her father and it is more appropriate for you to talk to her and find out what is troubling her. I hope she will be able to tell you, or Mum, or both. You have every right to know!" Simon started to walk away from his father, but Renato ran after him.

"Simon, wait a minute. I asked you because there is a chance she will confide in you more than she would in me. It's not easy for a young girl to talk to her parents."

Simon smiled, "Well, all right father, I will try, but I don't think she will tell me anything either."

Simon found the opportunity when he saw Angelina walking about the farm, all alone with a very sad face. He went up to her, and he asked, "Whatever's the matter with you, Angelina. We've all noticed, you're not the young sister we've come to know anymore?"

Angelina turned to her brother, cleared her throat and then said, "What do you mean I'm not the sister you've come to know?"

He looked at her for a minute and then he said, "Well it seems to me you're in a world of your own all the time."

"Oh, Simon, you're bothering me. Leave me alone." She said.

Now Simon was intrigued and wanted to know for himself what had happened to her.

He shouted at her saying, "No. I'm not going to leave you alone. I want to know. What is the matter with you?"

Angelina started to cry. "What's the point of me telling you, what the matter is? I know if I tell you, you will only burst out laughing."

This made Simon more determined than ever.

"Listen to me Angelina. Don't be ridiculous. I can see that this is not a laughing matter. You are unhappy and I want to know why?"

Angelina looked at her brother. She knew if she said anything to him it was likely that he would go and tell their parents and that would create more trouble than ever. She dried her eyes, and said,

"Look Simon, I don't understand what came over me, but I'm very sorry if my behaviour is not acceptable to you and our family. I promise I will do my very best not to upset my family anymore."

Simon realised then that she was not prepared to tell him anything. He patted her on the shoulder, and said, "Well whatever has happened remember that I'm here to help. You are my young sister, and I'm here to protect you all the time."

He knew very well that his sister was hiding something from him, but what?

Simon avoided his father after that because he knew how difficult it was for him and his wife to see Angelina so unhappy and he couldn't tell him anything even after trying his very best to find out.

Then he thought, perhaps he needed to have a chat with Beatrice. Maybe she could tell him the reason why Angelina had changed from a very happy and bubbly young girl to a very grumpy, young lady.

A few days later he saw Beatrice in the vegetable plot. She was there to pick some fresh vegetables for her Aunt Mary. He went up to her and finding her, as always, happy and smiling, he tried to make a lot of fuss of his cousin.

Beatrice said, "Hi cousin have you had a big win on the lottery?"

Simon was surprised. "What makes you think I could have won the lottery? You know our father doesn't give us any money for the things we really need. He certainly wouldn't give us the money to gamble on the lottery. I'm happy to see you are well and happy, but Angelina is not herself anymore. We think she might be ill. She won't tell us anything. You must have noticed that there is something wrong with her?"

Beatrice stopped what she was doing and looked at her cousin.

She said, "If I tell you the reason why Angelina is not well, you have to promise you will never, ever, tell anybody. If you do, it would only make things worse. That would upset her and all the family."

Simon, feeling that at last he was getting somewhere, said, "I promise you Beatrice. What you tell me today I will not tell anybody."

Beatrice put her hands on her face and gave a big sigh.

"Well then," she said, "The problem is with aunty and uncle, because they want Angelina to marry a farmer, when Angelina and I, both want to choose a man that we fall in love with."

Simon said, "But you are both too young to worry about things like that. You need to grow up, and then when the bell rings, you'll know who is the love of your life."

Beatrice's eyes lit up and she said, "But the bell has already rung, and it is very loud, especially in Angelina's case."

Simon looked at her and felt worried. "But this is impossible. She's far too young to understand what love is. And anyway who is this imaginary love?"

Beatrice said, "It's Domenic, the fellow with the guitar, but he doesn't know anything about Angelina being in love with him."

Simon laughed, "Is that all? Oh well, this is only teenager trouble and in no time at all, she will forget all about him. Before you know it, she will tell you she is in love with somebody else." And he walked away.

The next day while Simon was working on the farm, Renato went up to him and said, "I saw you talking to Beatrice. Did you have a chance to find out what was troubling your sister?"

Simon looked at his father and said, "Father, what I learned from Beatrice is that Angelina is just suffering from a teenage fantasy. There is nothing for us to worry about. Before we know, that will pass way and something else will crop up.''

The father folded his arms and walked away, murmuring to himself. Teenagers...teenagers, what she needs is a good telling off."

Chapter 28

Simon promised his father he would do whatever it took to find out what exactly was wrong with his daughter. Who was Domenic, the young man with the guitar, and why were the young girls attracted to him?

He went to the Town Hall to inquire about this new family that had come to live in their district, and what kind of property they held in the village now. He soon found out that Domenic's father was Mr Francesco, his wife, was Concetta, the oldest son was named Edward and the second son was Domenic. A young daughter, Marianna, was his youngest child.

However, that wasn't enough for Simon. He wanted to know about the family background. His visit to the Town Hall had told Simon, that the only information they had was that the family lived in the area of Naples, and had a villa there. The father had been the proprietor of many watermills, but because of the arrival of electricity, the watermill was no use to him anymore. Therefore he had decided to start a new activity, and now Mr Francesco was a merchant of forests.

Simon said thanked Mr Lorenzo, his informant, for his help and started to make his way out of the Town Hall office. Then the clerk, Mr Lorenzo called to him, "Just a minute," Simon turned around. "Why are you inquiring about Mr Francesco's family?" asked the clerk.

Simon touched his head with his hand in an affectation of concern, and said, "I met his son, Domenic in the church club, and I was interested. I'd never seen a young man play that musical instrument in such a way since Pasquale's sons left our village. Now out of nowhere this 'Domenic' appears."

Mr Lorenzo frowned, and said, "Simon, I do believe it is something more than that. I can read it in your eyes. You had a reason to come here and enquire about the position of Mr Francesco, now didn't you?"

Simon smiled and sighed. "You are right, as always. You know me so well. I can't ever tell you 'porkpies' can I? You know when I'm lying."

Mr Lorenzo patted him on the shoulder and said, "Come on Simon, spit it out. What is the real reason you've come here today to enquire about Mr Francesco and his family?"

Simon felt embarrassed, "Yes, you are right. I came here because my silly young sister has only met this young man about a couple of times, and now she doesn't eat or drink anymore. I've been told that the reason is because she's madly in love with this young man. If our father gets to know what I have just learned I don't know what will happen? My father has it in his mind that his precious daughter is only to marry a farmer and he thinks he already knows who this young man will be."

Mr Lorenzo, burst out laughing. "Okay Simon, today you have made my day. Go home. This secret will remain here with me."

Simon went home, and his father said, "Simon where have you been all this time?"

He faced his father nervously, and said, "Father I needed a long walk, and now I feel better for it."

His father was annoyed, "I don't understand you. I thought you knew better than that. Knowing your brother and I needed your help on the farm, you thought a long walk was much better than giving us a helping hand."

Simon's temper was rising and he shouted at his father, saying, "Father, I don't understand you. You asked me to find out all about Domenic's family and how do you expect me to do that if I don't make it my business to enquire about them?"

His father was taken aback for a moment, and then he said. "If that's the case, tell me all about it."

Simon related to his father what he had learned.

"Domenic is the second son of Francesco and his wife Concetta. They have an older son named Eduard, his second son is Domenic, and there is a young daughter

131

Marianna. He's a forestry merchant".

Renato drew in a sharp breath and his features tightened. "Well Domenic, he is certainly not the right man for my dear daughter. I know Angelina is a teenager; we've all been young once, and know what it's like to indulge in fantasies. We also know that it will probably pass like it does with all young people."

Simon said nothing. He just put his head down and concentrated on helping his brother with his work. Then he saw their neighbour coming towards them.

"Hello boys! I heard today that we now have a forest merchant with his family, living in our district and apparently he needs people to work for him. If that's true, it will be a good thing for us, to work and be able to support our families."

Renato said, "Oh, yes, I've already heard of this man. I would like to meet him and see what kind of man he is, have a chat with him."

Luigi, the neighbour said, "Oh, well, he lives in our district so no doubt you will have a chance to meet him one of these days."

He lifted his hand up and said, "Well I'll say goodbye to you for the time being, and I'll see you soon." He went away along the path singing softly.

Simon and Robert looked at one another, and Simon said to his brother, "What Mr Luigi told us today, I already knew that."

Robert looked surprised. "How can you know all about them when I often go to the village and have never seen or heard of anything about this new family?"

Simon said, "While you were digging the ground, I made it my business to find out about the new family in our village."

Robert looked at Simon and said, "Maybe because I'm the older one, our father gave me the responsibility of working with him, so I have no time like you, to go around with Angelina and cousin Beatrice and enjoy the music at the church club."

Simon did not reply. He continued digging. In the evening he had a chance to see his sister by herself, and he asked her,

"Angelina, do you remember Christmas Eve. While we were in the church club, two young men came to wish us a Merry Christmas. Then after that, they played music until the midnight service started?"

Angelina blushed, and she said, "What about them?"

Simon said knowingly, "I think you had met them before that."

Angelina looked at him and she said, "Yes, I had met them once or maybe twice before. If you think I had a chance to speak to them the answer is no! But I like one of them very much, and I will do whatever it takes to let him know I'm madly in love with him."

Simon looked her in the eye and said, "Angelina you have only seen him once, or twice and you don't know him or his family and now you tell me you are madly in love with him? You are very young to know what love is. And if our father gets to know about this, I do not know how he will deal with you."

She looked at Simon, and said boldly, "I'm not afraid, I'll take one step at a time."

Not knowing what to say, Simon walked away from her. He had no idea how their parents would react when they got to know how their daughter was thinking. He did think it might be wise to tell his mother before news reached their father, but he knew he needed to wait for the opportunity to see his mother alone.

A few days later Simon saw his mother by herself, in the kitchen.

He asked, "Mum, where's Dad?"

Maria answered "He went to the County Hall, to do some business. Why? Do you need him?"

"No Mum, I need to speak to you about Angelina before father gets to know what is troubling her."

Mary looked up at him and said, "Now what has she done?"

Simon gave a deep sigh. "Angelina will soon create a lot of problems for you and Dad, and it will affect us all.''

Mary experienced a stab of apprehension and tried to imagine what her daughter could have done to cause her brother such concern. Looked straight at her son she said, ''Simon, I don't understand. What are you trying to say?"

Simon was feeling very uncomfortable and was regretting his decision to get involved at all.

"Mother, what I mean is, that Angelina doesn't eat or drink anymore because she is in love.''

Mary was speechless, and after the shock she said, "But this is impossible. She is much too young for that. And if it is what you just said, how do you know that?''

Simon found it difficult to answer his mother because he knew it would be another shock for her, but he had no choice. He needed to let his mother know what was going on in their family before her husband found out.

"She has met a young man at the church club, but so far has only spoken a few words to him, and he doesn't know anything about how she feels towards him.''

Hearing this news about her teenage daughter caused Mary to explode.   "It's impossible. I can't believe it. She's too young to fall in love with a young man without knowing exactly who he is. Simon, if this is true it's senseless. It could only happen to a girl who is mad, but not to our dear daughter, Angelina. She has always been a very good child.''

Simon said, "Mother, most young people at this age start to create imaginary love. Hopefully, in time she will tell us she's forgotten all about her first crush and is madly in love with someone else. What we need to worry about is how father will react, because in his mind Angelina can only be allowed to marry a farmer. It will send him into a fury when Angelina refuses to listen to him, but he does need to come to terms with the fact that Angelina doesn't want marry a man chosen for her. When she is old enough she will choose the man she loves herself and father will just have to make the effort to understand the situation."

Simon saw that his mother had tears in her eyes.

"Mum, don't worry," he said, "Everything will be resolved in time."

Simon left her and went to find his brother. "Roberto, we have a problem with our young sister.''

Roberto raised his eyebrows in curiosity and waited for his brother to speak further. When he'd heard the explanation, he said, "Brother, don't worry about it. It will pass. Our father will realise that she is just a young girl and needs to 'eat much more bread' before she knows what love is.''

He turned his back on his brother and went out of the room.

Simon was very annoyed with his brother, and wondered how he could be quite sure his parents wouldn't tell him who to marry.

Their father was an obstinate old man. He wouldn't stop and think that he was once a young man himself and Simon was sure he wouldn't have allowed his parents to tell him who to marry. He never listened to anyone, so how he could he expect his children to listen to him now.

However, he thought, when Angelina comes out of her fantasy, she will realise that she can't fall in love with a man, when she knows nothing about him or his family. And when she is old enough to understand what love really means she will realise that the wrong choice could be disastrous not only for her, but also for all her family.

Chapter 29

Simon thought he needed to go and investigate more deeply into the background of Domenic and his family. There was a rumour in the village about a merchant in the area who needed men to work for him in the forest, cutting down trees and making sleepers for the railway. With the tree branches they were making charcoal to sell for domestic use.

Simon wanted to meet Domenic's father so he went to the village and asked a passer-by, "Please can you tell me where the family of the merchant lives, the merchant who needs men to work for him?"

The passer-by said to Simon, "It's not very far from here, just after the church club there is an office with a brown door. You knock there and you may find him or one of his sons there to help you."

The passer-by turned back and said, "But you are Simon, Renato's son, and if I'm not mistaken, you don't need a job."

Simon blushed "Well you never know what the future holds. I thought since I'm here now I will inquire."

The passer-by said, "Yes, you are right. It's always better to know what is available. You never know." The passer-by went on his way.

Simon eventually saw the brown door and he knocked. A young girl came to open it.

Simon said, "My name is Simon and I would like to speak to one of your family."

The young girl called out, "Eduard, a man is here to see you."

He answered, "Well, ask him come in."

The young girl took him to her brother. Eduard lifted his head from his work and said, "How can I help you?"

Simon blushed again. "I heard that you need men to work for you."

Edward scratched his head and said, "Yes, we need two

men for manual work. But wait a minute. I think I know who you are. My brother told me he met you at the vineyard when all the members of the village came to help your father gather the grapes, and he told me what a wonderful time they all had. He mentioned the banquet your mother had prepared for them after they finished the gathering of the grapes. My brother Domenic couldn't stop talking about what a wonderful woman your mother is.''

While they were speaking, Domenic came into the office.

Eduard turned to him saying, ''Domenic look who is here.''

Domenic was speechless at first and then said, "Simon it's very nice to see you here, but how can we help you?''

Simon was so embarrassed. He waved his hand nonchalantly and then said, "Well, I heard we have a new merchant in our district that needs people to work for him, and I came to enquire what it is all about.''

Domenic realised there must be another reason for Simon to be there but he couldn't think what it was. He knew Simon's father was always short of labour and had ask for help from the people of the village, so how could it be that the son had come here to enquire about possible work?

However Domenic smiled and said, ''It is nice to see you. The last time we met was in the church club. You were with your friends, and your sister and cousin.''

Simon said, "Oh yes, but we only spoke for a few minutes and we didn't have enough time to introduce ourselves.''

Domenic said, "Well, Simon, next week my friends and I will be having a concert in the church club and it would be very nice if you and your friends, and maybe your sister and cousin could come and join us.''

Simon answered, "That's very kind of you, Domenic. If we are free, of course we would all like to come, providing our parents allow us. I'm sure we will all enjoy hearing you and your friends' music.''

Simon then shook hands with Domenic and his brother Eduard and he left to go back to the farm. When he returned home, his brother, Robert, asked him, "Where have you been?"

Simon answered." I've been in the village, to find out more about Domenic and his family."

"Have you?" Robert said to his brother.

"Well, I have done better than you," he said.

Simon was puzzled." What do you mean, you've done better than me?"

Robert laughed, "This morning I woke up with a toothache, and I decided to go to the village of Mignano to see if the dentist would see to my tooth. I sat next to two middle aged women and I couldn't help hearing the conversation they were having."

"One of the ladies said, "Do you know Caterina, a few days ago I came here to make an appointment with Doctor Wilson. Today I've come here and I have been told by the receptionist that he is not available."

Aileen replied, "I'm not surprised. Doctor Wilson has been needed in court again for the last few days."

"Catarina nearly jumped out of her chair. "What do you mean he was needed to attend the court again?"

Aileen said, "Oh Catarina. I'm astonished. You live in this village and you tell me you don't know what happened here a few months ago?"

Catarina couldn't understand what her friend was talking about.

Aileen said, "You know as well as I do, today to be a dentist, or a doctor doesn't mean you can make a living just on your profession because only very rich people can afford to go to see doctors or dentists. With the deep recession we are in, the poor people just can't afford to see them. For that reason the doctors don't have many patients and struggle to make a living. Therefore some of them need take other work to keep up the living standards they had before the War and the Spanish fever."

Catharina said. "Okay, I know all that, but you didn't

tell me yet why Doctor Wilson needed to go to the court.''

Her friend Aileen said, "This is a long story, but I will try to tell you what I know. Doctor Wilson, besides being a dentist, is also a merchant. He buys whatever he thinks he can trade to make a deal. You know in this district there is the Town Hall, and we have a mountain and a big forest nearby. When the trees of the forest are ready to be cut the head of the administration puts the forest up for auction. Then the one who bids the most money is the one who will get the forest. Doctor Wilson wanted to buy the forest. His intention was to buy the forest and employ the local people of the village to cut the trees and then to export the wood, but there were many more people at the auction, and one of these men was Mr Francesco Di' Catto, and he was the most successful bidder. The Doctor was very disappointed because he couldn't bid more than Mr Francesco Di' Catto, and he was even more upset because Mr Francesco Di' Catto came from a different district, and the doctor felt he had no right to acquire the forest of Mignano.''

Still looking puzzled, Catharina said "I still can't understand why the doctor needed to go to the court.''

Aileen said, "The reason the doctor needed to go to court was because one day a man came to his surgery with a very bad eye. The doctor asked the patient how it happened and the man answered,

''Today is the first day I started work in the forest of Mignano. While I was cutting a tree a piece of wood went in my eye.''

The doctor asked him, "Who is your employer?''

The man replied "Mr Francesco Di' Catto.''

The doctor said, "Your eye is very badly damaged, and I can't do anything about it.'' And he asked him, "How many children do you have?'' The man replied, "Twelve, sir.'' The doctor thought for a minute and then he said, "Well, did Mr Francesco Di' Catto pay the insurance for you?'' The man replied, "He couldn't have done because I just started work today, and I didn't have any documents to give to him to register me.''

The Doctor laughed, "Ha....ha you don't know how much that pleases me, because now he is the one who needs to support you and also all your children until they come of age.''

The man was very upset, because he knew he wasn't able to work any longer, but at the same time he felt sorry for his employer, knowing it wasn't his employer's fault.

When Mr Francesco Di' Catto learned what had happened he flew into a rage. He knew now he was ruined for life. He knew the doctor very often went to his friend's house in the evening, to play a game of cards, and when he finished, he would return to his own house. So one night, Mr Di' Catto, waited for the doctor to came out of his friend's house, and then hit him on the head with an iron bar.

The police arrested Mr Di' Catto, but not for long. The family applied for bail on his behalf. His first son Eduard always needed to be alongside his father in every court session because his father was illiterate. Meanwhile his young brother, Domenic needed to work alongside his employees.''

Roberto said. "You see, brother, without any effort, I found out much more about this family than you have, and without anybody's help."

Simon, said, "I'm amazed how you happened to hear all that, in the Doctor's surgery in Mignano through these two ladies gossiping about that poor family's situation. I'm astonished that the people of this village don't know anything about their neighbour.''

Roberto said, ''Now you know all about Domenic's family, what you think about them?''

Simon answered, "I think that is nothing to do with us. Actually, I feel very sorry about the way these two women were gossiping about the incident."

"So, what about Angelina?" asked Roberto.

Simon said, "Angelina needs be told that she can't fall in love with a young man she doesn't know, and also doesn't know about his family either. That is not on. I personally think in time she will meet somebody else and she'll forget all about this young man with his guitar.''

They both laughed.

"Simon," said Roberto. "Next week I'm sure our priest is expecting us to cut some branches of olive trees for the religious ceremony on Palm Sunday. As you know, a procession will go round the village streets carrying the olive branches, with everyone praying and singing, 'Hosanna, Hosanna to the King of Kings', and other religious songs as they walk round.''

He continued, "I expect our mother will also want us to put out the big long table so that our priest can come and bless it before she puts the food on the table. Then later, when mother, with the help of Angelina and Beatrice, have prepared all the Easter dishes to place on the big table, the priest will come to bless it. Then she will cover the table with a white table cloth and she will thank the priest and give him a basket of eggs for Easter."

Simon said thoughtfully, "I do hope mother doesn't have any trouble with Angelina because she really needs both girls to help her to prepare the menu for Easter Sunday.''

Roberto was puzzled and he said, '' Simon what do you mean Mum could have trouble with Angelina?''

Simon made a gesture with his hands, and said, "What I mean is that these days Angelina is very difficult, and Mum needs help from both girls. Can you imagine how much food she needs to prepare for all our family, and then mother's family? If that is not enough, our father has also invited all his relatives, and of course the Easter menu is not an easy one. Some of the dishes take a very long time to prepare.''

"Well if necessary, we might need to step in and do whatever mother asks from us,'' said his brother.

Simon looked at his brother and said, "Do you know what mother said a few days ago? She said in Holy week most people fast from Holy Friday to Easter Sunday.''

Roberto replied, "This is exaggerated. Not everybody

fasts. Some do, and some don't. I can only manage one day, and sometimes none at all.''

Roberto and Simon were amazed and relieved, to see Angelina and Beatrice, helping Mary in the kitchen for two days in perfect harmony in every possible way. After Mary had put all the beautiful food on the table, even the priest was astonished to see all those beautiful dishes full with traditional food cooked by Mary with the help of the young people.

On Easter Sunday morning the bells of the church rang out to tell the people of the village to rejoice for the dear Lord Jesus had risen from the dead.

All the people went to church to hear Mass and, returning home, all sat round the table with the head of the family giving thanks to The Lord and blessing all his family and the relatives sitting round the table, rejoicing for Easter Day.

Chapter 30

On Easter Monday, there was a tradition that most people filled a basket with good food and go into the country for a picnic. Usually, the young people organise a big concert and many go to listen to the music and have a good time.

When Angelina and her cousin heard about the concert, they began to get very excited, knowing that it was likely that Domenic and Giuseppe would be there. Better still, they would be the ones playing music with their friends on stage.

Roberto said to his brother, Simon, "Oh, that's why Angelina and Beatrice were so helpful. They must have known something about the concert. Without a doubt the girls would do whatever it took to get our parents' permission to go to that concert."

So then, Mary called her two sons and said,

"Roberto and Simon, you know that today is the traditional countryside picnic? You probably know too that there is a concert not very far from here. I'm sure your sister and Beatrice would like to go. If that's the case, you need to go with them."

The brothers groaned, and said , "Ok, mother, if that is what you want us to do. We'll go to the concert and take the girls with us. Perhaps John and Jimmy can come with us too."

Mary said, "Yes, why not, the more you are together the better it is."

Not long after the mother had spoken to her sons, they saw Angelina and Beatrice running towards them with their arms up in air, screaming and saying, "Roberto, Simon, this afternoon, there's a big concert not far from us and we want go. We're sure our parents will only let us go if you come with us."

Simon said, "Ok, we will take you there, but you have to promise you will both behave yourselves."

Angelina smiled, "Of course we will behave

ourselves.''

Roberto looked at his brother and said, "Simon did you notice anything?"

Simon answered, "Yes, Angelina is very excited because she knows Domenic will be there with his friends.''

Roberto laughed, "Well, I expect his fans will be there to cheer him, and I can assure you, that will make Angelina very jealous, because he will appreciate all the fuss that the other girls will make over him.''

Simon said, "I do hope Angelina will come to her senses and forget all about this young man. It will be much easier for our parents because in their minds they will only let the girls marry farmers.''

Roberto said "I'm not so sure. I have been told that love at first sight mostly has a happy ending.''

Simon said,'' Yes, I do hope that's so in Angelina's case. In time, as she grows older, she will forget all about this young man and his guitar.''

They both laughed, and said, ''Come on, let's go and see if these two young girls are ready for us to take them to this concert.''

A few minutes later Angelina and Beatrice came running downstairs, yelling, "We're ready and we need to hurry up, otherwise we'll be late for the concert.''

Robert said, "We've been waiting for you. Have you brought some pullovers with you? You may need them later on, when it gets cold.''

They both answered, ''Yes,'' in chorus.

"Mother has made sure we have enough pullovers with us, and money if we need it,'' said Angelina.

Both girls jumped happily into the carriages but as they travelled along the road they realised that John and Jimmy were there waiting for them. The brothers pulled the reins of the horse to stop, and let John and Jimmy climb on their carriage.

"Thank you all for inviting us," said Jimmy.

Simon, said, "We've been told that there are some very

talented players who are going to be there today. Some of them play classical music and others play opera. We also have been told that some of the young musicians appreciate it if the audience join together to sing with them, and there will be dancing all around the grounds to make this Easter Monday more enjoyable for young and old alike."

As they approached the concert they could hear that the band was already playing loud music and the audience were joining in. Some people were already dancing round the grounds to the beat of the music. They noticed most of the audience were very young people. Roberto and Simon were looking for a place to sit down, but they noticed there was nowhere, and everyone was standing up, clapping their hands and dancing.

Then suddenly, Domenic and Giuseppe appeared from nowhere, and came up to them. "Hello Simon, and Roberto, how nice to see you here with your friends and family."

Roberto lifted his hand in response and said, "We're very pleased that you and your friends are here too. We can see that most of the people are very young, and that most of them dancing all the time, but we would just like to find a place where we can sit down to enjoy the music while we have a picnic."

Domenic and Giuseppe laughed. Then Domenic said, "If you look around you'll see there is plenty of room and if you have a rug with you to put on the grass, you can sit down and have the picnic. At the same time you can all join in with the music when you are ready to sing and dance."

Roberto and Simon smiled, and said, "Yes, while we have the picnic we will listen to the music, and later we'll join in with the crowd and enjoy ourselves."

While they were sitting down with their picnic they heard a young girl scream and, looking out into the park, they saw Domenic with his guitar, with his other friends, singing a song with the words 'She was too young to fall in love, and I was too young to know'.

Angelina burst out crying because she thought it was meant for her. It took the brothers a long time to get her to understand that it was just a popular song in the charts and it meant nothing.

The concert went on and on and, as predicted by the brothers, the girls were jealous at the fuss Domenic and Giuseppe received from the many young girls who were in the show and as well as many other girls in the audience.

Speaking for them both, John said to Roberto and Simon, "This is ridiculous! We've both had enough of watching the behaviour of these girls. It's not worth us staying a minute longer than necessary. We want to go home."

The brothers agreed, "You're right. It's time for us all to go home.''

Angelina and Beatrice were disappointed, but they knew they had no choice but to obey their brothers and follow them to their carriage to go home.

The next day, Mary asked the girls, "Angelina and Beatrice when you came home last night it seemed to me you didn't enjoy the concert at all... what happened?''

Angelina said, "The music they played was very boring. There were many girls there and when the young musicians played, they screamed and screamed and made a lot of noise. The musicians made a fuss of them, but not of us. They didn't pay any attention whatever to us, no matter how much we tried to bring their attention towards us. They just didn't look our way, and that wasn't fair.'' Mary understood and said, "My dear girls, if there were so many of you there it would have been impossible for them to give attention to everybody. Be sensible now. Angelina was very annoyed. She slammed the door, and was going towards her bedroom when she met Simon.

He said, "Whatever is the matter with you. Even if we gave you all our attention, for you, it is never enough. For example yesterday we made a big effort for the two of you. We even took John and Jimmy to make sure you wouldn't get bored with just the two of us, but no, you don't even like them.''

Angelina raised her voice and said, "Simon that is enough! If you want to know the truth, I only wanted to go to see the concert because I hoped Domenic and Giuseppe would be there, and they would notice we were there to support them, but no, they didn't notice as at all. Oh yes, they made a lot of fuss of all the other girls, but they didn't even acknowledge us, and Beatrice tried very hard to let them know we were there to support them, and for that we are very annoyed with them.''

But Simon and Angelina didn't know that Renato was round the corner of the house and he heard all that Angelina said to her brother. He followed Angelina upstairs and said, "Angelina, why have you been arguing with your brother Simon?''

Angelina didn't really like to tell her father about the concert. She knew it would make more trouble for her and her cousin Beatrice, knowing his expectations for them both. "Dad, there is nothing for you to worry about.''

Then she walked away from him. He was annoyed but he thought it was better to leave her alone for the time being. He would eventually find out from his wife or from his sons what was going on.

Two days later he was sitting with his wife on the terrace when he said, "Mary, two days ago, after Easter Monday, I saw Simon and Angelina having a very unpleasant conversation. It was the sort of conversation that you wouldn't like to see between brother and sister. Do you know what it was all about?''

His wife blushed, and answered, ''How can I possibly know what is going on with these two young people?''

He looked at her and said, "Come on Mary, I know for a fact that mothers always know much more than fathers.''

Mary looked at him and she said, "Go on with you, maybe if you sat down with your family and listened to them they might have more confidence in you, and they might surprise you at how easy it is to discover what troubles them.''

Renato lifted his arms up in the air and went out of the room, uttering a few words to himself. After a few days however, he was curious to know what was going on in his family, and thought it was time for him to find out what was troubling them. So he called both his sons and said. "Roberto, Simon, I heard that in the village we have a new family. What do you know about them?"

Simon answered, "Yes father. The father is a merchant and he has a wife and two sons and a young daughter.''

The father said, "I have been told one of their sons is a very good businessman, and the other one works and supervises his father's employees, but is the opposite of his brother Eduard."

"Well, father," answered Simon, "The younger brother's name is Domenic and the young girls of the village are all excited, because he is very good looking and he plays music just like Pasquale's sons did when they were here.''

Renato's mouth twisted a little as he spoke again. "You boys need to keep an eye on our girls for us. I wouldn't like to think of them getting infatuated with this young fellow.''

Simon couldn't help saying, "I'm afraid it's too late father. Angelina has already met him, and I think she likes him, but the good thing is he doesn't know anything about it. Of course, Angelina is not the only one feeling like this. Nearly all the girls of the village feel exactly the same.''

Renato said, "Then you boys definitely need to look after your sister and your cousin. We are farm people and we only want what is the best for the girls and our family, do you understand me?''

Robert and Simon looked at one another and said, "Yes, father we can only try."

A few days later, Angelina said to her parents. "Mum, next week is Pentecost day (Whit Sunday) and we need to gather flowers to decorate the road for the procession which will go around the village. You know we must take a part in this special event because it's important for us to do the utmost for our church.''

While Angelina and her cousin were trying to have a conversation with Mary, Simon burst into the sitting room and said, "What is going on here?"

"Simon whatever is the matter with you? She asked.

He answered, "Mother, I hope Angelina and Beatrice don't ask you about me accompanying them to the dance in the church club, because as you know, father said that Roberto or I need to go with them wherever they want to go. We have been working all day, while those two girls only think about going out and enjoying themselves. Well that's not on with me, or my brother.''

Mary understood the frustration that the brothers suffered by having to accompany their sister and their cousin everywhere, after they'd worked hard all day in the fields.

She answered, "But this time you are wrong Simon. Your sister was only asking me if she and Beatrice could go into garden and the fields to gather flowers for decorating the village streets, to celebrate Whit Sunday.''

He lifted his arms in frustration, and said, "That is news to me. Now they need to gather the flowers. Surely there are more than enough people in the village who could do that. Why is it that we are always needed more than anybody else?''

Then she knew he was very tired. She looked at him, and said. All right, Simon, don't worry. We understand. Go into your room and have a rest. I know that tomorrow you and your brother will have a very hard day.''

The girls looked at Mary, and Angelina said, "Mother, why does our father insist Roberto or Simon need to escort us wherever we go?''

Mary said, "I don't know how to tell you this, but the point is you are both very young to be going out by yourselves. There is a lot of danger out there.''

Angelina looked at her mother and said, "Mother, we are young but we aren't silly. We know you and our father have a fixation on not letting us go out by ourselves in case we meet a stranger but we have already met one. It's not what you think. He is a good man, but he is not interested in me and that is it.''

The mother suddenly felt very apprehensive and then she said, "That is the reason why your father and I are very concerned about your future.''

Before the mother could finish what she was trying to say Angelina slammed the door and ran out of the house. Beatrice heard the door bang and went into the sitting room where her aunt was embroidering the name on something for the bottom drawer for her daughter. Beatrice went in and said, "Auntie, I heard the door slam, what is going on?''

Maria didn't know how to answer. She folded her arms and said, "It's the same old story. You youngsters don't understand how much we worry about your future. We only want what is best for you all, especially as Angelina doesn't do anything else but rebel at everything we say.''

Beatrice gave her a strange look and said, "Because we are young doesn't mean we don't appreciate the love and good intentions you have for us. What we can't understand is why we can't choose the man we will fall in love with? Why do we have to marry someone we don't love?"

Mary was surprised at her niece's answer. "Beatrice, you have been here with us since you were a very little girl. We love you like we love Angelina, and that is the reason why we would like you and your cousin to have a better future."

"Auntie, I do understand that you love us," said Beatrice, "You and Uncle want what is the best for us, but what would you have said, if your mother had come to you and told you not to marry Uncle Renato, but the man they had chosen for you, because they believed he would be the best one for your future?"

Her aunt was flustered and didn't know how to answer her niece. She drew in a deep sigh and said, "We didn't have the same opportunities you both have now. Our parents had many children and every one of us just had to get on and marry the person we liked, but that didn't mean we made no mistakes. I was fortunate that I met and liked Renato, but many others had a very poor life and we would like to prevent an unhappy marriage for you two."

Beatrice looked at her aunt and said, "But if we do make a mistake and we have a poor life, then we can't blame anybody but ourselves, otherwise we could blame our parents for our bad fortune."

The aunt give another deep sigh: and said, "It is no use talking to you now, because you are both very young, but we will have this conversation when you are both old enough to understand."

Beatrice smiled and said, "Auntie, I see you are making some beautiful embroidery, what is it?"

The aunt looked at her niece, and said, "This is a sheet for Angelina's bottom drawer, and I will do the same for you. What I'm making is very simple, but for more sophisticated ones I need to ask the Nuns of Santa Catherina. They can do marvellous work for special brides like you and Angelina when the time comes."

Beatrice was speechless. She just waved her hand to her aunt and went out of the room, to go and look for her cousin. After a long search, she found Angelina sitting near the pond and she seemed to be very upset.

Beatrice shouted, "Angelina, I've been searching for you for ages, and here you are. What came over you?"

Angelina turned round and said to her cousin, "You ask what came over me? You jolly well know. I'm fed up with my parents. They keep on and on, about our future and you know that makes me very stressed. There is not a day that goes by without the mention of our future. I have heard that the American government has opened their ports. If I had 100 lire I would willingly run to America."

Beatrice laughed, "Well first you are not old enough, second you haven't any money, and third what about Domenic?"

Angelina answered, "You have some idea about my

151

feelings towards him, but as far as I know I'm only a good friend to him.''

Beatrice smiled. "Angelina, it's about time you stopped worrying about your parents. As we said before, we will not allow them to make us marry the man of their choice. Anyway, have you forgotten what we need to do?''

Chapter 31

Angelina gave her cousin a strange look and then said, "What do you mean, have I forgotten? What have I forgotten?"

Beatrice was getting exasperated with her cousin. She said, "Next Sunday is Pentecost Day. It is our duty to gather as many rose petals as possible for our church. Don't you remember when we were little girls, after the evening service we had to go to Sunday catechism?"

Angelina answered, "Of course I remember, how could I forget?"

Beatrice said, "Then you know how important it is to keep up our traditions."

Angelina said, "I remember the Sunday school teacher told us all about Pentecost day. She said, "About forty days after Easter the disciples were gathered together in an upper room, and they were all sitting down. Suddenly there came a sound from heaven as of a rushing mighty wind, which filled the room. And then tongues of fire appeared that came and sat upon their heads. They were all filled with the Holy Spirit, and began speaking with each other in different languages."

Beatrice said, "Our tradition is to follow what we have been taught. The priest will organise the people of the parish to cover the road with petals of roses and other flowers so that the procession with the Corpus Domini(the Sacred Host) will walk on it."

"That is what I remember, and now let us get on and gather as many flowers as we can, as that is part of our duty."

Angelina picked up the basket that Beatrice was holding and said, "All right, let's start!"

Together they went into the rose garden on the farm, where Mary had a special interest in roses, and also many other flowers. They didn't have enough to fill the baskets they had with them, so Beatrice said,

"How about, if we go into the cornfields and look for flowers. Before the harvest there are lots of poppies in flower, and they are red so they're just right for our needs."

Angelina said, "Why not? I think that's a good idea, but we need to be very careful not to damage the corn, otherwise there will be more problems for us."

They both had a good laugh and off they went.

After an hour or two the baskets were full to the brim. They went home, very excited to show their parents what they had achieved. Mary was very happy, but Renato was more concerned about the possibility of his corn being damaged.

He said, "Girls, for your sakes, I hope you haven't damaged the corn, otherwise you will need to go to church and pray to the Good Lord for safety!"

The girls folded their arms and Angelina spoke for them both. She said, "If we did, we have very good protection from the One above. He knows that we have done our best and we took every precaution not to damage the corn".

The church club was held every week and was very enjoyable for the young people. For Domenic it had become a very sad time, because he had been called to do his National Service. However, his friend Giuseppe was not fit for the army. Most girls of the village were all around Domenic saying, "You will write to me, while another one tried to tear her hair out saying "No, he will write only to me and not to anybody else."

Angelina was broken hearted. She stood quietly and wasn't able to go and express her feelings for him, or be comforted by her cousin. She went home and shut herself in her bedroom, refusing to have any contact with her family, except her most faithful cousin. Now her family realised how deep her attraction was for that young man. At the same time they were happy, for now he was far away there was the possibility that she would forget all about him, and John had a chance to conquer her heart.

With the passing of time, Angelina began to accept that she had no chance of knowing to which part of Italy he had been sent, to do his National Service. Once a year he could have two weeks' leave.

Then one day Beatrice received a letter postmarked from the Alpine province of La Spezia. Beatrice was disturbed to receive a letter from the Alps. She kept looking at the envelope and tried to remember what she had been taught in Geography at school. Then she hid the letter under her pillow and crept into the bedroom where her Uncle and Aunt were asleep. She tip-toed to the desk, took his pen knife, and quickly returned to her bedroom. Before she opened it, she first made sure that Angelina was sleeping, then with great care she opened the envelope, and saw that inside the envelope there was another one addressed to Angelina.

Beatrice was taken aback, and very carefully she went over to Angelina's bed and gently tried to wake her up. Angelina didn't like to be disturbed, and said, "Beatrice, will you please leave me alone."

Beatrice put her finger to her lips and said softly, "Keep quiet! I have something for you."

Angelina lifted her head and said, ''Oh don't be silly, whatever's come over you?''

Beatrice said, "There's a letter for you. Let's open it and see who it's from".

"Angelina's hand began to tremble and as she opened it and then she gave a very loud squeal of excitement. Luckily enough her parents didn't hear.

"Oh Beatrice, I can't believe it. It's from Domenic."

Beatrice nearly fainted but managed to pull herself together and said, "Read it out, but quietly, otherwise uncle and auntie might hear you, and that would be disastrous."

The letter said:

'Dear Angelina. Here I am at the top of the Alps; it is a

beautiful place, but I can't help missing the church club, and Giuseppe, and you and Beatrice and not to mention my guitar, and my accordion. I look forward to being on leave so that we can all have a good time together. Please write to me, and tell me the news from our village and all the gossip going round, which I miss so much. I send love to you both.

Domenic'

Angelina said, "The letter is very short but very nice. I'm astonished, I wasn't expecting that! I wonder if he has written to all the other girls who begged him to write to them."

Beatrice said, "Yes, the letter is very brief but it's a start. You never know what the future holds. But it's important that nobody in our family gets to know anything about this letter or any other ones if more arrive."

Angelina was very happy and she said, "Tomorrow, I will write to him and say how happy I was to receive his news, and how wise of him to address the letter to you and not to me directly."

Beatrice said, "It was very good thinking, and he must continue to do so in the future."

Angelina smiled, ''Oh Beatrice I'm so happy because he wrote to me. It makes me think he's not completely indifferent to me. I do hope in future we'll have a chance to get to know one another better, and maybe fall in love with one another."

Beatrice smiled, "But you don't need to fall in love with Domenic because you are already in love with him. He is the one who needs to fall in love with you."

Angelina said, "You're right. I loved him from the day I first met him. Tomorrow I will write a letter to him, but I promise you I will not let him know my feelings towards him, otherwise there is a chance he might not write to me anymore, and then....?"

Beatrice smiled, walked away towards the terrace and

then she said, "Why are you waiting for tomorrow? Do it today!"

Angelina went into her father's room, opened his desk, and took out some writing paper and an envelope. Then she went back into her room to write the letter:

'Cave Of Conca Campania
24-July 1925

Dear Domenic,

When Beatrice came into my room with a letter in her hand, we were mystified about the contents and then surprised and delighted when we opened it and saw another envelope inside with my name on it. . When I opened my letter I started to get excited to read that you are at the top of the Alps. Thank you very much for writing to me. In the village all the young people are missing you, including us, and Giuseppe.

Since you left us, the church club has not been the same. Everybody is missing your music. People can't stop saying that since you left they feel an emptiness in the village, and we agree with them. Now we look forward to when you come on leave. We know it is for a short time only, but also we know it is not forever. While you are here our village will come to life again for me and Beatrice, and Giuseppe.

It was very sensible of you to address the letter to Beatrice, otherwise there was a chance that one of my family might have opened it, and I do not know if they would have given it to me. If they hadn't it would have been a pity because your letter is very special to me and Beatrice and Giuseppe. Everybody is missing you, especially me.

All my love to you, my dear Domenic, and also love from Beatrice.
Angelina. '

Before she closed the letter she thought she'd let Beatrice read what she had written to Domenic. But just then Mary came into her room and Angelina hastily tried to hide the letter. Her mother realised that something was going on and she asked Angelina what she was doing.

"What is the matter with you," she said.

Angelina shook her head, "Nothing mother." She said.

Maria gave her suspicious look and said, "You are trying to hide something from me."

Angelina's face was full of defiance as she faced her mother.

"Now mother, whatever could I possibly be hiding from you?"

Mary was very suspicious and curious too.

"What is that envelope you just had in your hand?"

"Oh mother, it's nothing for you to worry about."

While that was going on Beatrice came in from the terrace, and said, "Angelina, I need to write to my cousin and I left the envelope somewhere but I don't remember where I put it."

Angelina said "Here you are, I found it on your bed."

Beatrice quickly snatched the envelope from Angelina's hand, and left the room before Mary could say anything. She knew the girls were up to something, but what was it? As she left Angelina's room, she was shaking her head and muttering to herself.

Beatrice was out posting the letter, to make sure that her aunt didn't find out that Angelina had received a letter from the merchant's son, who was now doing military service and in the Italian Alps. Meanwhile, Angelina was worrying where her cousin had taken the letter she'd written to Dominic.

Half an hour later Beatrice returned home. She entered very quietly, to make sure no one in the family knew she had been out. Angelina was feeling uncomfortable. She had wanted Beatrice to read the letter before it was posted to Domenic.

Beatrice opened the bedroom door very quietly and

carefully. Angelina jumped and said, "Beatrice where have you been? I was very concerned about you, and by the way what has happened to the letter I gave to you when mother was here?"

Beatrice laughed, "I went to post it of course. Did you want Auntie to find out about the letter you had in your hand?"

Angelina was surprised. "But I wanted you to read it before it was sent."

Beatrice laughed again, "Do you think I'm silly? Of course I have read what you wrote and I changed the envelope and I rewrote the address, closed it again and posted it."

Angelina sighed with a sense of relief, "Oh thank you, Beatrice. I don't know how I would manage without your help."

Beatrice said, "We have been together most of our lives, but the day will come when we grow old, and maybe we will have our own family and live away from one another with many children."

Angelina said, "Maybe so, but we will never, ever forget one another. We are not just cousins, we are much more like two sisters."

A few days later, Beatrice spotted the postman coming towards her and she ran to meet him to prevent him coming near the house, in case he had post for her. The family would be very curious to know what it was all about. In fact, the postman said, "Miss, I have a letter for you."

Beatrice smiled and went towards him, saying "Thank you."

She took the letter, and hid it in her basket as she walked towards the vegetable garden, where Angelina was gathering some vegetables for her mother, to make a vegetable soup. Beatrice looked all around to make sure there was nobody about who could see or hear what they said. Then she went very near to her and said, "Angelina, I have a surprise for you."

Angelina began to get very excited and Beatrice said, "Angelina behave yourself. Somebody might hear us. Let's go away from here; and go somewhere where there is no chance that anyone will see or hear us."

Angelina said, ''Beatrice, where is it?''

Beatrice put her finger on Angelina's mouth and said "Be quiet! Let's sit down near this oak tree away from the farm house."

Then Beatrice opened Domenic's letter and gave it to Angelina. The letter said,

'Dear Angelina

I can't describe my excitement when I read the news of our village, and how all of you have been missing my music. I'm also missing you all... but the consolation is that after three months I will be back on leave for two weeks and after two years of service I will be back forever. To be a soldier is very hard, but at the same time very good that you learn to obey every word the Captain tells you, and if you don't you will be punished very hard. When it is time for dinner one of the soldiers calls us with his trumpet, loud enough to be heard all round the mountain, then says, ''Whether you are rich or poor, the soup is ready, come and get it.'' While we were all sitting at table and starting to eat, one of the soldiers stood up and said, ''Sir it is impossible for me to eat this soup.'' The Captain went up to the soldier and asked, "Why?" The soldier said, ''Sir there is a little bit of earth in my soup." The Captain laughed and then looked all around the other tables and said, "Listen all of you. This soldier is complaining, saying he can't eat the soup because he found a little bit of earth in it. What he doesn't realize is that he has come here to defend our country and to do so you all need to get on and eat whatever is put in front of you.'' The soldier stood up and said, ''Sir, I know we came here to defend our country but we didn't come here to eat the country.'' And all the soldiers laughed.

That was one of many things we have to put up with in our situation, and at the same time it is hard, but I like it. I have missed my family and my friends, and especially you Angelina, and also your cousin Beatrice, and my friend Giuseppe, not to mention my guitar. I look forward to the day when I'm on leave and with you all in the church club. We will have good times again. I need to go now because we have to march and train for tomorrow's show in the village down below the mountain.

All my love to you my dear Angelina, and Beatrice and Giuseppe.'

Angelina and Beatrice laughed to read about the soldier pointing out to the Captain about the earth in his food. And above all that he was looking forward to the time when he would be on leave and with them and all his other friends again, playing the guitar and having good times like before he had left for the army.

Angelina said, "I will write to him now."

Beatrice started laughing, "Angelina, make sure auntie or anybody else doesn't see you write. If they see you, they will want to know who you are writing to, and if they realize it is Domenic, I do not know what will happen to us."

"Oh Beatrice, of course I will be very careful. I know that if my father comes to know anything about Domenic I'm afraid we will both be in deep trouble."

Chapter 32

Angelina was in the vegetable garden while Beatrice was looking for her in the rest of the farm. At last she spotted her coming towards her.

"I have been searching for you, where have you been?" said Beatrice.

"I was in the vegetable garden, gathering some carrots and onions and any other vegetables I could find for making soup. Mother needs to make the soup for this evening so let's sit under the oak tree, and talk about Domenic and Giuseppe."

"Then after a while Angelina said, "Oh Beatrice, I think we'd better make our way home now or Mum will send Simon to look for us. If that happens, I think he will never stop interrogating us until he finds out the reason why we are sitting here under this oak tree.''

They began to run, and ran until they were out of breath and needed to sit down and rest. Then they realized Simon was walking along the path nearby and had spotted the girls sitting down and catching their breath.

He stopped and he couldn't understand what was wrong with both of them. Why were they here and not where they should have been, in the vegetable garden.

He came over to them. "Whatever is the matter with you two?'' He asked.

Angelina spoke, "We just fancied going for a walk.''

That didn't go down well with Simon. He made a gesture with his hand in dismissal of her explanation. "If I have heard right, our mother asked vegetables for the soup tonight.'' you to go and gather some

Angelina was annoyed with her brother, and she said, "You heard right, but since Mother doesn't need to make this soup until tonight, we thought we had plenty of time to go for a walk .Is there anything else you want to know?''

Simon gave Angelina a peculiar look and walked away.

Later on Angelina asked her mother where Simon was.

"I sent him to the village to do some shopping for me," said Mary.

Soon after that Angelina spotted her brother coming from the village and could see that he seemed distracted as if he had something on his mind and was trying to avoid her. He went into the kitchen, where Mary was making minestrone with the vegetables Angelina had gathered earlier from the vegetable garden.

He went up to his mother and gently tapped her on the shoulder indicating that he had something very important to tell her, but at the same time not wanting anybody else to hear.

Angelina was curious about her brother's behaviour and very quietly hid behind the kitchen door straining to hear what her brother was trying to say to his mother. She saw him sit next to his mother's chair in the kitchen and began to quietly whisper to her about the church club and the merchant's son. She could just hear what he was saying.

"Mother, Domenic was called to do his military service and in the church club there isn't anyone else who can play the guitar like him, so all the young people were feeling very sorry for themselves."

Mary answered, "Oh that is good news."

Angelina quickly ran away from the door and into her bedroom.

Soon after that, both girls realized that John and Jimmy were being invited more frequently to the farm; sometimes to do odd jobs, and other times for dinner with the family.

Angelina's oldest brother, Roberto was becoming a little mystified when he realised that they were seeing rather a lot of John and Jimmy around the farm, much more than was necessary.

He asked his mother why the two young men were coming so often. He commented that he didn't like to see them strolling around the farm like two black flies as though they were searching for something, but for what he couldn't think."

Mary felt obliged to explain. She said, "Well Roberto, your father and I are very fond of these two young men and we have two young ladies who may have an even chance of falling in love with them."

Robert had a strange expression on his face as he said, "What do you mean they might fall in love with them? Who are they?"

Mary smiled and said, "Your sister and your cousin of course."

He exploded, "What! Surely you don't mean it?"

She looked Robert in the eye and said, "And why not?"

Now Robert began to get very angry with his mother.

"Mother, this is an outrage. I do hope you and Father are not planning the same for me and Simon, because we will not permit you to do that."

Robert slammed the door behind him as he left the room.

Mary sighed sadly, realising that her son didn't understand the love that parents have towards their children, and that they only want what is best for them.

As Robert was coming out of the room he met his brother Simon, who, realising his brother was annoyed, asked him, what was wrong.

"Mother is sometimes so unreasonable," he said.

Simon was very curious. He wanted to know what it was all about.

Robert, still angry, said, "It seems that our parents intend to choose a wife for us. I told her that it was an outrage, and I think it is, but our parents say they only want the best for us."

Simon laughed, "This is not new to me," he said. "I didn't tell you because I thought that idea was only for the girls, but now I see that it applies to us too."

Robert shook his head, "I don't understand what you mean."

Simon hesitated and said, "This is not so easy to explain, but I will try. As you know, Beatrice and

Angelina go to church for the evening service and, one evening, after the service, the priest announced that the Parish had decided to start a church club for the young people with the help of their parents. They could come to the evening service, and afterwards get together and have a good time. Angelina and Beatrice came home and told our parents all about it. They agreed and contacted the other parent, and together they arranged a buffet for the young people to enjoy. After a little while Angelina and Beatrice met two young men, one playing the guitar and the other one playing the trumpet. It seems to me that Angelina fell in love with the one playing the guitar and our cousin with the one playing the trumpet."

"However, as you heard today, our parents have other ideas. They already think they've found a match for the girls. They have chosen John for Angelina and Jimmy for Beatrice. As you can imagine, the girls have rebelled at the plans our parents have decided for them.''

Robert was open mouthed with shock. "Goodness me! I would never have thought our parents could be so naïve as to think like that. I tell you now, that I wouldn't like that to happen to anybody, especially to our sister. What a good job she has a mind of her own and is as stubborn as a mule, rebelling at anything our parents say to her.''

Simon said, "So, you don't blame Angelina, because now you also know what you heard from our mother. She just told you what they have in their minds, so now you know what is going on.''

Roberto said, ''I find it all ridiculous. I will never agree with them."

Chapter 33

By now the correspondence between Domenic and Angelina was becoming more and more frequent, but to make sure the postman did not deliver Domenic's letters to anybody else in her family, Beatrice and Angelina decided that one of them would always be outside the farmhouse to wait for the postman. Renato, like many farmers, was accustomed to getting up early in the morning and liked to go round to his stable and make sure that all his livestock were present and well. He was amused to see Beatrice strolling round the farmhouse early one morning.

He shrugged his shoulders and continued on his way. Every morning he began to notice one or other of the girls always out there waiting for the post man to arrive. Renato was amused but at the same time he was curious to know what was going on.

He said to his wife Mary, "I really don't understand why one of the girls is always waiting for the postman. Why can't he deliver the post to one of us? What's going on?"

His wife said, "Why don't you ask him?"

He nodded his head, "Right, I'll do just that! I must know what these two girls are hiding from us."

Mary laughed, but she was concerned because in her mind she already knew something of what was going on. She also knew that soon or later the girls' secret would be revealed, and then there would be trouble in the family.

A few days later, Renato thought he would meet the postman some way before he arrived at the farm house so that Angelina or Beatrice wouldn't know what was going on. Perhaps then he would be able to find out from the postman why one of these young ladies was always waiting outside the farm house for him to arrive?

Later on, the postman appeared, and Renato went up to him and asked if he had any post for his family?" The postman said, "Yes, I have a letter for Miss Beatrice Di

Simone.''

"Well as I'm here, you might just as well give it to me. I need to go home and I will be able to give it to her,'' said Renato.

"Well, I believe we've had this conversation before, and I told you then, the reason I can't give it to you is because I must give it to the person whose name is on the envelope. It's for your niece, Beatrice. That is my job, and that is what I will do. Good-day, Sir.''

The postman went to where Beatrice was waiting for him and said, "There you are Miss. I have a letter for you. Your uncle asked me to give it to him so that he could pass it to you, but I couldn't do that. It can only be given to the person it's addressed to."

The postman went away muttering to himself 'I'm sure there is a young man writing to her and that nosey old man wouldn't have delivered the letter to her until he'd found out what the letter contained. But I didn't give to him. Ha-Ha'.

Renato was very angry. It didn't take his wife Mary very long to realise that he was in very bad mood. So she waited for a little while and then she asked him, "Renato whatever is the matter with you.''

He looked at his wife and seemed more than angry than ever. Then he gave a deep sigh and said, "I ask myself, is it right that a postman can't give the post to me because it is addressed to Beatrice and he can only give it to the person whose name is on the envelope. She is a young lady and it seems that she can receive post from anybody. That makes me very angry.''

Mary was beginning to feel very anxious herself at seeing her husband so stressed. She knew that sooner or later there was going to be trouble in the family.

She waited for the right moment to have a word with her niece and find out was going on, but in her mind she already knew more or less what to expect. Nevertheless she still hoped she was wrong.

The next day, Mary saw her niece all by herself near

the Sycamore Tree, so she approached her and said "Beatrice, you know how much we love you and until now we have always been a wonderful and happy family, never hiding anything from one another." If there was something to be said, it was said, and the problem was resolved. "This morning your uncle was walking along the path in the farm and he met the postman, who had a letter addressed to you. Your uncle offered to bring the letter to the farm house to give to you, but no. The post man insisted he needed to deliver it directly to you. That upset your uncle very much. Can you tell me who it is that is writing to you? And why the post man refused to give the letter to your uncle?"

Beatrice was taken aback by her aunt's direct approach.

"Auntie," she replied, "I'm not in a position to tell you anything at the moment, but trust me this is very personal and I can't say any more than that. When the time is right, you and Uncle will be the first ones to know."

Mary was confused and realised that the situation was even more serious than she had thought. It was going to be very difficult to resolve the problem when she didn't know who was writing to her niece, but she promised herself that she would find out.

The following day she went to visit her sister and she told her about the letters Beatrice was receiving.

"My dear sister," she said, "As aunt to your daughter and my very dear niece, I have become very concerned about her. Beatrice is still a very young, and much loved girl, inseparable from Angelina, and she needs to be protected, but we do not know from whom."

Giovanna, sister of Mary, said, "Mary, send Beatrice back to me and then I will see if I can find out what is going on, and who this person is who writes to her."

Mary said, "I will do my best."

A few days later Beatrice received a message from her mother saying she was not well and needed to see her. Beatrice was shocked because it was very unusual to be sent for by her mother unless she was very ill and wanted to see her. Beatrice went to her aunt and asked, "Auntie, I have had a message from my mother, asking me to go home because she needs to see me. I do hope there is nothing seriously wrong with my family."

Mary looked at her niece and said, "My dearest child, I've been in the village and went to see my sister. I can assure you there is nothing wrong with your mother or your brothers and sisters".

Beatrice looked puzzled, and then said, "But Auntie, if you have been to see my mother, and you tell me there is nothing wrong with her or my family, why must I still go to see the?"

Mary was expecting these questions and explained to her niece. "Remember, you will always belong here, with all of us. You and Angelina are like sisters, but you still have your own family. They have every right to see and love you just like we do, but you will come back to us. We need you to come back to us. Angelina would be very sad without you. She would die of a broken heart if you didn't come back. So you go to visit them like you've always done before, but remember, this is your home with all of us." Beatrice felt comforted. "Ok, Aunt Mary, I'm sure Angelina won't mind if I go tomorrow to visit my parents, for a little while, but as you said, I will be home with my beloved Angelina very soon."

Her Aunt nodded her head, and said, "I'm pleased you're going to see your family, but remember we are here waiting for you." Beatrice smiled and went to tell Angelina all about what had happened. Angelina was surprised but she smiled at Beatrice and said, "Beatrice, you go to see your family and have a nice time with your brothers and sisters, but you make sure you keep our secret: do you understand?"

Beatrice nodded and then said, "Angelina, we are almost like sisters, and I promise you we will be friends always, even when we are married and have our own family, but for now I need to go to my family and see why my mother needs me," said Beatrice.

"Well Beatrice" said Angelina, "You go now, but promise me you will come back to me as soon as you can, do you understand?" Beatrice said, "Of course!"

Then they hugged one another and Beatrice went to tell her aunt and uncle she would go, but she would be back as soon as possible. Her aunt and uncle kissed her and said, "Beatrice we do love you more than we can say, and we will be waiting for you." Mary gave her niece a hug and Beatrice ran down the stairs to Simon, who was waiting to walk her to the village and her own family.

After twenty minutes' walk they arrived, and Beatrice saw her brothers and one of her sisters, running towards her. They hugged one another and they all went into the house, where their mother was sitting near the table, writing to her brother, who lived in America.

Simon announced their arrival and his aunt immediately got up from her chair to welcome them. "Oh Simon, are you alright?"

"Yes Auntie, I'm fine, thank you."

"Thank you for bringing Beatrice here. It will be dinner time soon. Will you wait and dine with us?"

"No thank you aunt," said Simon, I need to go to back because my father needs help on the farm."

He hugged his cousin and his aunt, and then said, "Please don't let Beatrice's brothers and sisters spoil her, because when she comes back home, our parents will be very strict with all of us and that makes it hard to understand them."

Beatrice's mother smiled. "Now Simon, you're telling me porky pies. Your parents are nice people and remember I know them well. Your mother is my sister and you will never find another person as soft as her. She is the opposite of me. I'm the one in the family who was, and still is very strict." Simon just smiled, and said, "I must go now."

He hugged his cousin and his aunt, and he said to Beatrice, "You take care now and I'll see you soon." They hugged one another and Simon left.

Beatrice went to her mother and with tears in her eyes she said, "Mom, it is lovely to see you, but more than ever because Aunty Mary said you felt the urge to see me and hug me. That made me feel a part of my bigger family, but I must confess that living with them and my dearest cousin, Angelina, has been a very enjoyable time. That doesn't mean I don't miss you, because I do, but now I'm here I want to know what you want to talk about."

Beatrice's words were now causing her mother to feel guilty about the real reason for her request to ask Beatrice to visit. She was starting to get extremely stressed and she said, "Not now, my dear, not now, this is a time to enjoy your visit with us. Wait until your father comes home tonight. He is going to be so happy to see you sitting at the table, dining with the rest of the family."

Beatrice said, but Mum, you aren't being very fair. I have been almost every day."

"Ah yes," agreed her mother, "You have been near every day, but you haven't slept in the same room as your brother and sisters, and you haven't been sitting at the same table."

Beatrice was finding it difficult to understand what her mother was trying to say. After all, she knew that Beatrice lived with her sister Mary so what she was on about. Then she saw tears running down her mother's face.

"My dearest girl, I know you can't understand what I'm trying to tell you, but I must explain to you why you've been living with your Aunty Mary and your Uncle Renato and their family."

Before her mother could finish explaining Beatrice said, "But I know, Mother. Aunty and Uncle have already told me and I have accepted it."

Giovanna was getting herself in a muddle and was keen to straighten everything out as quickly as she could. "Now listen to me," she said sternly, "I need to tell you myself."

"After the war of '15-'18, and the Spanish 'flu, Italy and the rest of the world went into a deep recession, and is still suffering it. Having a big family, we realised we weren't going to be able to feed all of you. My sister Mary knew about our situation and offered to bring you up alongside her own daughter. She said that would be good for both you girls. Having two older brothers it would be better for Angelina and also better for you. She promised us that she would always respect the fact that you live with them but would always be our daughter. We agreed that as you grew older, we would have the opportunity of explaining the situation to you; that you would have a better chance in life, living with my sister Mary and her family. We knew we could see you at any time we wanted to. It was all for your benefit and what comforted us was that you always knew you were our daughter, even though you lived in the farmhouse with Mary, and her family.''

Beatrice threw her arms round her mother and said, ''Thank you Mum.''

After a few days Beatrice felt the urge to return to her Aunt Mary and Uncle Renato, but above all she missed Angelina and really needed to see her. She went to her mother, smiled and then said, ''Mum, it was wonderful to be here with you and Dad, and all my family, but now it is time for me to return to my aunt and uncle, and more than ever I want to be with Angelina. By now she'll want to know why I didn't return earlier.''

Giovanna asked herself why Beatrice needed to go so soon. She was aware that she hadn't been able to find out anything that her sister wanted to know. Who was the person who was writing to her daughter?

She stood up from the chair and started to walk round the house. Then she took a deep breath and called Beatrice to her.

"By the way, your Aunty Mary said your uncle was surprised to see the postman up at the farmhouse, because he doesn't usually come to them. They don't even know the postman's name, and your uncle was even more surprised when he told your uncle that the letter was for you.

Chapter 34

Giovanna said, ''Now do you understand why your Aunty Mary and your Uncle Renato are very upset, because they only wanted to protect you.'' Beatrice shrugged her shoulders and said, ''Yes mother, you are right, that they want to protect us, and in their minds Angelina and I should marry the men they choose for us. But neither Angelina nor I will permit them to choose. We believe not even you, or my father, would allow that, would you Mum?''

The mother was thoughtful for a moment, then she said, ''You are a young girl and you make up a lot of fantasy in your brain; even so you haven't yet told me who this person is, who has been writing to you?''

Beatrice felt herself getting annoyed. She said accusingly, "You didn't answer the question I asked you."

Giovanna gave her a curious look. "I can't give you the answer if you don't tell me who the writer is.'' She replied.

Beatrice was getting more annoyed. "I can't tell you what my Aunt and Uncle wanted to know, we are only prepared to reveal that when the time is appropriate.''

Her mother took a deep breath and said, "Beatrice, if you don't tell me what I need to know, your Aunt and Uncle will be very cross with us, with you, and that poor cousin of yours. I tell you now, they can make your life and Angelina's, very difficult.''

Beatrice stamped her feet on the floor in frustration. "Mum, you can't say that because, if I tell you who the person is it would create more problems for all of us. I will tell you, and Auntie Mary and Uncle Renato only when the time is right.''

Giovanna was exasperated. "If you don't tell me now there is a chance your uncle and your aunt won't let you stay with Angelina any longer.''

Beatrice said, "But that's not fair. Angelina and I have

always been like sisters to each other. We belong to one another. Surely they wouldn't do such a terrible thing?"

Giovanna said, "You live with my sister and I've known Mary all my life, yet you've never seen how merciless she can be when she doesn't get her own way."

Beatrice began to whine.

Her mother knew she had to try another way. She said, "If you tell me what has upset them, I promise you I will find a way to make them understand. After all, it is not a crime for a young girl to receive a letter; maybe from a friend or a young admirer. I'm sure they'll understand. Of course it would depend on what the letter is all about."

Beatrice said, "Mother, now you are beginning to understand. It was just a letter from a friend of both of us and no more than that. We can't see what all the fuss is about, but Auntie and Uncle are frightening us because of it. In their minds we must not befriend anybody but the men what they would like for us, because we can only marry young men whose parents have a farm. Angelina and I are friends with two young men. One is Giuseppe, the son of the shoemaker, and the other one is Domenic, the son of the merchant. We are only friends and they have no romantic feelings for us. Feelings like that are only in our minds."

Giovanna said, "Don't worry dear. I will have a few words with them and you can rest assured I will not reveal anything you have told me. I was young once. I will make your Aunt and Uncle understand that this young man writes to you both and is only a friend for now, and no more than that."

"But Mum, that won't please Auntie and Uncle, because in their minds the only friends we are allowed to have are John and Jimmy. We know and respect them, but they are our family friends and no more."

"Well, Beatrice, go back there, if that is what you want, but if at any time you find it difficult to live with your Aunt Mary, then you must come back home and that is that."

Beatrice was distraught, "But what about Angelina?" she wailed.

Her mother grimaced, and then she said, "Angelina is my niece and I'm sure my sister Mary and her husband are nice people, but I'm afraid Renato has always been a stubborn man and my sister obeys him in everything. If he says his daughter can only marry the man he wants for her, there is nothing we can say, but you don't need to do anything he says because at the end of the day we are your parents and he doesn't have any power over you. If life becomes unbearable, you must come back home and that is that. I'm quite sure Angelina will stand her ground, and she will win her battle. So it's up to you. Go back if you want and tell Angelina what her Aunty Giovanna says."

"Ok Mum, I'll go back to the farmhouse, but I know now that if Aunty Mary and Uncle Renato insist we must do what they command us to do, and we don't agree, I have the opportunity to come back home. But I can't say that for my poor cousin Angelina. She has no chance of leaving her parents, but like you say, she is strong willed, and she will put up a big fight. No doubt she will win, no matter what her parents say or do. Angelina is a character who always defeats any obstacle that gets in her way."

Giovanna said, "This is your home, Beatrice, and we will not stop you marrying the man you love when you are old enough to do so."

"Thank you Mum," said Beatrice. "I'd better make my way back to the farm now because I'm concerned about Angelina missing me. I'll just say goodbye to my brother and sister and I promise you and Dad, I'll be here any time you need me. I know that if in future I have any problem with Aunty or Uncle I can always come home and stay with my family."

And with that, Beatrice left her family, and went back to the farmhouse, to her aunt and uncle. When she arrived, her cousin's joy was immense.

"I thought you had abandoned me," said Angelina. Then she added. "While you were away I received more letters from Domenic.''

Beatrice didn't understand, "Do you mean Domenic put your name on the envelope, knowing that Aunty and Uncle could take it from the letter box and read it before they gave it to you?''

Angelina explained. "Beatrice, you have been away from us less than a week, and you've already forgotten what my parents would have done?''

Beatrice smiled, "Certainly not. What I thought was, that they would read the letter and then put it on the fire and that would be the end of it.''

Angelina was hysterical. "What you just said makes me realise, that if my brother Robert hadn't been there to see the postman, no doubt they would have done just that. You see, Angelina, the postman asked my brother if he knew where I was. My brother told him I was in the village with Aunty Giovanna and family. The postman said, "Well I need to go back to deliver her letter." Robert asked the postman to give it to him, and he would give to you when you came back. He thought about it, and then he said, "I shouldn't give it to you because on the envelope it says to only deliver it to the person named, but I trust you to do just that, thank you.'' My brother Roberto said, 'Don't worry. I will do as I said.'' He thanked the postman and came straight up to me. He said to me. The postman has given me this letter. It belongs to Beatrice. Make sure you keep it in a safe place for when she gets back from Auntie Giovanna, then you can give it to her.''

Beatrice said, "That was a bit of luck, the postman giving it to Roberto. If Uncle had got hold of it, it would have created a lot of trouble for both of us. By the way, auntie went to see my mother because she wanted her to find out about the mysterious writer. I promise, I said he is a friend of both of us, and that is all. I also told her about Uncle wanting us to marry only farmers. She said that I can marry the man I love when I am old enough. She knows you are a very strong girl and Aunty and Uncle have no chance of having their own way, so, dear

Angelina, you will have a fight to look forward to when the time comes.'' They both burst out laughing.

Chapter 35

Two months later Mary asked her son to go to the village to get some shopping for her. "Simon, I need you go to the baker's shop to buy two kilos of the special flour I need to make a cake for your brother's birthday tomorrow. The flour I have here is not good enough."

Simon started to grumble. "Why me?" he complained. "Surely you could send Angelina or Beatrice."

Mary was annoyed with him. "Don't be ridiculous. I'm asking you because I need the girls to help me in the kitchen today." She gave him the money and said, "Now get on and don't take all day."

Simon slammed the door as he went out.

When he reached the shop and entered he saw there were a few girls there talking to one another about the church club. The shop assistant was serving as well as listening and wanted to know what was going on at the club. One of the girls said, "We are very excited because there is a rumour going round our village that two young soldiers will be coming home on leave from the army for two weeks and one of them is Domenic Di Gatto. We shall soon have two weeks of entertainment to look forward to. It's been so quiet since he's been away."

The lady shop assistant laughed and said, "I quite agree with you. Young people in the village need a little bit of distraction. "So far we've only had war, Spanish fever and the recession, so I hope you will be able to have a bit of fun for a change."

The girls went out of the shop laughing and singing on their way home.

Simon was standing there thinking only about how to prevent his parents organising the future of their children.

Then the shop assistant startled him by saying, "Wake up Simon, I'm waiting for you to tell me what you came to buy, but it seems to me you are in a world of your own."

Simon came to his senses abruptly. "Sorry, Giulia you

are right, I was. I have a few problems with my parents and I don't know how to resolve them.''

Giulia was immediately curious. "Oh yes, why don't you tell me what the problem is. I may be able to help?''

Simon gave a deep sigh and said sadly, "The problem is, it can't be resolved because of the way my parents behave towards their family.''

Giulia was taken aback and obviously curious, "Oh, I see, so what is the matter with your parents now?''

Simon knew he shouldn't be talking to Giulia about his family problems and was aware that he'd already said too much. She was staring at him in an enquiring way and he heard himself stutter as he tried to find the right words to answer her.

"Never mind, Giulia thanks anyway. They are family problems and must be resolved in the family.'' He then paid his money and said goodbye. "Give my regards to your parents," she called after him.

On the way home, Simon wondered if it would make trouble for Angelina if he told his mother what he'd heard in the shop about Domenic coming home from the army for two weeks leave. Just before he arrived home he met his brother Roberto.

"Thank God I've seen you before I arrived home,'' said Simon.

Roberto could see that his brother was troubled and asked him what the problem was.

Simon told him what he'd heard. "I don't know if Angelina and Beatrice know that their friend Domenic will be back in the village for two weeks leave soon.''

Roberto could see the problem immediately. "I'm sure Angelina and Beatrice will want to go to the club and one of us will have to go with them. Our parents will never, ever let those two girls go anywhere by themselves. We both know how stubborn our sister is and unlucky too. Father hasn't changed, and there is a chance it could make family life very unpleasant for all of us. We must do whatever it takes to see that this situation doesn't erupt

179

into a big row with our parents. We need to do something to avoid that."

Simon agreed at once. "You're right of course Roberto, but our parents have this fixation in their minds that the only men they can see as suitable for the girls are John and Jimmy. So what can we do?"

Then they looked at one another and then burst out laughing.

Robert said, "We are very silly talking about all of this, when we don't even know if the girls have already forgotten about Domenic and Giuseppe. Let's go home. We can deal with this problem if it arrives."

As they entered the house and were going upstairs, they heard such a racket coming from the girls' bedroom that they knew they were up to something. They were obviously very excited.

"What on earth?" Simon exclaimed.

"I haven't the faintest idea," said Roberto. He shook his head and sighed. "Those two rascals are up to something for sure?" He went on, "I think they already know what you've just heard in the shop. We need to investigate."

Simon said, "We'll knock on their bedroom door, but before they answer we'll go in and say, 'we heard all your excitement, can we join in?'

They did just that and the girls were shocked and speechless.

Then Angelina found herself and stood up. "Well brothers mine, you can't join us now, but you soon will because we have found out that Domenic Di Catto will very soon be on leave from the army for two weeks and can we beg you both to come along to the church club with us. If you don't come along with us we can't go because our parents won't let us enjoy the two weeks of entertainment. It would be very sad for us, and it is unfair that you men are free to come and go when you like, and we can't. Please help us, otherwise it will create a lot of disagreement in the family and you don't want that. What do you say dear brothers?"

Roberto and Simon stepped back, shocked, and looked at one another. Robert said ''Oh, goodness me. I can't believe you two girls. How can you behave so badly and create so much trouble, when you can't have your own way with our father and us? We know our father can be an unbearable man and it's not easy to live under the same roof, with him sometimes, but even so, we need to escort those girls to the church club."

Simon looked at his brother and said, "Do you think it would be easier if we invited John and Jimmy to come along as well. Then our father would be much happier, knowing that those two young men would be there with us as well? We'll have the opportunity to take these two rebels to see the show, and our father will think he's achieved what he always wanted for his daughter and for his niece, which is to have John for Angelina, and Jimmy for Beatrice.''

After a few days Angelina and her cousin knew Domenic had arrived in the village, and it was time to approach the two brothers again.

Angelina informed Robert and Simon that the coming Saturday was to be a big day for her and Beatrice and reminded them of their promise to go with them to the club. She added, "You know our father he won't let us go by ourselves, we need your help.''

Later, Robert discussed it with Simon and they planned to go to their father and tell him that they wanted go to the church club and take Angelina and Beatrice with them, and if their father wanted them to, John and Jimmy as well.

Simon waited for his father to be in a good mood, before approaching him and said, "Dad, I heard that there is to be a musical concert in the village tomorrow evening. Roberto and I are going and we would like to take Angelina and Beatrice with us."

His father snapped at him. "What do you mean, you want to take the girls with you?''

Simon said, "Roberto and I are going and we thought it

181

would be good for Angelina and Beatrice to come with us. After all they can't go anywhere on their own so we thought we'd give them a chance to come with us.''

Renato wasn't convinced. He said, "Young ladies should stay at home with their mother, and embroider linen for their bottom drawer.''

Now Simon was getting annoyed with his father, "There is plenty of time for them to embroider, but it is not very often we can go out as a family.''

Renato said, "Ok, but tell me, are John and Jimmy coming with you?"

"I don't know father, but, no doubt they know all about this big musical concert. It is good fun for young and old alike. Renato smiled and said "Yes, all right, if the girls want to go.''

Simon was happy to get his father's permission to take the girls to the church club. Now he needed to tell his brother Roberto. Simon waited for the opportunity to talk to his brother and tell him the good news. A few hours later Simon spotted Roberto coming towards him. Simon said, "Roberto, at last I have managed to convince our father to let us take the girls with us to the church club.'' His brother laughed, "Well done," he said.

Angelina and Beatrice were over the moon, knowing that Roberto and Simon were able to escort them to the church club, so that they could see and hear Domenic and Giuseppe and their friends, playing music together. It would be spectacular music with Domenic's accordion and guitar and Giuseppe with his trumpet; plus many other young people with different musical instruments.

On the evening of the church club, Angelina and Beatrice put on their best frocks and helped one other to arrange their hair. Then when they thought they looked more sophisticated than any of the other girls would, they went to the brothers to tell them to prepare the horses and the carriage so that they could all go together to the church club. But they had a surprise when they went downstairs, to see John and Jimmy talking to the brothers. They had their own transport and they all went to the village for the evening concert.

When they arrived, the hall was already nearly full. Domenic and Giuseppe spotted Angelina and Beatrice with their brothers, and their friends, and soon made sure that six seats were prepared for them. The concert went on until twelve o'clock midnight. It was a big success. Domenic and Giuseppe went up to Angelina and Beatrice, their brothers and friends, shook hands with them, and said, "It is an honour for us that you all came here to see us playing tonight. We don't know how to thank you all for giving us the privilege of having such an audience here this evening."

Angelina and Beatrice were moved to tears, to hear Domenic and Giuseppe talking to the brothers in such manner that made both girls relax.

Angelina said to Domenic, "We enjoyed being here with you, but we will enjoy it so much more when you finish in the army and return to us permanently."

Domenic said to Angelina "We need to talk."

Angelina began to tremble and she said, "I look forward to that, but I don't know how, since my father will not let Beatrice and I come to the village by ourselves."

Domenic looked worried. Then Angelina said, "Domenic, we will arrange something before you go back to the army, but now my brothers are waiting to take us back to the farm."

Angelina and Beatrice hugged Domenic and Giuseppe and went on their way to meet the brothers who were waiting in their carriage to go back to the farm.

Chapter 36

Next day Angelina said, "Beatrice, did you realise what Domenic said, before we left, 'Angelina we need to talk'. I didn't expect that. I was shocked, but at the same time I was overjoyed. I told him I didn't know whether my parents would let us come into the village by ourselves, but I said I would think about it and let him know if somehow I could meet him before he goes back to the army."

Beatrice said, "I did realise Domenic was eager to talk to you, but I also understood he didn't know how he could get to talk to you, when we were all there, especially when your two brothers were there with us."

Angelina said, "It was impossible for me to get to sleep last night. All night I was thinking about how I can have a chat with Domenic when we both have such a big problems with my parents. Then I decided I must do something about it. I took a page from my old exercise book and started writing:

'Dear Dominic and Giuseppe: We would very much like to have a chat with you both, but my parents won't let us come to the village by ourselves. We will try to go to my aunt's house. On the way home from there, about a mile from the farm, there's a lane on the left of the road and a post with the name 'Catone' on it. If you walk down the lane, it will take you to the orchards which belong to the farm. I will send a letter to Giuseppe to give to you and we hope that you can both come and meet us there. All our love, Angelina and Beatrice." '

"I haven't put the letter in the envelope yet, because I wanted you to read it before sealing it."

"Now we need to make a plan to enable us to meet Domenic and Giuseppe."

"You go to my mother, Beatrice, and say, 'Auntie, last

night I had a terrible dream. I dreamt my mother was very ill and repeatedly calling my name. In my dream it seemed that she needed me badly. She was delirious. I'm very concerned about her. I can't relax until I know if it was just a dream or she is really ill and needs me. I would like to go and visit her." Now if my mother says 'yes', you will ask her if I can come with you. If she says 'yes', then you will come and ask me if I want to come with you. Of course you know that my answer will be 'yes'. If she says we need to go with the carriage we can ask one of our brothers to take us to your mother, and then we shall try to make our own way back."

"Now, when we reach your mother's house, you need to tell your mother exactly what you said to my mother. While you're talking to Auntie, I'll try to bribe your brother with 5 lire, to take the letter to Giuseppe. He only lives three doors away from your mother. Giuseppe needs to go to Domenic, give the letter to him and him only. When the time is right, we will tell your mother we need to go home and we'll make our own way back, without bothering our brother. This is our only chance to see Domenic and Giuseppe for a few hours by ourselves."

Beatrice looked at Angelina in admiration.

She said, "You amaze me. How can you work that all out? This plot that you have in your mind is big, devious and mad, but at the same time very clever! But I'm as mad as you, and I will support you all the way."

Angelina laughed and then said, "Tonight we'll ask Simon if he will take us. Then tomorrow morning we'll take the first step in the plot we have prepared .I shall take the opportunity to have a chat with the one of your younger brothers to see if he knows Giuseppe. If he does, he can give the letter to Giuseppe. Then we will be on our way to having a chat with the men of our dreams."

Beatrice said, "I tremble all over at the thought of all this. I can't imagine what will happen to us, if our family discovers the plot we've made."

Angelina said, "We need to do it, otherwise our

parents will eventually make us marry men that we don't like and, my dear cousin, we need to take this chance. We mustn't have a negative attitude if we want to continue with our dream.''

"Nevertheless I'm still afraid,'' admitted Beatrice quietly.

Angelina was beginning to feel annoyed with her cousin and sensing this Beatrice said, "Alright then, I will do whatever it takes to make this plot succeed. We need to look for Simon and we need to tell him we have permission from your mother, to take us to the village to visit my mother."

Angelina went round the farm, looking for Simon and after a few minutes she spotted him near the cherry tree. She called him and said, "Simon, Beatrice and I have permission from our mother to go to the village to visit Aunt Giovanna, Beatrice's Mum, will you take us there?''

"Of course I will," he said, "What time do you want to go?''

Angelina smiled and said, "About nine o'clock in the morning, is that alright with you?''

Simon said, "Yes, that will be fine''.

The next morning about eight o'clock, the two young ladies both jumped out of bed, very carefully washed themselves, and dressed in their prettiest frocks and fashionable shoes. Then they both ran downstairs as fast as they could to the carriage. Simon gave the command to the horse to gallop towards the village. After twenty minutes the carriage stopped in front of Giovanna's house. They pressed the doorbell and a young boy came to open the door, He was very pleased to see Simon, Angelina and Beatrice. Then the boy ran into the house, shouting ''Mum, Mum Simon is here, with Angelina and Beatrice.''

Giovanna was surprised and couldn't understand the reason for their visit. She said, "I'm astonished to see you all this is so unexpected. I do hope there is nothing wrong with my sister Mary or the rest of the family?"

"Angelina and Beatrice looked at one another and they

knew they needed to start telling their story, but only when Simon had left his aunt's house and gone back to the farm.

A few minutes later Simon said, "Auntie, as far as I know there's nothing wrong with our family, but I need to go back, because Father needs my help round the farm. The girls can stay with you a little while longer."

Angelina said, "Simon, go home and don't worry about coming back for us, we can come home on our own when we are ready."

Simon said, "That's okay by me. I know that father needs me today, and I'm sure he doesn't mind if you come home by yourselves." He kissed his auntie and cousins and went back to the carriage to go back to the farm.

Now Angelina made Beatrice understand that she needed to sit near her mother and tell her all about the dream she'd had, which was the reason for coming. She needed to see if it was just a dream. Angelina had suddenly spotted Beatrice's younger brother, the one who had opened the door when they arrived. Angelina beckoned him and said, "I know you are Mario, and how old are you?"

"I'm eight years old," he said.

"Mario, do you know Giuseppe, the son of the shoemaker?"

He looked at her and said, "Yes, he lives only a few doors away from us."

"If I give you a letter, would you be able to take it to Giuseppe? You need to give it to him and nobody else. This is very important and it needs to be a secret between you and me. Don't tell anybody else. If you do that for me, I will give you 5 lire, but you need to promise you will never, ever tell our secret to anybody, otherwise I'll demand my five lire back from you, do you understand?"

Mario said, "I promise you I will never, ever tell anybody."

Angelina gave him the letter. "Now you go and give the letter to Giuseppe and when you come back I will give you the 5 lire I have promised you. Is that alright?"

187

The boy looked seriously at Angelina and said, "I will do just as you say, and I promise I will never, ever tell anybody about the letter."

Mario took the letter and off he ran. A few minutes later he was back, and said, "I gave the letter to Giuseppe and he said I'm a good boy, and he gave me a sweet and patted me on the head.''

Angelina gave him a 5 lire note and kissed him. She went to see Beatrice, still sitting near her mother. She turned round, saw Angelina and said, "Angelina, one of my sisters is making dinner for the family, and she has asked us to stay so that we can have dinner together. I think we should."

"Of course we'll stay." said Angelina. "That would be lovely." Two hours later they were all sitting round the big table with plates of Spaghetti Bolognese, and for dessert, a nice sponge cake. All the family was happy to have their older sister and their cousin with them for dinner and Giovanna was over the moon at seeing her niece and especially her beloved daughter Beatrice.

After dinner Angelina said to all the family, "We'd better make our way home now, because it is a long walk and it will be some time before we reach home."

With tears running down her face, Giovanna thanked her daughter and her niece for being concerned about her health. She said, "Will you thank my sister and my brother-in-law for letting you both come and see if I was ok?" They kissed one another and Angelina and Beatrice left to make their way home.

Along the way they looked for the lane and the post with the name 'Catone'. It wasn't a problem for them to find the place, because they had been there before and the orchard belonged to their family. Giuseppe knew the place well because he had been there many times to give a helping hand to Angelina's family. After twenty minutes' walk, they got to the lane and ten metres along the lane they reached the Orchard, but there was no one there. They sat on the grass in despair and Angelina said, "It hasn't worked. We took a lot of risks, and now what? There is nothing to be done, but to make our way home."

Suddenly there was a loud shout coming from the fig trees further down the orchard and at the same time there was another loud noise as Giuseppe climbed down from the apple tree. The girls were shocked and surprised, but full of joy, and went towards them, hugging, shouting and then smiling, saying "We've done it. We've done it."

They all sat on the grass, finding it difficult to believe Domenic and Giuseppe were really there and with tears in her eyes, Angelina said to Domenic, "You are my life's dream."

Domenic burst into tears and said to her, "As soon you walked in the room I knew you were the girl for me."

Then Angelina said, "When I heard you playing the guitar and I saw your lovely blue eyes my heart nearly jumped out of my breast".

And then Giuseppe said, "I've been in love with you, Beatrice, since the last day of school, but I was not brave enough to tell you. Now here we are, and at last we know we belong to one other forever."

They sat and talked for a long time, then realised the time had arrived for them to make their way home, otherwise they would find themselves in great trouble and their plot would be discovered. With tears in their eyes they embraced one another, and said, "We'll see you both in the church club next Saturday." The girls said goodbye and made their way home.

Angelina and Beatrice were full of joy because they'd met Domenic and Giuseppe. Angelina said, "I can't believe what happened to us today. It almost seems unreal that the plot to meet Domenic and Giuseppe actually succeeded. What we did today is beyond any dream I would believe could happen. We always knew we had very deep feelings for them, but for them to declare their love for us is much more than we expected. I can't contain myself. It seems to me that my heart is bursting with joy and happiness, and I'm afraid when we reach home it will be written all over my face. Our family will never stop asking us why we look more relaxed and happy then we've ever been."

Beatrice said, "We must appear like we were before, otherwise the plot to meet the men of our dreams will be revealed, and the happiness we have will turn very sour in no time, It would be worse than a nightmare."

Angelina said, "Oh no. Our family will make us marry the men of their choice. But we won't let the cat out of the bag. We will act, and I'll pretend to be always very grumpy and miserable, even more than before."

Beatrice laughed. "Angelina, you are so clever. I know you will go to any lengths to do what you want and nobody will ever get in your way."

About an hour later they reached home and went upstairs. Mary was in the kitchen, and she said, "Angelina and Beatrice, I'm so happy you spent a day with my sister and her family. When Simon came home earlier, and told me how well my sister Giovanna looked, it was a great relief for me. Beatrice's dream was just a dream, but it was nice for both of you to spend a day with my sister and all her family."

Beatrice said, "Yes, Aunty, my mother and father, and all my brothers and sisters were pleased to see us. It was a very happy day with all my family and it was also good for them to see their nephew Simon and their niece Angelina. We had Spaghetti Bolognese for dinner, which was very nice."

After a while Angelina said, "Mother, we are very tired, and we need to get up early tomorrow morning, because father said many people from the village are coming to help him with the farm and that means we need to get up very early to give a helping hand."

Maria said, "You haven't had any supper."

Angelina said, "Don't worry, Mum, maybe later on, if we are hungry, we will make some sandwiches."

They both went off into their bed room and could hardly contain their joy of knowing that, at last they'd both realised their dream, and their feelings were reciprocated, but it was going to be very difficult to keep the secret.

They both felt like going to all their relatives around the village and the whole world to tell them, that they were in love, and they dreamed of being in the arms of their handsome men, Domenic with his guitar, and Giuseppe with his trumpet, shouting and singing and telling them that they would love them forever.

But it was difficult to keep their secret and their true feelings would never be disclosed to their parents until Domenic come out of the army and the girls were over twenty one years old.

Chapter 37

Angelina and Beatrice tried very hard to hide their secret, for they knew, if their family saw any change in their behaviour, after they had been to the village to visit Beatrice's mother, they would want to know the reason why. So the act continued.

Beatrice said to her cousin, "Angelina, this Saturday will be the last day for Domenic and Giuseppe to play in the club together until the army grants Domenic another two weeks' leave, so we won't be able to see them for a long time."

Angelina said, "Not a moment passes without me thinking how hard it will be, not to be able to see him for six months or maybe more."

Beatrice said, "You need to ask one of your brothers or maybe both of them to come with us on Saturday evening to the church club."

Angelina looked at Beatrice and said, "Beatrice, this time it's me trembling all over."

Beatrice said, "I don't understand what the problem is. After all Roberto and Simon have met Domenic and Giuseppe many times and shaken hands with them. They're just friends like us. How can they refuse to come and say goodbye to Domenic. I know it's not the same for Giuseppe because he remains in the village. Anyway, I know you are very clever and you can make your brothers believe and do whatever you want. Domenic and Giuseppe will be playing music at the church club on Saturday, and as I've just said, they are just our friends. That's why we all need to be there this Saturday evening and you need to make them understand they have no choice but to be there with us."

Angelina looked very concerned at the thought of not being able to see Domenic for six months. Just the thought of that gave her a deep pain in her heart.

Two days later Angelina saw her brother Simon near

the gate of the farm and she approached him.

"Simon, you know Saturday is the last day Domenic will be playing his guitar with Giuseppe at the club, and you know Father won't let us go there by ourselves, well, we thought that it would be nice for you and Roberto to come with us. It's not just for us. You and Robert have both met them, and it would be nice for you to be there with us to wish them well until next time?" Simon smiled and said, "Ok, sis, I will tell Roberto, and convince him we should go all together as a family."

Next day Roberto approached Angelina and said, "Yes, Simon and I will come with you and Beatrice. I know Saturday evening is the last evening Domenic will be able to play because he has to go back to the army, and I know, my dear sister, the way you look at one another tells me he is much more than just a friend. But I tell you, my dear sister, you are much too young, and you must understand Domenic needs to go back to the army, and you could easily fall in love with somebody else, suitable for you, that what our parents would like."

"Angelina said, "Roberto, I will not fall in love with anyone else. Domenic is and will remain my love forever, and our parents can't do anything about it because I do not intend to get married before I'm twenty one, when I will be old enough to be in charge of my own destiny."

Roberto looked at his sister and was not at all surprised, as he and his brother Simon had known for a long time that Angelina and Beatrice believed they had both met the right man for them. But they were very concerned, because they were much too young to fall in love. Angelina could easily fall in love with another young man, but if their father had his way it would be John who would take Angelina to church; and Jimmy would take Beatrice, but time would tell.

However on Saturday they would take Angelina and Beatrice to the church club to say good bye to Domenic, while Giuseppe remained in the village to help his father with his shoe shop.

Angelina said to Beatrice, "My brothers realise I'm in love with Domenic, and you with Giuseppe. I only hope they never, ever let our parents know anything about it, otherwise I don't know what will happen to us." Beatrice looked at Angelina and said, "Well, you must beg your brothers not to reveal anything to your parents, because they know how difficult your 'old man' can be. If they let your father know it will be disastrous for all the family. I mean all the family will suffer only because their daughter fell in love with a person they didn't approve of."

Angelina said, "Yes, I know the whole family will be dismayed, and life will be impossible, but that wouldn't be just for me, but you also."

Beatrice said, "Ha, but at the end of the day, I'm just his niece. If your father makes life very difficult, you'll be the one who suffers the most. I can always go back to the village to my parents' home and, although my father was very strict with us when we were children, I can rest assured he will not be the one to choose a partner for any of us. When he knows I'm in love with Giuseppe, he will rejoice, because he is our neighbour and a family friend for many years."

Angelina looked at Beatrice and said, "That is even better, because then we have the opportunity to fight our ground with my parents, for they have no right to be matchmakers for the future of their young family."

They both laughed. On Saturday afternoon the brothers said, "Angelina and Beatrice, we will come with you, but we must make sure we are home just after eleven o'clock. Tomorrow we have a very busy day on the farm, and if we are late there could be trouble with Father".

The two young ladies lifted their shoulders and Angelina said, "Ok brothers, eleven o'clock it will be."

They dressed up in their best outfits, did up their hair and set out to look their best and to be as attractive as they could make themselves. Then they went to the brothers and Angelina said, "Dearest brothers, we do not know how to thank for coming with us tonight. It means the world to us, and please, please, don't say anything to our parents. If they get to know, we can't tell what will happen to all of us. We are very frightened.''

Then Angelina and Beatrice jumped onto the carriage that was waiting for them outside the farm gate. The brothers were very concerned in case their parents discovered the secret of the young girls, and got to know that their two sons had helped their sister and cousin to defy their father.Nobody knew what would happen to all of their family, because they knew their father sometimes behaved like a wild animal, flying into a rage, when he couldn't get his own way.

Roberto and Simon said to the girls, "Before we enter the club, we need to have a very serious talk with both of you. You must stress to Domenic and Giuseppe that both your relationships need to be absolutely secret until Domenic comes back from the army, otherwise your life will be not worth living and a big war will break out between the two families of Mr Renato Caccia and Mr Francesco Di Catto. Do you understand?''

The young girls looked at one another and they were very frightened. They both started shaking and Angelina said, "We promise we will make sure nobody will ever know anything about it until we are old enough to be responsible for what we doing."

As they went into the club Domenic and Giuseppe were nowhere to be seen.

Angelina said to her cousin, "You talk to Roberto and Simon, and tell them I need to go out for personal reasons.''

She went outside the club, and she noticed Domenic and Giuseppe in the corner of the square, near the church, waiting for them to arrive. Very quietly, Angelina went towards them, and when they saw her they became very excited.

Angelina said, "We need to talk very quietly. Beatrice and I are with my brothers, and as you know, we are both madly in love with you, but we are much too young; and our parents do not know anything. If they ever get to know about us we will be in dead trouble. We must be very careful not to let them know anything at all. Before you go, we shall meet in a secret place and we will plan how we can contact one another while you are away in the army, but until then it must be strictly secret until we are old enough to be able to look ahead for our future. For now we need to be very careful, otherwise we will have more trouble than we can ever manage. Now we should go into the club separately and don't let my brothers know we've already met.''

Domenic, with tears in his eyes said, "Angelina, I love you very much and I will do whatever it takes for us to be together, so today we will handle any obstacle that comes our way.''

Giuseppe said, "That goes for me too''.

They embraced each other, and Angelina returned to the church club by herself, then ten minutes later Domenic and Giuseppe entered and pretended to be surprised when they saw Angelina and Beatrice with the two brothers.

Domenic and Giuseppe went towards them and said, "Oh, Angelina and Beatrice, how lovely to see you both here with your two brothers this evening.'' Then they turned to Robert and Simon, shook hands with them and said, "Thank you all for coming here this evening. It's an honour for us that you've all come to hear our music, because it's my last day before I go back to the army.''

Roberto and Simon were amazed to hear Domenic, and Giuseppe talk to them like two mature gentlemen. They replied, "The honour is ours, to have the privilege of coming to hear the lovely music you play for us and the many young people who are here this evening. We can assure you we look forward to the time when you will be back home at the end of your military service and when we can continue to have the pleasure of your music again.''

Domenic and Giuseppe smiled and thanked them again and they went on stage to start playing. The evening was very enjoyable and the music indeed was more entertaining than ever, but unfortunately for Angelina and Beatrice eleven o'clock soon came and they needed to leave the club to go back home. They waited for the interval and then the brothers, Angelina and Beatrice went towards them and again thanked Domenic and Giuseppe for the lovely music, shook hands and wished Domenic all the best for the rest of his army service. They told him that they were already looking forward to his return, when he would keep the village well entertained with his lovely music.

Angelina and Beatrice had been very brave and not let their brothers know how upset they were. During the carriage ride home, Roberto and Simon didn't stop praising Domenic and Giuseppe at how well they entertained all the young people with their music, and how much they looked forward to seeing Domenic back when he had finished his service in the Army.

Chapter 38

The next day Angelina looked at Beatrice and said, "Beatrice, my heart is throbbing so much that it's very painful. I can't let Domenic leave without saying goodbye to him. We must find a way to meet the boys again so that I can tell Domenic how much I will miss him, and give him a big, big hug."

Beatrice said, "Last week you made a plot and I was amazed how successful that was. Now I want to tell you something, but you know I'm not as clever as you are and my ideas are not usually as good as yours. Yesterday I heard Auntie say to Simon. 'Tomorrow is Sunday and after the church we need to take Roberto with us to see the Renato family so will you tell Angelina and Beatrice that after they return from church they need to go down to the vineyard to gather some white grapes for me. Tomorrow I need to go and visit a friend of mine in hospital so I would like to take some grapes from our vineyard to her."

Beatrice continued "We always go to the village for Mass, and I'm sure they will be there, and we'll be able to see them. We could tell them we need to go the vineyard to gather grapes for auntie and it would be nice if they could come and meet us there."

Angelina said, 'Yes but if they are not there, then what will we do?"

Beatrice said, ''If neither one of them is there, we can write a note, put it in an envelope and give it to one of Giuseppe's family to give to him. I can assure you, as soon as Giuseppe receives it, he will go straight to Domenic and they will come to the vineyard. They know where it is, because they have been there before and it will be safe, because auntie and uncle and Roberto are out together visiting friends."

On Sunday morning Angelina said, "Well, before we leave for church we'd better write a note and put it in an envelope, as you said yesterday."

Beatrice nodded her head and said, "As always, you are one step ahead and that's a good idea. We need to walk all the way to the village, because we are not able to go to the ten o'clock Mass but we'll arrive in time for the eleven o'clock one."

When they reached the village, they saw Domenic and Giuseppe walking towards them. Angelina found it difficult to contain herself for the joy of seeing them. Immediately she said how happy they were to see both of them there.

Angelina explained the situation, "This afternoon we need to go to the vineyard to gather some grapes for my mother, who needs to visit a friend in hospital. It will be just the right chance for you both to come and meet us there, so we can spend a little time together. I'll be able to tell you, Domenic how much I will miss you."

Beatrice said quickly, "And I would also like to tell you Giuseppe, how lucky I am to know that you live near my mother's house and we have more chance to see each other, even we can't let our family know yet about the feelings we have towards one another. Angelina's father is not an easy man, and we are not old enough yet to make our own decisions. Uncle Renato wants us both to get married to farmers. We will fight for our right to choose our own husbands, and he will never, ever, succeed. That's the reason we need to wait until we are old enough to be able to do what we want and not what he wants for us."

Domenic said, "We'll be there this afternoon after lunch and then we'll able to talk about our future. We are so happy we met you here now. I really thought we would not be able to meet one another before I left for the army, and that would be very sad for us."

Angelina and Beatrice both had tears in their eyes, and Angelina said, "Now we need to go into church because the service is starting, but we will wait for you both there this afternoon in the vineyard."

After the service Angelina and her cousin needed to walk all the way home because their family needed the

199

carriage to go and visit Renato's relatives. On the way home they sang romantic songs, and both were very happy. One hour later they arrived at the farm and noticed Simon was waiting for them. He said, "Dinner is ready for you two, but I need to go and visit one of our neighbours. I may spend some time with them, but after you've finished your dinner, remember to go to the vineyard to gather some white grapes for Mother, and I'll see you both later on."

He ran down the stairs, as fast as he could, and off towards the neighbour's farm.

Angelina and Beatrice rubbed their hands together and jumped for joy.

"This is marvellous," said Angelina. "It couldn't be better. Not for one minute did we think it would be as easy as this. Now we can spend some time with Domenic and Giuseppe and we can plan how we can keep in contact without our parents having any idea about what we are up to."

They grabbed some food and ran out of the house, as fast as they could towards the vineyard, in the joy of knowing that they would be able to meet Domenic and Giuseppe and spend some time with them.

Domenic and Giuseppe were eating white grapes and behaving like two school boys when they spotted the two young ladies running towards them. They all hugged each other until they were breathless. When they came to their senses they sat down and began to make plans for their future.

Angelina looked seriously at both of them and said, "Domenic, I love you much more then I can say, but I have a problem which I've already tried to explain to you. My father is a matchmaker, and in his brain he is the only one who knows what is good for his children. Therefore he expects me and Beatrice both to marry farmers but we won't do that in a million years. We would rather die from starvation then marry a man we don't love, so until we are twenty one our love must remain secret, otherwise my family and yours will suffer.''

Domenic looked sadly at Angelina and said, "Well we can't last another year, or more, without any communication with each other.''

Giuseppe suddenly said, "Wait a minute. You can write to Angelina at my address, and every Sunday when the girls come to church I will be able to give your letter to Angelina and you will be able to communicate with each other.''

They kept saying how marvellous it would be when they could say to their parents and to all their relatives, 'we are in love and will marry and that is that.' It doesn't matter what they say, because we will be able to tell them we are old enough and they need to accept what is right for us, and they can't do anything about it.''

Chapter 39

Angelina's parents had noticed a change in their daughter's behaviour towards the family.

Renato said to his wife, "Mary, I think we need to speed up the embroidery for the bottom drawer for our two young girls. Yesterday I had a chat with John's father and he told me that John likes Angelina very much. That pleases me a lot. As you know, I have always liked John. That young man is good looking and he's a hard worker, capable of doing everything. Personally, I would like him to be our future son-in-law, and I wouldn't mind if Jimmy could be a future nephew. The families of those young boys own farms and in the future they will inherit the properties. If Angelina and Beatrice married those young men they would be secure for life."

Mary sighed. "Oh, Renato, how can you keep on, when we have already mentioned this to the girls and do you remember the problem we had with them?"

Renato said, "Yes, I know but at the time they were much younger. Now they seem more grownup."

Mary said, "I'm not sure. Angelina is determined and I don't think she gave in to you very much. She is very stubborn, like you, and if she doesn't like the idea, there will be nothing you can do or say to change her mind."

He sat down heavily on his chair and continued mumbling to himself. "Women don't understand anything. I went to America to earn money to buy myself a farm, and provide security for my family. Now, the girls have every opportunity to enjoy a secure future, but they won't take it! Well, I will not give in to them. At the end of the day they need to do what they are told."

His wife leapt from her chair and faced him angrily. "You are as stubborn as a mule, but you have forgotten, they are just as bad as you are and you will not succeed."

By chance, Roberto overheard his parents' conversation, and he didn't like it. He thought that children needed to make their own destiny. They had already approached that subject and it had created a lot of bad feeling between them for a few days. He was very annoyed. He left the house, and straight away bumped into his brother, who could immediately see that something had happened to upset him.

"Whatever is the matter with you?" He enquired, "It looks like you've had an argument with someone and lost."

"Yes brother," he replied angrily, "I think we will be having a lot of arguments in our family if our parents don't change the way they think about the future of their children."

Simon looked at his brother curiously and asked, "Why?"

Roberto said, "I've just overheard a conversation between mother and father and what I heard will create a lot of trouble which makes me very unhappy."

Simon said, "Come on, let's find a place to sit down where our parents can't hear us or see us, and then you can tell me all about it."

Roberto run his fingers through his hair nervously, and said, "Did you notice anything different about Angelina and Beatrice, the last time we went with them to church?"

Simon said, "Yes, of course, I'm sure by the way Angelina behaves, that she is madly in love with Domenic, the young man with the guitar. The good thing is that he's gone back to finish his national service and hopefully when he returns that little romance will be all over and done with. She's still very young and you know what young people are like at that age. They fall in love so easily and then out of love just as quickly. It appears to me that Beatrice may be in love with Giuseppe, but she is a little bit older and maybe she has more sense than Angelina."

A few days later, Simon saw Angelina jumping and singing love songs as she worked around the farm.

"I think I know what's making you so happy," he

remarked.

She smiled and said, "I can't tell you, because for the time being my happiness needs to remain a secret until the time is right, and then, dear brother, I will make an announcement to all our family, relatives and the whole world, but I know that my happiness might not please everybody. In fact, I believe it will have a terrible effect on our family, but I don't care. It's what I want and nobody can take it away from me."

Simon shuddered in premonition and said, "It won't shock me because I have an idea what it is all about, but if it is what I think, you will find it very difficult to win this battle with our parents."

Angelina looked at him and said, "Yes, I know, but I will fight until I win. Simon, please, I ask you not to disclose anything to anybody. The conversation we had here today is between you and me until the time comes when I can reveal the choice I have made for my life."

She kissed Simon and said, "Simon, I trust you."

Simon saw Robert later, and said to him, "I have had a word with Angelina, and I promised her that although we both think we know what her secret is we will never say anything to anybody, because in reality we haven't anything to say. She didn't tell us anything. What she is saying is whatever we suspect, will we please keep it to ourselves, so that we can keep peace in our family."

Roberto nodded his head in agreement. "We don't think we know what is going on. We've had a talk about what we do know, but we need to keep quiet until the balloon goes up, and then we'll see what happens."

They embraced one another with tears running down their faces, and continued walking down the valley of the farm.

Domenic continued writing love letters to Angelina and sending them to Giuseppe's address as they'd planned and Giuseppe was able to deliver them to her on Sundays after Mass. Angelina replied with the most romantic letters she could to impress on Domenic the deep love she felt for him. She often told him how hard it was for her not to be near him. Her love was so deep that sometimes she wrote to him in very dramatic words like, 'Damn the railroad. Damn the steam engine!' because they have taken my love away to the Alps for service in the Italian army."

And so it went on until she received a letter from Domenic telling her that his national service was over and very soon he would be able to return to the village. Angelina couldn't contain herself after she'd finished reading his letter and a loud shout came from her room.

Mary ran into the room to see whatever had happened and found both Angelina and Beatrice hugging each other, and weeping tears of joy. She didn't understand what had come over them.

Angelina looked at her mother and said, "Domenic's national service is over and at last he's been discharged from the army."

Mary was confused, not understanding why this news would have such an effect on the girls. She said, "Whatever is the matter with the two of you? Who is this young man, and what is he to do with you?"

They both looked at Mary, and remained silent.

Mary repeated her question. "I need to know why you are both so excited. After all he is a just a young man from the village who has finished his national service and what is that to do with you two?"

Angelina stood up and faced her mother boldly. She said, "Well, I might as well tell you now. I'm in love with Domenic."

Her mother put her hand to her mouth and ran out of the room. She was shocked and horrified, knowing how much trouble this would cause in her family. She went into her room and shut her bedroom door, and she was trembling. How would her husband react when he realised that his beloved daughter was in love with a merchant's son. She was sure that he wouldn't accept it when his precious daughter told him she would never be a farmer's wife but instead she wanted to marry the son of a merchant who always works together with his brother in their family business. Renato had decided a long time ago that Angelina and Beatrice would marry farmers and be like his wife. He had not considered at any time that they would oppose his wishes. He certainly wouldn't be expecting his beloved daughter to tell him something like, 'no father, I will not marry John, but I will marry Domenic, the son of Mr Francesco Di Catto'.

Mary thought that the shock might kill him, or worse, that his behaviour would be uncontrollable and shocking. What would happen to her family? Mary was afraid.

Chapter 40

When Mary heard a knock on her bedroom door, she froze and then began to shake like a leaf. She called out, "Who is it?"

Roberto answered. "Mum, it's me."

He opened the door and realised immediately that something was terribly wrong with his mother.

He said, "Mother, whatever is wrong with you today?"

She lifted up her teary eyes and said, "I don't know how to tell you this, Roberto but Angelina just told me, that the young man who plays the guitar in the church club is returning from army service and now she wants to tell everybody she is madly in love with him. I don't know how your father will react to this news. He may think it's just a joke and his daughter's gone absolutely mad, or it could make him very angry and he could lose his temper. Believe me, Robert, I think there will be a lot of trouble in our family and it could be unbearable for all of us."

Robert looked his mother in the eye and said, "Mother, you mustn't say anything at all to our father, because we all know what he is like but, given time, he will surely realise that he is not going to be able to make Angelina do what he wants, or what he thinks is best for her. I'll shall go to her room and tell her that for the time being, she must not say anything to our father or to anybody else. Hopefully, in time, he will come to his senses and then slowly he will reason with himself and understand that his children need to be responsible for their own future."

His mother agreed with him. Robert went to Angelina's room and challenged her. "Angelina, you did say you wouldn't reveal your secret until you are twenty one, so why now? Do you realise, if you say anything to our father now, there is a chance that the shock will give him a heart attack, or that he will go absolutely mad and then, who knows what will happen to our family?"

Angelina looked a little shamefaced as she tried to

explain herself to her brother. "Unfortunately, I couldn't help falling in love with Domenic, but I will promise I won't say anything for the time being. In time, Father must realise that I will not marry John or anybody else except my Domenic. Our parents need to understand, once and for all that their children need to be responsible for their own destiny."

Roberto said, "Yes, but for now you must keep quiet. In time we will try to convince him. His ideas are absurd. If they really want the best for you they must let you choose which man you want for your husband."

Satisfied that he had Angelina's assurance that she would keep her secret a bit longer, Roberto went back out into the fields to help his brother.

Alone again with her cousin, Angelina said, "Now, I am beginning to realise how difficult it will be for me to meet Domenic and for us to know more about each other, but I promise you this. I will fight tooth and nail with my parents to convince them of my decision. As I said before, as soon as I'm twenty one I will tell them who I want to be my future husband. For now though I need to find a secret place where we can meet and get to know one other, to find out if our love is what we both want for the rest of our lives. Then I will be able to offer him my love for all eternity. Remember Beatrice, you are in the same boat. My parents want John for their son-in- law, and Jimmy for their nephew."

Beatrice shook her head and said, "Oh no. If my uncle wants that for me he will be disappointed. I will return to my parents' house, because they will not make me marry to a man I don't love. My mother has already said to me, 'Beatrice, she said, you will marry the man you love' and she said that if uncle gets very stroppy, my father will have a word with him."

Angelina said, "Hey, what about me. Are you telling me if that happens, you'll go back to your parents' house and leave me here all by myself to fight my corner?"

"You won't need me here any longer," said Beatrice,

"because you will be so busy making up ground with your family, there will be no time to miss me. You will have Domenic to help you and support you until you have both achieved what you want and uncle comes to his senses. When the time is right, he will take you to church on his arm, right up the aisle and deliver you to Domenic himself.''

Angelina laughed bitterly, "Ha! This is a dream, and you are very romantic. I'm afraid that I can only dream in the moment, because I know I will have a very long battle with my family and I know I need to shed many tears, but I will not give up until the victory is mine.''

Beatrice said, "I know you will win, but remember you always have my support even if I'm not near you like now. When you need me I will be where you are at all times.''

Angelina smiled warmly at her cousin. "We have been together since we were very young, and we will always support each other, I know that.'' said Angelina. "You are not just my cousin, you are my best friend, and no matter what the future holds for us, good or bad, we will fight together, until we have success.''

Beatrice said, "Now that you have told auntie you are in love with Domenic, I wonder what will happen to our Saturday church club?''

"I haven't the faintest idea" said Angelina, "Because Mum and Robert know, and I've been told by him to keep quiet. If nobody else knows, there is a chance that everything will be as before, and we must hope we can still do as always and take it from there. I need to write a letter for Giuseppe so that he can get it to Domenic.''

"Well, we usually go to Mass on Sundays so we can hope we'll have a chance to meet them both there, and then you can give him the letter yourself,'' said Beatrice.

Angelina said, "If we have a chance to meet them both, I can't express my joy at seeing him but it will be absolutely marvellous to see him more than ever now, that I know neither my mother, nor my father can make me marry any farmer. Even the thought of that makes me feel ill.''

Beatrice smiled, "And fortunately I can escape this situation, because my parents will have the last word.''

Angelia said with feeling, "Thank God for that.''

While they were talking, Simon came into the room. "Can I join in your conversation''? He asked.

Angelina and Beatrice both smiled, and Angelina said, "Of course you can, but you know we are very boring.''

Simon replied, "You maybe, but I'm not. I need to discuss something very important with you two now.''

Angelina raised her eyes in surprise, and thought 'what now?'

"Well," said Simon. "Robert has told me what you said to Mum, and like Robert I'm very concerned for your future. Unfortunately, we know for certain that if father gets any idea of this, it will be very difficult to deny it. We can beg him but, as you know, he can be very stubborn, but we shall have to try.''

Beatrice said to Simon, "Yes, try we must, but that is easier said than done, because, as you have just said, he is so difficult.''

"Yes, yes, but if we go to John, surely he will understand, because no man wants to marry a woman who doesn't love him? And that goes for Jimmy as well, because we also know you love Giuseppe although I know your parents will not oppose him and will be happy for you to marry. In your case, the choice is yours, but our father's ambition is to see both of you get married to the men he chooses. Robert and I will have a talk with both John and Jimmy and explain the situation to them. We are sure they will understand.''

Angelina said, "It will probably be a shock for them. Our father has convinced them that we were the right girls for them and now you're going there to tell them that it isn't so, that it was just our father's fantasy. How they will take that, do you think?''

Simon said, "Yes, but the facts are as I said before, that it was his idea to see his precious daughter and his beloved niece get married into prosperous families with big farms, in the hope that one day they would inherit the family fortune and became like his own wife.''

"You are probably right, Simon," said Angelina. "You must go to them and explain. That it is the only way we can get out of the situation we are in now. The family knows what is going on, and to prevent bad feeling between our families, we must try for everybody's sake.''

A few hours later, Simon met with Roberto and said, "I have had a discussion with both girls, and they've agreed for us to go and explain everything to John and Jimmy.''

The following day, John and Jimmy were passing near the farmhouse, and seeing them Simon decided to use the opportunity to speak to them. He called out to them, "Hi, John and Jimmy. When you are free, Roberto and I would like to have a word with you both.''

John said cautiously, "Is anything wrong?''

"Of course not", said Simon reassuringly, "It's just that we need to have a friendly chat.''

John said, "Okay, I tell you what, tomorrow Jimmy and I need to go to Orchid village, where there's a nice restaurant called 'The White Horse'. We could meet there at about two o'clock for a cup of coffee, or a beer if you both like.''

Simon said, "That will be fine with us. We'll see you there tomorrow at two o'clock.''

Simon went to his brother and told him he'd made arrangements to meet with John and Jimmy at a restaurant called The White Horse, near Orchid, the next day.

Roberto said, "That's fine by me!''

The next day, both brothers went to the White Horse, and found John and Jimmy already there, waiting for them.

Roberto and Simon joined them and Roberto said, "At last, we have a few minutes to ourselves.''

John said, "You boys don't know how lucky you are. You have a marvellous father who lets you do what you want. Our fathers, as you know, are brothers, and they are very domineering. Sometimes they can be aggressive

211

towards us and the personnel who work for us, and even more so if they can't have their own way."

Robert raised his eyebrows and said, "Go on with you, we've known your fathers for a long time and they are both very good gentlemen. You say that your fathers' behaviour is bad, but you don't know anybody until you live with them. Yes, our father is a kind man and helps everybody as much as he can, and, yes he has a good heart, but as long as people understand him and they do what he says, they are his best friends. But if anybody crosses his path, no matter who, then he can change very quickly and become a man you would not wish to meet him or even smell. We tell you, our father is more than dominant towards us, he is controlling. When we were children we obeyed him, but now he tries to control us and he thinks he has the right to choose wives for us, and husbands for Angelina and Beatrice, whether they are in love or not. It doesn't matter if they have no feelings towards the chosen wife or husband. For him it is not important as long they have big farms. Only then can they be part of our family. But tell us, what good would it be if there is no love between wife and husband? We all know that property is a necessary part of our existence, but love and tranquillity is also essential for a family with children. We came here because we want to help both you and our sister and cousin. We believe he wants you to marry the girls for business reasons only. For young people like you two, love needs to come from both sides. We believe that young people must choose their own destiny we all know what the proverb says, 'You make your bed and you lay in it.'"

John and Jimmy were a little taken aback at Robert's long speech and John said slowly, "Are we to understand that you came here to tell us that you would not be happy, if in time, we would like to court your sister and your cousin?"

Robert said hastily, "No my friends, we would be more than happy if they responded to your love. My father wants all of us to get married into wealthy families like

212

yours, but if there is no love what good is it for anybody?"

John and Jimmy looked thoughtful and John said, "We do like your sister and your cousin, but we haven't yet had a chance to get to know them. At the moment we are just good friends and we don't know what our future holds, but it seems to us that we may need to look further afield. That doesn't stop our family being friends, as we've always been."

Simon said, "Of course not, our families have been good friends for many years and we'd like to continue being so for many years to come. What we don't want to see is, that one day we discover that our family has been mixed up with the wrong partners, just because our father was so selfish that he wanted his daughter and his niece marry two nice men like you. His ambition, as we said before, is the inheritance the girls would get if they married into a rich family. If our father keeps pushing you both towards his daughter and his niece, say to him, 'for the time being, we are ok, but in the future we will see. We want destiny to take control of our life, and we hope that our parents will let us choose the future for ourselves. We hope that we will remain friends as we've always been, for many years to come'."

John and Jimmy had understood exactly what Robert and Simon meant. They held out their hands, and Jimmy said, "Thank you for putting us in the picture. Now we understand what you meant and for that we are very thankful to both of you. You are very good friends."

John and Jimmy left and went to their business, and Robert and Simon went back to the farm, knowing their job was accomplished.

Chapter 41

On Saturday morning, while they were all at table, Angelina let Roberto know that she wanted to have a private word, without anybody else in the family realising. Roberto left the table and a few minutes later Angelina followed him.

She said, "Roberto, I know, even more now, how important it is to keep my secret from father. I'm asking you and Simon to give me a chance to meet Domenic and explain to him, the position I'm in. Now if there is any chance it could stir up conflict between Domenic and our family, it can't be allowed until I'm old enough to do so."

Robert said, "Yesterday, we met John and Jimmy and we don't think you and Beatrice need to worry about them any longer. We explained the situation with father to them and we think they both understood. If our father keeps telling them to pursue you, they need not take any notice, and at the same time they must not tell our father that we have had a word with them. I can assure you they do not know anything about you and Domenic, you have my word. Tonight, Simon and I will come with you and Beatrice to the church club, and we'll give you both the chance to have a long chat with Domenic and Giuseppe, but you must both be very careful of the people of our village or before we know it, they will start to gossip, and in no time our father will get to know and then what...?"

"Roberto, I'm very grateful to you and Simon. I promise you both we will be very sensible, and whatever we do, we'll take great care not to let anybody know until I'm old to announce it."

Roberto then went to his mother and tried to explain the position to her, and to see if it was at all possible to avoid any conflict in their family. Through no fault of their own there was a chance of losing the peace and tranquillity they'd had until now. It was frightening to know that if they let the cat out of the bag, and their father got to know, there would be a big problem to resolve, especially if their father ever found out that all along, his daughter and niece had been seeing the young men when they were not old enough to do so, and mother knew about it. But Angelina had promised him that nobody would ever know anything about it until the time was right and nobody could stop her. Come what may, her father, family and friends would in time, know of the romance between her and Domenic, the son of the merchant Francesco Di'Catto.''

Mary listened to her son Robert and with a tremble in her voice, she said, "This is very scary, but we must try to keep it secret. If we don't, we will have a very difficult time. It will be like a time bomb ready to explode in our house, because Renato can't achieve what he wants. He has fought all his life to see his children in a better position than he ever was himself, until he went to America and earned and saved money to achieve what we have now. In his mind he would like us, his family to be even better off than we are now.''

After talking with his mother about Angelina's secret, Roberto remembered he'd promised Angelina that he and his brother Simon would both accompany them to the church club. He knocked on their bedroom door, and Angelina said, "Roberto, we won't be long, I'm just finishing writing a letter and then we'll be ready.''

He replied, "Take your time, it's too early yet. Be ready in an hour's time.''

She was pleased, because she had time to explain the situation in the letter she was writing.

'My dearest Domenic,' she'd written, *'I can't explain the joy I feel to know that your military service is over and I'm now able to tell you how much I love you. Tonight will be difficult for me because the people in our village will start gossiping if they suspect anything and it would soon reach my parents which would be a big problem for me. First, because I'm not old enough to make my own decisions and also because I have very strict parents who, even when I*

am old enough, would only permit me to meet you if they had approved you first. If Mum and Dad don't approve, don't worry, we'll keep our secret and can still love one another. When the time is right we will be able to let the whole world know that we belong to each another and they can't do anything about it, because we will be old enough to get on with our own lives.'

'Beatrice is my cousin and we've lived together since we were babies. She will be able to explain everything to Giuseppe and then he can talk to you about the position I'm in. As the proverb says, 'Where there's a will there's a way'. Nobody can stop the deep love we have for each other.'

'Tonight, Beatrice and I, with my two brothers, will come to see you playing your music, but unfortunately, as much as I would like to embrace you and hold you near me, whispering all the love I feel for you, my beloved Domenic, it will not be possible. Beatrice and I will try to find a secret place so that we can meet, until we can look for a future together and overcome any obstacle in our way.

All my love

Angelina xxxx '

Before putting the letter in the envelope, she let Beatrice read it and then she said, "Roberto and Simon are very concerned that if the people in the club notice we are in love with Domenic and Giuseppe and start gossiping, our parents will get to know and then what will happen? So I'll give the letter to you and you give it to Giuseppe. Eventually he will give it to Domenic, but we must find a secret place to meet them both, without our parents knowing anything about it, until we are old enough to get married, whether they like it or not. For now we'll make ourselves as pretty as we can and we'll be with them, but without giving people any idea about what is going on between us and Domenic and Giuseppe. We'll only let people think it's the music we are interested in and nothing else.''

Five minutes later Angelina heard her brother Robert telling his parents about the concert and that they'd invited Angelina and Beatrice to go with him and Simon.

Angelina said, "Mum and Dad, Beatrice and I are going with Roberto and Simon to the concert. We'll see you later if you're both still awake.''

They smiled and Mary said, "I very much doubt that your father and I will be awake as we're very tired. We'll see you all tomorrow. Good night."

Then the girls left the house with their brothers.

When they arrived at the club, the music was already playing loud and the young people were dancing to the beat of 'Tango Italiano'. Domenic and Giuseppe stopped playing and announced ten minutes of interval. Domenic put his guitar in a safe place in the corner of the room, with Giuseppe's trumpet, and went towards Angelina and Beatrice, shaking hands with Robert and Simon then turning towards Angelina and Beatrice.

While they were talking, Beatrice very carefully gave the letter to Giuseppe, explaining to Domenic the situation they had with her family. Domenic would be able to read it later on, when he was at home. When Angelina's eyes met those of Domenic, she had a job to contain her tears, but she did! Then the show continued without a break until the end. Domenic and Angelina were careful not to talk when they were near each other. They both knew their hearts were bursting with joy, but they also knew they needed to conceal their feelings in front of Angelina's brothers and the village people. Only one little sign would be enough to spread gossip all around the village. The family of Renato would be thrown in turmoil and affect not only Angelina and Beatrice but also Roberto and Simon.

Renato would accuse his sons of knowing all along what Angelina and Beatrice were up to and kept quiet. But if that was not enough, they had gone against their father and helped the girls, when they knew all along what their father wanted for his precious daughter and niece. That was to be happily married into a well off family. Luckily the girls managed to control themselves and, as far as they were concerned, everything went smoothly. The next morning Angelina and Beatrice were very happy to know that Domenic was home and they would find a secret place to meet, away from their parents' knowledge.

Chapter 42

Two days later, Beatrice was surprised see her young brother Mario strolling round the farm. She immediately went out to meet him and asked what he was doing there. He looked relieved,

"Our mother sent me here to see you, but I have been told by Giuseppe, our neighbour, to give this letter to you. You need to be very careful not to let anyone see me give this to you."

Beatrice took the letter from Mario and realised that it was addressed to her but was really from Domenic to Angelina.

Mario said, "I also wanted to tell you that yesterday there was a knock on our door. When I opened it, there was our neighbour, asking me if he could see our parents. I took him into the kitchen, where Mum was preparing dinner for all of us. I heard him telling our mother that the postman who delivers the post round the district is not well enough to continue with his job. Then Dad walked into the kitchen and smiled at him. Our neighbour went on to say that, for that reason, the job had been offered to their son, Giuseppe and they were over the moon. When they told Giuseppe he was pleased, but he said, "Father, I will only take the job if I can go to see Mr and Mrs Forino and have a word with both of them, because I want to have their daughter Beatrice beside me." Our father said, "I can't see why not. That can be arranged, and we will let you know as soon as possible."

Beatrice went to ask her aunty and her uncle if it was possible to go home to stay for a few days with her parents. She was astonished when they said, 'yes, of course you can go, and take Angelina with you'. Beatrice went back to her brother Mario and said to him, "Go back to mum and dad and tell them that Angelina and I will come home for a few days as soon as we can."

Mario went back to the village and Beatrice went

looking for her cousin in the rose garden. Beatrice stood there and beckoned, to let Angelina know she needed to speak, but then she couldn't. Angelina saw her cousin standing there without saying a word and said, "Whatever has come over you? It looks like you've seen a ghost."

Beatrice began to stutter, "I need... to speak....to you now..."

Angelina was startled and ran towards her cousin. Quickly looking around the garden she spotted an old bench. Then she grabbed Beatrice by the hand and made her sit down.

"Now, tell me what is going on."

Beatrice looked at her cousin, "It isn't easy for me to explain it to you, but I must try. While you've been here, my young brother came to the farmhouse looking for me. I was surprised to see him there and I asked him if there was anything wrong at home. He said, 'No, but Giuseppe gave me a letter to give to you.' When I opened it, I realised there was another closed envelope inside, with your name on it and here it is. Giuseppe's father says his son Giuseppe has been offered a job as postman because the one there now needs to retire because of poor health. They offered the job to Giuseppe and he said 'yes', but only if I will be beside him, and together we can go and talk to my parents. Mum and dad said, 'We don't know what he means. We are Beatrice's parents, but she's lived with her uncle and her aunty since she was a baby. We need to arrange something, and then see what this is all about.' "

Angelina said, "I'm confused, but I tell you what, there is only one way to find out."

"Yes, I know," said Beatrice, "So I went to your parents and they said we can both go and visit my family for a few days."

Two days later, Giovanna and Mathew, her husband, arrived at the farm to have a talk with Renato and family about their daughter Beatrice.

They said, "We came here because our neighbour's son has been offered a job in the post office, and we think he is very fortunate, but he said he would only accept the job if he can come to speak to us at our home with Beatrice by his side. We don't understand what he means and we need to find out.''

Renato was sitting near the table and banged his fist on the table, jumped out of his chair, and with a loud voice said, "How dare the two of you come here and tell us your neighbour can't take the job if Beatrice isn't beside him! I want to know who this young man is to demand such a thing. Beatrice has been with us since she was a baby and we are the ones who have the right to say what is good for her. We need to make sure her future will be as good as possible. She needs to marry someone from a family like ours, in farming, and then she will know that, no matter what the world throws at her, she will always have food to put on the table for her and her family, for the rest of her life.''

Giovanna turned to her sister Mary, "Yes, it is true that you and Renato and all your family have the right to speak out, but at the end of the day, Beatrice needs to choose for herself who will be her future husband. If you remember, we said to both of you, we will give our child to you, with the understanding that you will never be able to adopt her. She is still our daughter, no matter what, and we have every right to take her home and decide what her future will be.''

Mary stood up, looked at her sister, and said to her. "Giovanna, how can you take Beatrice away from Angelina, when you know they are so very close. They have lived and grown up together and it is cruel and merciless for you to take this precious child away from us.''

"Look, Mary, we have not come to take Beatrice away from you, but you need to understand, sooner or later that these two young girls will get married and they have the right to choose their future companion for themselves. Then they will be able to have a happy family, like we've done. We have come here to ask you and Renato to let

221

Beatrice come home just for a few days. If you like, Angelina can come and stay as well, and then both of them can return to you happy and refreshed. Believe me Mary, a little change doesn't do any harm to anybody. We are family, and we will find out what this young man means by having Beatrice beside him. We'll make sure nobody makes her do anything she doesn't want to do, until she is old enough to get on in life with the man she chooses herself. For now, she must come home and see what this young man wants from her.''

Renato was very angry. He left, slamming the door behind him. He went looking for his sons for support. He was sure that he had every right to object to what he was being asked to agree to, and he thought that only his sons could stop their aunt and uncle from taking Beatrice away from him and his wife in such a cruel and ruthless way. Indeed, they loved their cousin and they couldn't allow her to marry a poor man like Giuseppe, who would always just be a poor postman. In his mind Beatrice must be a farmer's wife and then she would never need to worry about how to feed her family in the future. Also, it was cruel to take her way from Angelina.

As soon as they saw their father arrive, Roberto and Simon knew something dramatic had happened at home. Roberto said to Simon, "Oh...oh. Look out. I see trouble coming our way."

As soon as Renato got near his sons, he started shouting and making desperate movements with his arms, saying, "Come home. We have a problem. They've come to take our girls away from us. We need your support.''

Roberto went up to his father and tried to calm him down, saying to him, "Father, calm down, and tell us who wants to take them away.''

Renato was in such a state that he wasn't able to talk. Roberto and Simon took him over to the shed and got him to sit down. Then they asked him again, "Dad, who are these people who want to take way your girls?'' Renato heaved a big sigh, and then said, "They, are your Uncle

Mathew and your Aunt Giovanna, and they want Beatrice back in the village.''

Robert and Simon were astonished and found it difficult to understand why their father was so worried about it. After all Beatrice was his niece and Angelina was his daughter, and if his in-laws wanted to take their daughter away for a while, where was the harm? They decided to go home with him and find out what was going on in their family. Robert took his father's arm said, "Come on Dad, we'll go home with you and find out what this is all about.''

Ten minutes later, they arrived home, and heard their mother talking to their Aunt Giovanna. They went in and greeted their uncle and aunt, and then they asked what was going on.

Their uncle explained, "There is nothing wrong. We came here because we would like to take Beatrice home for a few days. Our neighbour has a son called Giuseppe, and he has been offered a job as the postman. However, he says he will not take the job until he's been to talk to us, and he wants Beatrice beside him. We want to find out what this young man wants from us and why he needs Beatrice beside him''

Neither Robert nor Simon, were surprised when they heard their uncle's explanation for their visit because they already knew that Beatrice and Giuseppe were madly in love with each other and were waiting for the opportunity to tell their parents. The air was charged with emotion and Roberto and Simon both knew that they needed to calm everyone down before things got out of hand.

"Mum, Dad," said Robert, Please let Beatrice go, and Angelina too if she wants to, with uncle and auntie for a few days. A little change would do them good.''

Renato was very angry but he knew he had no choice but to let them go. However, he emphasised that it was to be only for a few days and then they should return home to where they belonged.''

Roberto then drew his uncle and aunt aside and said,

"Please don't be too hard on the girls. Giuseppe and Beatrice are in love, and it is right for Giuseppe to want Beatrice beside him, but be careful not to let our parents know anything about Beatrice and Giuseppe. It needs to remain a secret until their love is so strong it is impossible to conceal any longer and no matter what problems come their way, nobody can ever stop them, not even our stubborn father. He can shout, he can insult Giuseppe, but in the end he needs to come to terms with it himself. He must surely remember how, many years ago when he was young himself, he rejected his own parents' wishes for his future and married the woman he loved."

Giovanna and Mathew stood quite quietly listening to what their nephew was saying to them. They were speechless and could hardly take in what they were hearing. After a little while, Mathew spoke.

"So, you and Simon have known all along what was going on, and we knew nothing. We can't deny that we knew that Giuseppe, being our neighbour, liked Beatrice, but as a friend only. We never realised that deeper feelings were developing between them. Now that we know, we're very happy for them to get to know each other better and we will do whatever it takes to help them in any way we can. We promise that we will not let slip anything to Renato and Mary until the time comes right and nothing can stop the two young lovers getting married. They could become a very lovely family and that will bring joy to all of us."

Once this understanding had been reached, Mathew and Giovanna embraced their nephews, said their goodbyes and went back to the village taking Beatrice and Angelina with them.

Chapter 43

The joy of the two young girls was indescribable when they realised the battle had begun much earlier than they had predicted, with the help of Beatrice's father and mother. As they arrived in the village, they spotted Giuseppe on the corner of the road. Beatrice's heart began to beat very fast, and her mother noticed her face was as red as a very ripe tomato.

"Beatrice", she said, "We've noticed there's a young man waiting for you.''

Beatrice was surprised at that remark, but of course she didn't know her cousin Roberto had had had a quiet word her parents. Beatrice glanced at them curiously and answered, "Of course, it's Giuseppe.''

Her heart beating so hard that it was difficult to contain her emotions, but she knew she had to control herself so as not to let her parents know what was going on between her and Giuseppe. So she said again "It's Giuseppe, our neighbour.''

Her parents glanced at each other and then her mother said, "Beatrice and Angelina, tomorrow is a special day for our family and we were thinking of inviting Giuseppe and his family for a special dinner.''

Beatrice and Angelina stared into each other's eyes. Did Beatrice's parents somehow suspect that something was going on between Beatrice and Giuseppe? "Why are we having a special dinner tomorrow? What is going on?" asked Beatrice. Her parents smiled knowingly.

"We thought it would be nice to celebrate you both being here for a few days and how nice it would be to share the excitement with our neighbour.''

Angelina gave her cousin a little nudge. Beatrice turned to look at her, and saw Angelina make a sign to her to keep quiet.

As soon they were in the house, they ran into one of the children's bedrooms, and before they spoke to each other they looked all around the room to make sure there was nobody who could hear them.

Beatrice looked at Angelina and said, "Angelina, I know you've understood as much as I have. My parents know what is going on between me and Giuseppe. That's why they came to the farm and brought us home to find out more, and if that is so, what do we do now?"

"We don't say anything," said Angelina. "We just act as normal as possible. If they know what we think they do, sooner or later they will interrogate us, and then we must answer them accordingly, as best we can."

Beatrice looked up into the sky and said, "Oh no. I think there will be a lot of trouble between my parents and yours, because they have a different view about their children's future."

Angelina suddenly felt very grown up and serious. "We always knew that one day there would be a big battle between our parents, but we can't deal with them. However, we will continue to fight for our future until they understand that they can't organise their children's lives once they are adults. They must let them get on with their own lives."

Beatrice said, "Oh Angelina, I've always said you were much braver than me, but I'll try my best to be strong, because I know you are beside me. Together we can handle whatever destiny throws at us."

Angelina said, "For now, we'll talk with all your brothers and sisters and then we'll take it from there. Don't worry.

The next day they were aware that Giuseppe and his mother and father had arrived. They all went into one of the rooms to have a private conversation. A few minutes later they all came out and went into the dining room. Giuseppe shook hands with Angelina, gave Beatrice a big smile and she smiled back at him. The family, with their guests, sat round the table, and while they were eating dinner one of Beatrice's younger sisters turned round to Beatrice and said, "Giuseppe won't take the job he's been offered unless he can have you beside him."

Giovanna drew a sharp breath and said, "Be quiet, Elizabeth!"

Then she turned towards Beatrice and said, "Your father and I need to talk to both of you, but for now let's all sit down and enjoy the dinner."

An hour later, Giovanna and Mathew, called Beatrice and Angelina into the dayroom, and made sure none of the younger children were in listening distance.

Mathew spoke first. He said, "Now then, young ladies, we know a little bit of what is going on between you, Beatrice, and Giuseppe and we also know about Renato and Mary's ambition for you both. Like every father and mother, they want what's best for their children. Unfortunately, it doesn't always go the way that the parents want. It seems to us that's what has happened to you now, Beatrice. Angelina's parents are not aware of all this and I want to make it clear that nobody, must say anything to them about today, because it would doubtless trigger a big war between Renato and Mary and us. The two of you know we would never be able to see one another again, and that must not happen. Do you understand?"

Beatrice started crying and said, "But we must marry the man we love when we are old enough."

"That is the reason we came to the farm, because we agree that you and Giuseppe, when you both are old enough, can be officially engaged."

Then Giovanna spoke to Angelina and made sure none of their younger children were about.

"Angelina", she began. I know Beatrice is not just your cousin, but also your best friend, and so more than ever, this needs to remain a secret between the two of you. We know Beatrice and Giuseppe are in love with one another, and we are not at all surprised that he is here with his family today. We also know that your father and mother are anxious for each of you to marry only a farmer's son. We think differently. We believe that young people should

227

be responsible for their own destiny but we can't let Beatrice's brothers and sisters hear what is being said. Angelina, do you think you could distract them while we are talking so that they don't know what is going on? If they find out, before we know it, in no time at all, the news will be all round the village. Your mother and father will get to know. Then you know what will happen.''

Angelina understood the problem completely and suggested that she take her young cousins out into the village to buy ice-cream.

While the youngsters were out, Giuseppe was able to speak to Giovanna and Mathew and he said, "Beatrice and I have known that we belong to one another since the last day of school. We kept it secret because we were too young. We're still not old enough to get married and we don't have the means to support a family. However I have been offered a job in the post office which is secure, and I will save as much money as I can for our future but I can only do that if I know Beatrice will be beside me for the rest of my life."

Mathew said, "Giuseppe, you have just said, you are both very young, and it is much too early to promise such a commitment now. Your feelings may change as you both get older, and then what will happen?''

Giuseppe, with Beatrice at his side, said, "No, our love will last forever. I can only take this job if I know that Mr Renato Caccia Capo will never be able to make Beatrice marry the man he wants, just because his family have a farm, and his job is secure. If I know Beatrice will be at my side for the rest of my life, I promise you I will take the job in the post office, and I will also help my father with the shoe shop. We will be together forever and support one another. Because we know the situation with Angelina's parents, we promise that it will remain secret until we are old enough to do otherwise.''

Both sets of parents felt reassured by Giuseppe's promise that Renato's family wouldn't ever know anything about their romance until they were both old enough to get married without any trouble.

A few days later, the young ladies returned to the farmhouse. For many years Renato and his wife Mary had had the pleasure of inviting the families of John and Jimmy as guests, but lately the invitation had been turned down by both families. One day Renato said to his wife, "Mary, I don't understand. After many years of being friends with John and Jimmy's families, now every time we invite them, they turn down our invitation."

"There must be a reason why they refused to come to our dinner party," she said thoughtfully. "It is very unusual for them to do that after all these years I wonder what the reason could be."

Renato was furious. "Well, I am not going to accept their refusal without an explanation. I shall go to their house and demand to know what it's all about."

"Mary put her hand to her mouth in horror. "Oh no. Renato, you mustn't. You'll never change will you? You're as stubborn as ever. If they don't accept the invitation we've sent them, maybe they are not well, and I'm quite sure they will answer when they are ready."

Two weeks later, while he was walking along the road, Renato saw John with a young lady beside him and he was shocked. He hadn't expected to see that having always thought that John could never have anyone else but his beloved Angelina. He said to himself, "This isn't possible. I must be seeing things. John belongs to Angelina."

He gave them a hard look but he didn't have the nerve to say a word. Instead he turned back to the farmhouse and ran up the steps, two at a time. When he reached his room he flopped into his chair. When his wife Mary came in, she saw her husband on his chair in great distress.

"Renato what's happened to you?" she asked worriedly.

He looked at her and said, "I have just discovered why our friends haven't accepted our invitation to the family party."

His wife smiled at him quite unsuspectingly. "Oh, yes.

What is it then?'' She asked.

He found it difficult to find the words at first, but then he said, "The dream I've had since the birth of our daughter has just been dissolved in a flash.''

More curious than ever, Mary insisted on knowing what had happened, but again he was unable to tell her.

Mary stamped her feet on the floor and shouted at her husband, saying, "I don't understand you. Will you please explain yourself once and for all.''

Then she looked at his face, and saw that his expression was one of devastation, as if the whole world had tumbled down on him. Then finally, he said, "All the dreams we had for our daughter have faded into thin air.''

By now Mary was beginning to be exasperated and very annoyed with her husband.

"Renato stop playing games. Just tell me exactly what happened today?''

He looked at her with tears in his eyes, and said, "My heart is broken for our daughter. She will never be able to marry the man we thought was to be the man of her life because, today I saw another young lady beside John, and he was hugging her closely.''

Mary instantly felt a sense of relief. She knew now that Angelina would at last begin to see light at the end of the tunnel.

Mary looked at her husband kindly and said, "Oh, well. Don't worry Renato. There are many more fish in the sea ready to be caught.

He answered, "But it's not what we planned for our Angelina."

"Mary answered, "You are right that it's not what we've planned. Destiny has its own plans for her.''

Roberto and Simon soon realised that their father was not the same person they were used to. He'd always been sociable with everybody, but suddenly he appeared very quiet and subdued, and was obviously making some effort to avoid any contact with his neighbour.

Roberto mentioned it to Simon. ''We need to find out

what the problem is with our father, without him realising we are worried about his health.''

Simon looked at his brother said, "Surely our mother must realise there is something the matter with him?''

Roberto said, "Yes, tomorrow I will have a word with Mum, and see if I can find out what is wrong.''

The next day Roberto waited until his father went out of the house, then went into the kitchen to see his mother and find out why their father appeared to be unwell.

Before he spoke to his mother she said to him, "Robert, after you've had your break, you need to go and help your father in the orchard."

Robert looked at his mother and said, "Yes mother, I will, but not before you tell me what is wrong with Dad."

Mary looked at her son and said, "You all know your father is very concerned about the future of his family, but more than ever now. Yesterday he saw John with a young girl on his arm; and they were hugging one other, walking along our road not very far from the farmhouse. For a long time we thought that one day, John and Angelina would get married and have a long life together, blessed with many children. All that is impossible now and it's difficult for your father to accept the situation. It will take him a long time to get over that.''

Roberto said sternly, "Mother, you jolly well knew that it would never have happened, because both girls are already in love with somebody else and are only waiting to be old enough to do as they please.'' With that he left to go and help his father.

He spotted Simon in one of the fields and he went over to him and said, "Simon, the lecture we gave to John and Jimmy worked well, because yesterday our father saw a young girl on John's arm. I'm afraid it shocked him very much and the shock could trigger a heart attack. For a good many years he'd thought Angelina and John belonged to one other, but that was the wish of our parents not of their daughter. They should know what the proverb says, 'Man is born, but destiny is given!' Now we can only hope that Dad can get over it for all our sakes.''

Simon said, "It must be very sad for our father, seeing what he believed would come to be in time, was nothing but pie in sky. They had wished for their precious young daughter the same chance that our mother had, to be a farmer's wife.''

Roberto said, "But with one difference. Not many young ladies like to see little lambs, and little chicken slaughtered nearly every day.''

Simon said, "You're right, but unfortunately, most of us like eating meat.''

Roberto said, "Well, the only thing we need to do now, is to support our father and do our best to help him along until he gets over his disappointment and looks ahead for a better future for all of us.''

Chapter 44

Angelina and Beatrice realised Renato was a very grumpy old man, but with a difference now, that he didn't mind any more if Angelina and his niece went to spend some time with Beatrice's parents in the village of Cave. Giuseppe took the job in the post office, and now he was very pleased to be able to see Beatrice openly. Now and then Domenic took the chance to meet Angelina, but with the understanding that none of Beatrice's family should know that Domenic and Angelina were madly in love with one other.

Mr Francesco Di Catto, as mentioned before, had bought the forest and employed men to cut down the trees, exporting them around the country for carpentry, joinery and sometimes he supplied sleepers for the railway. He was very ambitious man and very proud of his job. He provided well for his family and in his mind he felt that his business had helped many young people around the district, giving them the possibility of helping their parents with their young families. Very often he ended up in court, because his attitude towards other businessmen wasn't always what it should be, and for that reason he needed the support of his first son Eduardo. He made sure he was well educated and could represent his father on every occasion. For example, once he made a contract with a firm that owned the lorries that transported the wood or whatever else, that the clients needed. The person in charge of this firm was a woman, but according to Mr Di Catto, the woman was never quick enough to transport the railway sleepers and that had created difficulty for his business. One day he lost his temper with the woman. He shouted at her and called her a prostitute and for that reason the woman pressed charges against him, but Eduardo, his son, said to him, "Father, don't worry, I know a very good lawyer who will represent you and he will be able to sort this problem out."

A week later, Eduardo said to his father, "Today is the day we need to be in front of the Crown Court, but as I said to you before, the lawyer will sort everything out and before you know it we will be going into the bar for a glass of wine, and put it all behind us."

"I'm very nervous." His father admitted. "I wish it was as easy as you say."

Eduardo smiled, patted his father reassuringly on the shoulder, and said, "This small incident today will soon be resolved, but pay attention, for next time it might not be as easy."

They took the carriage, pulled by two white horses, and left the village of Catailli to make their way to the Crown Court of Rocca, Monfina. Not long after they arrived, the court usher said, in a raised voice, "Call Francesco Di Catto. Please enter the witness box."

The magistrate asked him, "What is your name?"

He answered, "I'm Francesco Di Catto."

"Did you call this lady a prostitute?" the magistrate asked him.

"Yes Sir, I did."

The Magistrate said sternly, "Are you aware of how you have insulted this lady?"

Francesco said, "Yes sir, but I didn't call her a prostitute in the moral sense, but as regards business, because I have a contract with this lady's company, to transport the RERR sleepers to the railway using her lorry. She never did it in the time I requested. It created grave consequences for my business and we nearly lost the contract we had with the railway as a result. If the sleepers didn't arrive in time it would mean my men would lose their jobs and then what? I was very angry with the lady and that was the reason why I called her what I did. I repeat, it was purely a business matter."

The Magistrate said, "Mr Francesco Di Catto, the Court has taken consideration on your behalf and finds you not guilty. For that reason the case is dismissed."

Eduardo was very pleased for his father, because he

was free from the Court and the accusation of insulting a lady and causing defamation of her character. Now he could continue with his business. His second son Domenic needed to be at work, supervising his employees at all times, and he thought his father was unfair. Eduardo, at all times, wore a very posh suit and tie. He was called 'Sir', and went gallivanting everywhere around the country. According to his father, it was part of their business to be able to meet with people who were well off, and important, and it was necessary for him to make a deal to purchase more forests where he could find the trees he needed to continue with his work.

Domenic would go to his father and demand the best gents bicycle at that time when not many people could afford one. After that, he demanded an accordion to play music like a piano, because he liked to play and sing. Next he wanted a guitar and so on and on. Finally his father said, "Domenic, it is about time you stopped asking me for all these musical instruments. You need to get on with the business."

Domenic answered instinctively, releasing all his pent up grievances.

"Yes father, but I'm the one who needs to work all the time. I'm the one who works side by side with all the men we employ. It seems to me that you and my brother hardly ever come onto the premises and when you do come, both you and he, wear suits, and change into working clothes when it's nearly time to go home. Then you change back again to go home in your posh suits and with a sophisticated stick under your arm and you walk through the village like you are somebody very special."

The father glared at his son and spoke sharply to him. "That is enough! You have no right to talk to me in that manner."

Domenic continued and couldn't help himself. "Why? Do I really need to work all the time supervising the men who cut the trees down, saw the trunks and attach them with ropes to go behind the mules downhill in the forest, so that the lorry can transport them to the railway? Then prepare and cut the tree branches to make charcoal. I tell you father, I also have the right to take time off and, like every young man, I have the right to enjoy myself.''

The father replied tightly, and while trying to control his anger said, "Yes, and you do that every Saturday evening. You and the other young men make a hell of a lot of noise, sometimes with your accordion or your guitar, along with the other young man and his trumpet. Somebody whispered in my ear that there are a couple of young girls hanging around you and the other young men playing with you. I tell you, my beloved son, you jolly well know who these two young girls are that are pestering you, but look out. I've been told that the father of one of them thinks he is better than anybody else."

Domenic went red, and said, "I think her father is like one I already know! I've heard about the father of the young girl you're talking about but I haven't had the opportunity to meet this man yet. Now I have my beautiful bicycle and that gives me the freedom to go wherever I want, not just on Saturday night, but also when I have the opportunity to escape from our business.''

The father said in a calmer voice. "You, listen to me, my son. Be careful. As I have just said to you, I've been told that the father of one of those young girls is very difficult when anything concerns the future of his young daughter, and of his niece.''

Domenic answered, "My dear father, nobody can stop me meeting the girl of my dreams, not you or her father, and when the time is right, we will declare to the world the love we have for one another. Neither you nor her family can stop us. If any obstacle gets in our way, we will run as far away as possible and then we will get married.''

His father was astonished to hear his young son talking in that manner and he realised there was no point in saying anything more to him. Time alone would tell what the future of those two love birds would be.

He shrugged his shoulders and left, mumbling to

himself, "If it's true what I heard from other people, my son doesn't yet know how he can marry the daughter of such a stubborn old man who thinks he is above everyone else. He thinks that nobody is good enough for his daughter or his niece."

Domenic continued to work very hard, but at the same time he made sure that he played his music and the people of the village enjoyed every Saturday evening in the church club. He worked very hard in the family business and he was well loved and respected by the men who worked for them.

Then one day, word reached the people all round the area that Domenic had been involved in an accident whilst riding on his bicycle and they were all shocked. As he'd been riding over the bridge of Conca Campania, a dog had run out in front of him. Whilst trying to save the dog, he went over the side of the bridge with his bicycle and tumbled down below between the brambles and the water of the river. He lay there unable to move until a passer- by saw him and raised the alarm. Help arrived and he was brought up from the river and taken to his home where he was attended by the local doctor.

As the news spread the entire village was in shock. The news eventually came to the ears of Angelina's parents. Roberto and Simon were the first to hear about what had happened in the village, but Renato and Mary knew nothing until they saw their daughter's distress. Only then did they realise there was something going on between these two young people.

Chapter 45

The families of Caccia Capo and Di Gatto began to fight like cats and dogs, but still Angelina stayed madly in love with the son of Mr Francesco Di Gatto. Domenic and Angelina had managed to keep their secret for a long time, but after Domenic's accident with his bicycle, the rumours began to fly all around the villages of Cave and Catailli and inevitably reached Angelina's father.

Renato was in shock when he heard that his daughter was in love with Di Catto's son, Domenic. His dreams for his daughter and niece had vanished into thin air and he was so disturbed by all that had happened that he began to lose every human sense of justice. He'd thought it was impossible for his daughter to fall in love with someone like a merchant's son. In his mind that was not acceptable, and he started to behave in such a way that his wife and family were afraid he might commit an act, something so awful, that he would be put in prison for the rest of his life.

After a long struggle his sons Roberto and Simon managed to calm him down for a while. After a day or two he said to Angelina and Beatrice, "From this week onwards you two will not be going to church for Mass, and the church club is now history."

The girls were very upset, and after crying all night they decided to ask Roberto if he could go to their Aunt Giovanna and explain their position. So, Roberto went to the village of Cave to speak to his Aunt Giovanna and his Uncle Mathew, explaining to them what had happened, and to ask their advice. How could it all be resolved without any more trouble?

When he arrived he saw Giuseppe nearby. Roberto approached him.

"I think you already know what's happened to Domenic," he said.

Giuseppe said, "Yes, of course I know, as does everyone in both villages and people can't stop gossiping.

238

Before we know it, Mr Caccia Capo will get the news and what will happen to Angelina and Beatrice?''

Roberto said, "It's already happened. My father has ordered that both girls must not leave the farmhouse on Sunday to attend Mass or on Saturday evening to go to the church club.''

Giuseppe was shocked. "Oh no!" he said "Mr Caccia Capo can't stop Angelina and Beatrice from attending church on Sunday. That would be an insult to God and besides, the law of this country doesn't permit anyone to be deprived of the freedom to go to church. I will go and complain to the head of our church and the priest of our parish, and also to the local County Hall. They will advise me and I'll see what can be done about it.''

"Please, wait," said Roberto, "I need to consult with my aunt and uncle first and then we'll take from there''

They both went to Giovanna's house and knocked on the door. One of the younger children opened it, and when he realised it was his cousin Roberto, he ran inside, shouting, "Mum, Roberto and Giuseppe are here."

Giovanna said, "Well, let them come in.''

After embracing his aunt and uncle and the rest of the family, Roberto said, "I've come here today because I'm quite sure you've heard all the gossip going round the villages.''

They nodded their heads and then Giovanna said, "Well, we heard that poor Domenic had had an accident and ended up between the brambles and the river, but that he's okay and just needs to recover. The rumour is that Angelina is in love with Domenic.''

Roberto continued. "Well, I have come down from the farm because Beatrice and Angelina want to see you both.''

They looked at one another and Giovanna said, "Of course we'll come, but we don't know what we're coming there for.''

"Because Beatrice and Angelina are very upset and they want to see you both,'' said Roberto.

When they arrived at the farmhouse the two young ladies ran towards them with tears in their eyes.

Giovanna said, "Beatrice, whatever is wrong?"

Beatrice looked at her parents and said, "Mum and Dad, please take us away from here."

Before they could say any more Renato walked in and, seeing his sister- in-law and her husband, he asked them for the reason for their visit?"

Giovanna drew herself up to her full height and faced him. "We needed to come here today to take the girls away for a break that we've already arranged."

Renato tried to push his sister-in-law, her husband and Giuseppe out of the house, saying, "These girls are going nowhere and will not leave this house. I'm the father and my wife and Roberto and Simon are the brothers of Angelina. We're also the uncle and the aunt of Beatrice, who's been with us since she was a little girl. Beatrice and Angelina are now inseparable, and you can't come here and take them away from this house."

Mathew threatened to report Renato to the police because in saying that the girls were not allowed to leave the house or even go to church was tantamount to breaking the law and taking away their human rights. Even worse, he was preventing their daughter Beatrice from returning to the home where she belonged.

Beatrice said to her uncle and aunt, "I no longer need to be kept here in this place like a prison and I would like to return to my parents' home. Angelina will come with me."

Her Uncle Renato was furious. He roared, "Only over my dead body will you or Angelina move a centimetre from this house."

Despite his anger, Beatrice continued. "You are my uncle and I thank you and my dear aunty for loving me while I was small, but now I'm a young adult and I can decide for myself where I want to be and that's certainly not with you dear uncle, but I must confess I would still like to live with Auntie Mary and my cousins Roberto and Simon. I love Angelina but now I need to be with my parents. Angelina can come to live with me in my parents' house for as long as she likes.''

Her Uncle was beside himself with anger at Beatrice's bold statement. "How dare you speak to me like that," he roared. "I am, and I always will be, your uncle, and you will do as you've been told.''

Mathew said, ''No more, my dear brother-in-law. From today on, Beatrice will come home with us and she will stay for good. That goes for Angelina as well if she wants to come.''

Renato said, "Only over my dead body will you take these two girls out of this house.''

Mathew and Giovanna took Beatrice and Angelina by the hand and they ran out of the farm house.

A few days later, two policemen appeared in front of Mathew's house with a mandate to hand Angelina over to Mr and Mrs Renato Caccia Capo. Mathew had no choice but to send Angelina back to the farm house with her parents.

Beatrice and Giuseppe went to Domenic's house to see and report all that had happened after the incident he'd had with his bicycle. When Domenic saw his beloved friends and heard from them what had happened in the Caccia Capo household, and to his beloved Angelina, he was very sad and worried, knowing that she was all by herself without her most trusted cousin. He gave a howl and then broke down crying until a knot formed in his throat and made it difficult for him to breathe. Giuseppe and Beatrice were drawn into his emotional pain and began to do the same, until slowly he was able to say,

"I'm very deeply saddened for my poor Angelina, and now she is all alone without her beloved cousin, I can assure you I will do whatever it takes to see her and reassure her that as soon as she's old enough, she will be free from the situation she is in now. I can't do anything yet because of my injury. I only wish that somehow one of you could contact her, and tell her how much I love and miss her. As soon as I'm able, we'll meet and see how we can defeat all these obstacles. Young people get problems when it's time for them to leave the nest, but what our parents unfortunately don't understand is that children belong to them only until they are old enough to get on with their own lives and be responsible for their own destiny.''

Chapter 46

Beatrice was very concerned for her beloved cousin. The Court had decided that Angelina needed to return to the farm house with her family and it was very difficult to have any contact with her. Renato kept her in complete isolation and Beatrice felt very sorry for her. The situation was very grave and she wished she could have her cousin with her in the village to comfort her, in the hope that in time everything would be resolved.

At the same time, Giuseppe continued to visit Domenic and report daily. After a few days Beatrice received a pleasant surprise, when she heard a knock on her door and when she opened it, she saw her cousin Simon.

He said, ''I couldn't stay any longer, without knowing how things are here, and even much more telling you about Angelina.''

Beatrice, with tears running down her face, said, ''Simon, please tell me how is my beloved cousin is getting on? I miss her so much. My life is empty without her. I need her, but the situation is very bad between our two families and it's difficult to understand why this 'comedy' is necessary.''

"How right you are," he said. This is a real 'comedy' to entertain the whole village. They are enjoying the gossip and having a laugh about our father, imprisoning his only daughter, just because she fell in love with someone who he thought was unable to support her. Anyway, what did you find out about Domenic and his injury?''

Beatrice said, "Well, his condition is improving, but he is very upset for poor Angelina. He doesn't understand why we need go through all this pandemonium, just because my uncle doesn't agree with us. In his mind, only a farmer would be accepted in his circle.''

Simon said, "That goes for all of us. My mother has already said something similar to my brother and he has told her that he would resent any comment she that she made to him, about who he should marry and that he had no intention of letting anyone interfere with his life, especially his family''.

Simon continued, "Mother has never actually said that to me but I have said to her that when I meet the woman who I want to share my life with, neither she nor father will ever come between us. I impressed that on her and she nodded her head in agreement. Roberto thinks she understood the meaning of our conversation.''

A week later Roberto saw Domenic on his bicycle, not very far from the farm house, and he immediately went to tell his brother Simon to look after his sister while he went to see if he could find and talk to Domenic, to warn him to watch out. If Renato saw him on his territory he would be in great danger, and not just him, but Angelina also. Robert looked all around the fields but Domenic was nowhere to be seen. He went back to the farm house to tell Simon.

"Keep an eye on Angelina," he told Simon, "Because as I told you before, if Dad sees Domenic on our territory no doubt there will be a big tragedy for both our families.''

Simon said, "I think Domenic must realise that his presence round here would create a bad atmosphere for him and even more for his beloved Angelina. He probably went home, but undoubtedly he will do whatever it takes to contact our sister.''

Some days later, the boys noticed the village priest, along with two other men, coming towards the farm house. The priest asked Robert if it was at all possible to have a word with his father. Roberto said of course you can, and took them upstairs to his room.

Mary saw the priest with his friends coming into the house and not realising the purpose of their visit, said, "Oh what a lovely surprise. It's not very often we have the honour of a visit from our parish priest, unless it's Easter or some other feast.''

The priest looked at her and said, "This is a special occasion for me to come here with some friends of mine, because I need to have a word with you and your husband.''

Mary said, "Please come into our sitting room and make yourselves comfortable with your friends, while I go into his bedroom and wake him up. He went to have a little rest after a very busy morning and later on he needs to do more work in our vineyards.''

She left them and went to wake her husband, gently touched him and said, ''Renato, wake up. We have visitors.'' He said, ''Oh Mary go away... it seems impossible for me to have a little rest without being disturbed.'' He soon realised there was something odd about what she had said and then he said to his wife, "Mary, what do you mean, we have visitors?''

Mary said, "I said we have visitors, but the one we only see on very sad occasions or at Easter time.'' He jumped out of bed and said, "Just tell me who are these people?'' Mary said, ''I have already told you but like always you don't listen.''

She went out of the room and into the kitchen to make some coffee for the visitors. Renato came out of his room and went to meet the visitors who were waiting for him. When he realised it was the priest and men from the social services, he wasn't amused.

He looked at them, unsmilingly, and said, "Can I ask you why I have the honour to receive such authority in my house, at this hour of the day?''

The Social Services men replied, "Some people in the village have reported to us that you are keeping your young daughter incarcerated in your house, and we've come here to investigate.''

Anger filled Renato's senses and he became very agitated.

He replied with forced calmness. "May I know who these people are, who came to you and reported this lie to your office?''

The senior social worker spokesman said, "No, we can't tell you, but we want to know if it's true or not.''

Renato said angrily, "That is an absolute falsehood. How dare these people come to you and make this accusation against me."

The social said, "Well, can you prove differently?"

Renato answered. "Yes."

There was a brief contemplative silence, while the social workers looked at one another in silent communication, and then said, "Bring your daughter and her mother in, and let us speak to them."

Renato called his wife to bring in Angelina. Mary went into Angelina's room and said to her, "I don't know what's going on in the other room, but there are some people there who want to speak with us. Let's go in and see what it's all about."

When Mary and Angelina entered the room, the social workers noticed that the young lady looked frightened and very pale. They smiled at her reassuringly and one asked, "What is your name?"

She said, "My name is Angelina Caccia Capo."

Then he asked her, "What do you do all-day?"

She looked at them and said, "Nothing, Sir."

"What do you mean, nothing?"

With tears in her eyes she answered, "I have been told by my father that I must not go out of the house and that I have to stay in my bedroom."

The priest then said, "Is that why you don't come to our church with your cousin anymore?"

She said, without any emotion in her voice, "As I said before, I'm not allowed to come out of my bedroom. My father forbids me to do so."

The priest asked. "What is the reason for this imposition?"

She answered, "I've done nothing wrong."

The priest asked her again, gently, "Tell me, Angelina, why does your father behave like this towards you, if you haven't done anything wrong?"

With a trembling voice she answered again, "I do not know Father, but maybe because my cousin and I made

246

friends with two boys from the village, and my father disapproves of us making friends with any of the village boys, but we've never done anything wrong."

The priest understood that the young lady was afraid to speak, but he needed to know why Renato was behaving in such a manner. He remembered many occasions when Renato had invited the poor people of the village to come up to his farm to gather food for the young ones, so that the mothers could feed them. Renato and his family attended church regularly. What could have made this kind man turn against his own daughter in such a harsh manner?

The priest looked at Renato in an enquiring manner and then he asked him,

"Renato, we don't understand why your daughter can't come to church with her cousin and, even more, why you keep her indoors all the time?"

Renato answered, "Since the Unification of Italy, myself and millions of others emigrated to America and other parts of the world so as to be able to earn some money and then come back to our own country and make a better future for our families. I chose farming so that I could feed my family and build a secure future for them. I dreamed of a time when my children would be old enough to carry on with my work, and the girls would be married to farmers so that they would be like my wife, Mary and have no need to worry about how to feed their family. But no, I've been told that my precious Angelina is in love with the son of a merchant and I ask myself, 'how can a father permit his daughter to get married into a family of merchants'?"

Father Achilles sighed heavily and said, "Our God gives us children to love and cherish and help them to grow up and give them a Christian education, but after that, those children are responsible for their own destiny, so Angelina has done nothing wrong. You need to support her and bless her in the new life she has chosen."

At hearing this, Renato wasn't pleased at all with

Father Achilles, but he kept quiet.

Angelina had tears in her eyes. The priest asked her again, while the social workers listened carefully for her reply. "What do you want to do?"

With a tremble in her voice, Angelina said, "I would like to be able to go to church on Sundays with my cousin, as always, and to be free to live a normal life, like I've always done."

The senior social worker then said to the Priest,

"Sir, make sure this young lady goes to church every Sunday and to every feast and you, Mr. Caccia Capo, must let your daughter live a normal life, like every other human being. She must be free to go around without any restrictions whatsoever, otherwise you will see us here again, but next time it won't be as easy as it's been today. I hope you understand."

Angelina said, "Thank you sir, I very much appreciate your help."

They all shook hands with Renato who then went back into his room looking very angry and in a bad temper, because he knew that he needed to obey the law, or he would be prosecuted.

Chapter 47

A smile appeared on Angelina's face, and she actually laughed when she got back to her room. God was on her side and had given her the freedom to meet up again with her beloved cousin Beatrice. They could attend church together on Sunday or go to any other function the church had during the year.

Roberto and Simon, on the other hand couldn't help noticing how angry their father was. Having been away from the house when the visitors were there, they had no knowledge of the situation, and asked him what was wrong with him. He looked at them and said, "I hope you're not the ones going round the village spreading rumours about me forbidding Angelina from going out of our house."

They stared at their father with shock on their faces. Robert spoke. "Father, how can you say such a thing? We know you stopped her going out and you were successful in that, but we are your family, even if we don't agree with your ideas. We know that many times you get into a rage, but we couldn't, and wouldn't, go round spreading rumours about our family business."

Renato said wearily, "Okay, my sons, but someone did, and I think I have an idea who it may be. Somebody who doesn't understand that I love my family and I want to make a good future for you all. I don't like the thought of you suffering any hardship, like most of my generation had to do when we were your age. We needed to emigrate to earn a little money for our family, so we could come back again and make sure you would be well provided for."

The sons began to feel sorry for their father and Robert said, "Father, we do understand that how deep your love is for us. We try to fully understand the heartache you suffered in your youth, when you had to leave your dear family and your country to provide what we have here today. We know we need to follow your example and get on with our lives, and marry the person we love, just like you did with our mother.''

He looked at them, "Yes, now I understand that I've had a fixation about the need to see all you settled down in a wealthy family, but I must confess I'm finding it very difficult to realise that my daughter is in love with a merchant's son, when in my mind I thought a farmer would provide food for her and her family all year round.''

Simon said, "Father, it's time to take action. You're to let Angelina meet with Beatrice, let them go to church together, and let her be free like every other human being. She should be able to go round the farm and carry out her responsibilities in the house and cooking as she's always done. Then eventually she can go to the Saturday club with Beatrice, providing that Aunt Giovanna and Uncle Mathew give their permission. It will stop the people of the village gossiping and laughing behind your back.''

Renato didn't say anything, but just walked away from his sons.

They knew that the whole matter had been a shock and had had a huge impact on him. Having to overturn his decision and allow Angelina to be free to go out and about as she always had, was a bitter pill for him to swallow. It didn't go down very easily.

Chapter 48

A week later, while all the family were sitting at table having Sunday breakfast, Angelina turned to her brothers and asked, "Would one of you be able to accompany me to Auntie Giovanna's house, so that Beatrice and I can go to Mass together?"

Before either of them could reply Renato said, "This Sunday, we shall all go to church together."

Angelina stood up, turned to her father. "But father, it's a long time since Beatrice and I have been able to go to church together."

Her father answered very sharply, "Well, you will be able to see her in church."

"But we've always enjoyed having a chat while we walk towards church".

"Not today." He told her firmly.

Angelina stamped her foot on the floor and said, "That's not what the social services said."

Renato answered, "Go on then, tell me what they said."

"That I can go with my cousin to church and the priest has to supervise to make sure that what they said has been accomplished."

Renato then shook his head and left the table.

Roberto said, "It's all right, Angelina, don't worry. I will take you to Auntie's house and if Beatrice has not already left, you will be able to walk together to church. You will be able to have a lovely chat and tell one another all the news you've missed while you've been apart. Isn't that what you two wanted?"

Angelina gave a loud shout and said, "Yes, at last!"

It wasn't yet time to leave for church, so Angelina went to her room to put on her best frock and new shoes. She made every effort to make herself pretty, knowing there was a chance that Domenic would be well enough to attend the Mass. Later on Angelina saw her brother,

Roberto, waiting near the carriage. She ran downstairs as fast as she could, jumped into the carriage and they set off. As they approached the village, they heard the church bells ringing to tell people that Mass would soon start. Approaching their aunt's house, they saw Beatrice and Giuseppe making their way to church. Angelina jumped out of the carriage and ran towards them. When Roberto saw his sister and cousin together again, hugging one another, his joy was indescribable.

Beatrice said to Angelina, "Since we've been separated from one another, many things have happened, and it's impossible to talk about it all now, but the most important thing I need to tell you is that, when Domenic was feeling a little better he went on his bicycle towards your farmhouse to see if he could get a glimpse of you, but when he saw one of your brothers, he wasn't so sure if that was the right thing to do so he turned back towards the village. He thought that if he continued he could put your life and his in danger.''

Angelina said, ''I was amazed when I realised the priest and the social services were in our sitting room interrogating my father on my account. I didn't have the faintest idea who knew about my situation.''

Giuseppe said "It was me, who alerted the authorities to come and help you.''

Angelina said, "Oh, Giuseppe, I can't thank you enough for helping me. You didn't just help free me from my father's punishment, but as a result of what you've done, I've been able to come here today and meet with my dear cousin, whom I've missed so much. This is just marvellous.''

As they went into the church Beatrice noticed Domenic, sitting with his family, and she whispered in Angelina's ear, "Look out. Domenic is with his family sitting in the third row and we are in the fifth row on the other side of the church. We must warn Domenic not to come near us or your father will see him. If he makes a scene, many ignorant people in the village will enjoy laughing at us behind our backs and it could be their amusement of the day. That must not happen.''

Giuseppe said, "Don't worry Angelina. I'll go over to Domenic and we'll mingle with the crowd and when we are in a safe place, I will have a long chat with him. Then I will be able to tell him what happened to you during the time he was recovering. I promise you Angelina, we will find a way for you two to meet again very soon, but for today we'll leave it like that.''

Angelina and Beatrice went off together after Mass and slowly walked to Giovanna's house, where Giuseppe was already waiting for them.

Angelina felt very apprehensive and as soon as she saw Giuseppe she said, "First, I would like to know how Domenic is, and what he said when you told him you were the one to come and rescue me from my father's house, after he locked me in my bedroom.''

Giuseppe said, "Domenic had tears in his eyes and he didn't understand how a father could be so cruel to his own daughter." He said to me, "I will not just challenge Angelina's father, but anyone in the world who tries to come between us. If necessary we will run way as far as we can, and get married. Then we can build our life together away from everybody else.''

Angelina burst into tears and then said, "Giuseppe, you are the only one who can help us find a secret place so that we can organise things as Domenic said.''

"Slow down Angelina," said Giuseppe. "There is a saying that 'Rome wasn't built in a day'. Remember, you are still not old enough, as the social services said. If you two do anything stupid like that, they can intervene just as they did when you were imprisoned by your father in your room. They will find you both wherever you may be, and you will have to return home to a very angry father. Domenic will go to prison for kidnapping a young lady under the age of twenty one, and then what?''

Angelina began to shake all over, ''Well then, we need to do it as soon I'm old enough, but for the time being we

253

need to find a way to meet one another and continue fighting our family as best we can, but I tell you Giuseppe, they will never, never win.''

Giuseppe and Beatrice laughed and Giuseppe said, "Now you understand, never ever give up. Therefore be strong and you will win, and believe this, where there's a will there's a way. Nobody is more in love than you two, and it doesn't matter what they say or do today because in the end they will have to agree with you and then you will be a happy family.''

Chapter 49

After hugging Giuseppe, Angelina and Beatrice walked towards Beatrice's house and as they arrived, they saw Roberto with her family inside the carriage, waiting for her to go with them.

Angelina said, "I need to go inside to see my Aunt Giovanna and Uncle Mathew and all my cousins, so please wait for me."

Roberto was not impressed but he kept quiet. Five minutes later every one of Giovanna and Mathews' family came out and waved goodbye to them. Tears ran down Mary's cheeks to see her sister and all her family outside, when she couldn't go and give them a big hug. She didn't want to start another argument with her husband.

After dinner, as always, her mother and her father liked to go to have an afternoon rest, and Angelina started imagining what a joy it would be if Domenic could suddenly appear round the corner of the farm house on his bicycle. Together they could go behind the bushes where they wouldn't be seen by anyone, especially her family. She bent down and picked a daisy, plucking the petals one at a time saying, he loves me, he loves me not, until all the petals were completely finished and the answer was 'yes'. When she saw a bicycle coming towards her and realised it was Domenic, she couldn't believe it.

He put the bicycle on the grass and ran towards her. For a moment or two, Angelina thought she was hallucinating, because she'd wanted so much to see him and tell him how much she loved him. She couldn't believe it was him, until she felt his strong arms around her body. The joy of being embraced and feeling tremors all over her body when their lips met was more like a fantasy but in fact it was reality. Then she heard the family dog barking and she said urgently, "Domenic, take your bicycle and run over in that direction because my family are out looking for me."

Domenic ran as fast as he could to prevent her brothers

discovering them together and a few minutes later, Roberto appeared with the dog. As soon as he saw Angelina, he knew something had happened, but he couldn't understand what. He asked her what was wrong and it would have been her greatest joy to tell her brother, but she knew it wasn't safe to tell him. She was still shaking all over.

He took her back to the farmhouse and found their mother. "Mother, Angelina isn't at all well. I told her to put herself to bed and you will see to her.'' And he went out.

Mary immediately went up to Angelina's room to see what was wrong with her dear daughter. When she opened the bedroom door, her daughter didn't appear at all ill but well enough to go into the kitchen and help her. Mary said, "I think you're well enough to come to the kitchen and give me a little help with the supper.''

Smiling, Angelina said, "Of course mum.''

Her mother noticed a special smile on her face and wondered why she appeared more relaxed. Why could that be? Then she saw her daughter rub her eyes with her hand, as she began to peel the potatoes and then she started to sing, 'You can't ever forget your first love'.

Then Mary thought, perhaps that now her cousin is engaged to Giuseppe, she expects us to be like my sister Giovanna and her husband Mathew, in that we will let her marry whoever she wants. Well I, myself, don't mind, because, after all Renato and I had big arguments with our parents to prove to them that it was our life and not theirs. Now we must do the same for Angelina and it's about time my husband began to understand that it is right for her to marry the man she loves.

Roberto and Simon came home and went directly to Angelina's room, where they expected she would be very poorly and saw with great surprise that she wasn't in bed but in the kitchen, helping her mother to make chips for supper. Roberto said, "Ah, you made a quick recovery!"

She smiled and said, "But I wasn't ill.''

Roberto was confused and said, "When I found you near the woods, you were shaking all over and you found it very difficult to talk to me."

She shrugged her shoulders and said, "I don't know what came over me, but anyway it didn't last long."

Robert knew something had happened to her, and he said to himself, 'I wonder if I interrupted something special and Angelina found it very difficult to tell me or she was afraid of my reaction if I heard that Domenic was taking a gamble with his life and maybe Angelina's as well, so they could be together for a little while. After supper Angelina said goodnight to all her family and went to her bedroom to write a letter to her beloved Beatrice.

'My dear Cousin,

I can't tell you the joy I had yesterday to be able to embrace you again. I miss you terribly. It was very cruel of my father to separate us after we'd lived almost all our life together, not as cousins but almost like twins. But when I stop and think of the stupidity of my father, not everything is bad. By him doing what he did, you are now engaged to Giuseppe. Please thank him for alerting the social services and the priest. Now I can come to church with you as we've always done. Also thank Giuseppe for explaining to Domenic what had happened to us .That was a good thing because this afternoon I was strolling round near the woods on our farm and dreaming about Domenic when I saw a bicycle come towards me and guess what? It was Domenic! I can't describe the joy we both felt and if my brother hadn't come looking for me because of our dog barking, I can't tell what would have happened to us, but I'll let your imagination fill in the rest.... '

'Now I need to turn the light off, otherwise one of my family will see the light and come in to find out what I'm doing. Then I won't have a chance of reading what I've written to you.

All my love to you, my precious cousin. We'll see each

other in church on Sunday morning.

Xxxxxx Angelina'

Domenic kept coming up to the farm, on his bicycle, to see if it was at all possible to have a glimpse of the girl he loved so much; but it was very difficult to have any contact with her, because her obstinate father prevented anybody except her family and a few friends to go near her or the farm house. No matter what their sons or Mary said to him, he wouldn't give in to any pressure from anybody. Until she was twenty one, he knew he was in full control of her wellbeing. The law stopped him keeping her incarcerated in the house, but she was able to attend church on Sunday with her cousin. She could go round the farm and help her mother with daily chores in the house or garden, but other than that, there was nothing anybody could do for her. Poor Domenic was getting very frustrated.

His father, Francesco, thought it was time for him to go and have a chat with Angelina's father and see why these two young people weren't able to even have a friendly chat together. Mr Di Gatto put on his suit and his hat and his best shoes, and with his posh stick he went off to the market square in Conca Campania, where he thought Renato would be the with his stall of farm vegetables and fresh fruit.

When he arrived he spotted Renato with a few of his helpers and went up to him.

"Good morning, I'm Francesco Di Catto. Perhaps when you are free, we could go to the bar for a beer and a chat.''

Renato glowered at him and spoke sharply, "I haven't any time to spare for a chat, besides, I don't think we have very much in common and I have nothing to chat about. Goodbye."

Mr Di Catto felt insulted and degraded by Renato's attitude towards him. He went away muttering to himself, "Who does he think he is? He's just a merchant, no more than a peasant, and I will not be approaching him again, such a loutish man. The day will come, I'm sure, when he will come to me with his tail between his legs and say sorry for his behaviour towards me and my family, because I know that my son and his daughter will get married, no matter what he says or does. There is nothing anybody can say or do about it."

As he walked along the road, back to his village, he heard some local people gossiping about his two sons. They were talking among themselves, saying, "Do you know the two sons of the merchant? The older one is in love with one of the six pretty girls of Mr Benjamin, and there is no problem whatsoever. The second one is in love with the farmer's daughter, and it seems there is a lot of trouble because the old man doesn't accept his daughter's choice. He's not a farmer, like Mr. Cacciacapo. It is ridiculous. He's a good looking young man and is very much loved by the youngsters. He works for his father, and then plays for the young people on his guitar every Saturday night. This old man thinks nobody else is good enough for his precious daughter, unless he is a farmer's son.''

Mr Francesco Di Catto stopped and said to them, "Yes, you are right, but at the end of the day the heart doesn't give any commands. If their love is strong enough they will overcome any problem and they will win. Renato will have no choice but to accept what destiny provides for his daughter."

The people talking felt uncomfortable when they realised that Domenic's father had heard their gossip about his son and the farmer's daughter, and realised it must be very upsetting for him to realise there was so much gossip about the situation between the two young people. They felt sure that his son could easily find another pretty girl without any complications, like his brother Eduard had.

Chapter 50

Sometime later, Renato returned to the farm in a very bad mood. His wife Mary said, "Whatever is the matter with you today? You appear to be very angry? Did you have a poor return on the vegetables and lovely fruit we gathered from the orchards yesterday?"

He glared at his wife with an angry glare. Mary persisted. "Did you have a bad return on the vegetables and fruit you took to market? If not, what is the reason for your bad mood?"

He just slammed the door and went out. Mary knew her husband was no longer the man she'd married many years ago, because now he was a very grumpy old man and it was not easy to have a decent conversation with him. It seemed to her that in the last year or two it had become impossible to approach him without the fear of being attacked 'with an iron bar'. Mary was very concerned about him and she knew she must find out what had put him in such a bad temper. She knew that it was time to consult her sons to see if they could find out what was wrong with the man. He seemed to be in a more aggressive mood than usual.

Roberto and Simon approached their father, and Roberto said, "Father, since you came home from the market, you haven't had a break, and it seems to us you are more upset than usual."

He looked at them and he said, "Yes I am!"

"Why is that then?" asked Roberto.

When he answered, Renato's voice was gruff. "It's because that uncivilized merchant had the nerve to come up to me and invite me to go to the bar with him for a chat and a beer."

Roberto looked puzzled as he said, "So what's wrong with that?"

His father replied, "You all know he is our worst enemy."

Simon said, "Father, I don't understand. You confuse me. Why is this man our worst enemy? What has he done to wrong us?"

Roberto said. "He is the father of that vagabond, Domenic, who wanders round with his guitar and seems to have a great time, with the young girls going mad for him. You know that our sister is one of them, and you also know that it isn't what Dad wants. You have to help me make sure that our sister comes to her senses and leaves him well alone."

Simon answered, "Father, let me tell you something. Domenic is not a vagabond. He is a nice young man, and he's well respected by the people his father employs in their business. He plays music and he is loved by everybody in the village, and something else. It doesn't surprise me at all that Angelina has fallen in love with Domenic, because he communicates well with the young people and he's also very good looking."

Even as he was speaking, Simon knew that whatever he, or his brother Roberto, said about Domenic, their father would not listen, because he was so dead set against Domenic. They also knew that their sister was madly in love with Domenic, and whatever anybody said or did, it would not change that. Their father was a very stubborn old man and neither would he change his mind in accepting Angelina's choice of her future husband. It was unbearable to see his poor sister so unhappy. Angelina's mother and brothers resigned themselves to think that only a miracle would resolve this problem between the two families.

The next day, Simon went back to the village and met Giuseppe while he was collecting the mail from the post box. Giuseppe looked pleased with himself.

"Simon", he said, "I have very good news. This Sunday in church the banns of marriage between me and Beatrice will be published. As you know that will be for three consecutive weeks and then we will be sending out the invitations. We know that Auntie, Angelina, Roberto and you will be happy to attend our wedding, but we are concerned about Uncle Renato. We know he loves Angelina and Beatrice alike, and we know he doesn't approve, but I've always loved Beatrice, and she loves me too. We only hope you and all your family will come along to help us celebrate our marriage, because without your family it will be a very sad day for all of us."

Simon said, "I'm quite sure we will be there, even if we need to tie him to our carriage, but he will be there too."

Simon patted Giuseppe's shoulder and said, "Congratulations to you and to our beloved cousin Beatrice. I repeat. I'm quite sure we will all be there."

He said, goodbye and walked away into a nearby shop. On the way back to the farmhouse he thought, 'goodness me, as if we didn't have enough trouble, this will be the last straw. My father will go mad. He can't understand that Angelina and Beatrice will marry the men they love and not the ones he chooses for them. He is such a difficult man! I fear that we have a lot of trouble ahead, because I don't know what will happen when he hears the banns of marriage between Beatrice and Giuseppe being announced in church. How he will react? This is very frightening'.

When he arrived home, Mary could see straightaway that Simon was troubled. She asked him what was going on.

He looked at her and said, "Mother, this Sunday, the priest will read the banns of marriage for Beatrice and Giuseppe in church, and I'm very concerned about how father will react when he hears them."

Mary said, "Indeed. I need to talk to him. It's time he began to understand that Beatrice no longer lives under our roof, and we have no right to interfere with her or her family's lives.''

Simon looked a bit confused, "But Mum, Beatrice was brought up by us. Surely we have something to say."

"Yes, my son, but only because you and Roberto, both being a bit too old to play with Angelina, caused your father and I to beg Giovanna and Mathew to give us one of their little girls to grow up with our little Angelina. They had so many girls, and they knew if one of their girls could come to us, she would have a better chance than if she stayed with them. They agreed, on condition that if the child came to stay with us, she would always be their daughter and they would always be responsible if anything happened to her."

Simon shrugged his shoulders and walked away.

The next day, Mary tried to speak to her husband and found it impossible to make him see sense. She was thinking that if only she could somehow have a proper conversation with her husband, she might be able to make him understand that Beatrice is with her Mum and Dad, and they are the only ones responsible for her future now. At the same time, she knew he was a very stubborn old man and it didn't matter what she said to him, he would attend church that Sunday and when the priest was about to announce Beatrice and Giuseppe's banns, there was a chance that he would stand up and make a scene. It would be the gossip of the week for most people in the village. Then she thought, 'What if I bring one of the best bottles of wine up from the cellar, and let him have a few glasses of wine before we go to church in the presence of our sons. When the priest starts announcing the banns, he may keep quiet. Better still, if he drinks the whole bottle he will be so drunk he will stay at home and that will be better for all of us!'

When she told Roberto and Simon of her idea, they looked at her aghast. "Mum, are you insane? How can you even think our father would be so stupid as to not understand what you were trying to do to him? Surely he will come to know all about Beatrice and Giuseppe anyway. As you said yourself, the word soon goes round and then what will happen?"

Mary looked crestfallen. She said, "My only concern is the wedding of my niece. We need to carry on without any incidents caused by your father."

Roberto sighed heavily. "Well, mother," he said, "Let

me have a word with Dad. Surely that will be better than your silly way of stopping him being the talk of the village, with people laughing behind his back, knowing he is not Beatrice's father, but just her uncle.''

Mary said, "You can try, but it will be very difficult to make him understand that Beatrice is his niece by marriage, and there is nothing whatever that he can do. He needs to behave with dignity in the church."

Roberto was troubled when he left his mother in the kitchen and went to the fields looking for his father, trying to find the right moment to talk to him without annoying him. After ten minutes, walking along the vineyard, he heard his father singing an American song 'Oh, when the Saints, are marching in'. Roberto said to himself, 'Good, it seems to me that today is the right day for me to have a decent conversation with him, without the fear that he will bite my head off'.

Slowly he began to help his father attend to the vineyard, and then gently he began to start a conversation with him. "Dad," he said, "That song you were singing then. I've heard Angelina and Beatrice try to sing it but of course they couldn't and I don't know the meaning of the song."

Renato said, "It's a long story. When your sister and cousin were very little, they were both pests, and every day they kept asking questions about it. I explained to them that it was an American song, written after America was liberated from the English occupation."

Roberto laughed and said, "Now those two rascals have grown up, I think they are both much more difficult now than when they were little."

Renato said, "Yes, when they were little they were two little monkeys. Now they are stubborn young ladies who don't understand who loves them and how much sacrifice we parents have made for them."

Robert said, "They are grown up now and have more sense. Eventually they will get married and will settle down, as will Simon and I, and at last you and Mum can enjoy the rest of your life in peace."

Renato said, "I don't know about that, we are in a mess with Angelina. She is running after the merchant's son, and don't even ask me about Beatrice. We loved that child so much and now look what's happened. She's left us, and I heard that if she has her own way she will marry that postman."

Roberto burst out laughing, and said to his father, "Look, Father, I know we love Beatrice very much, but you and mum always knew Beatrice was your niece and not your daughter. Her mother and father have full responsibility for their own daughter and anyway, it's less upset for you two."

Renato straightened his back and faced his son, "Dear son, it is not so easy. If you have a child with you for a long time like Beatrice, that child becomes like one of your own."

Roberto said, "Dad please don't worry about Beatrice. The important thing is that she is happy, and what matters most is what is important for her, and for all of us. I heard that next Sunday will be the first week of the publication of their wedding banns in the church and it's very important for you to keep quiet for her sake and for all of us."

Renato laughed harshly and said, "Roberto, do you think I would stand up in the middle of the congregation and behave badly enough to embarrass myself and all my family. Entertaining the people of our village at our expense? Don't worry son, your father is not really as silly as he looks."

Roberto now felt more relaxed. His mother must have been over reacting, because of her husband's recent behaviour towards his daughter in the hope of stopping Domenic meeting her.

Mary began to think about Beatrice's bottom drawer For years she'd been accumulating linen for Beatrice and Angelina and had asked the nuns to embroider each one of the items with fine flowers with the girls' names on the sheets and pillowcases and all the items of underwear. Mary was very excited, because at last she could see that all the effort she had made had been worth it. Now was the time for one of them to get married and she hoped that it would soon be the right time for her beloved daughter Angelina, to do likewise.

Mary was very tense, not knowing if her husband would keep the promise he had made to his son Roberto, or have one of his impulses and embarrass all his family, plus that of Giovanna and Mathew and also Giuseppe. The people of the village wouldn't stop gossiping for a long time if that happened. Roberto realised his mother was trembling and gave her a nudge. "Be quiet, Mother, it's not Father I need to worry about now, but you. Please try and relax and everything will be all right."

At the end of the service, the priest announced to his congregation that Giuseppe and Beatrice would be married on the 20th of May 1927 in the Church of Santa Maria of Grace in Cave and Catailli. And all went well without any problems.

Chapter 51

Mary, Renato and all the family returned home and sat at the table for Sunday lunch. Not a single word was said about Beatrice and Giuseppe. Angelina went to her room and had started writing a letter to Beatrice when there was a knock on her door. It was Simon.

He said, "We are very pleased that Sunday is over for another week. Robert and I think that from today on, Father will begin to understand that his dreams are finally over. We're quite sure, because now it's impossible for him to still believe that one day you will fulfil his dreams. Nevertheless he's still dead set against Domenic being his future son- in- law, so you need to pay attention to what you do and say, until he comes to his senses, otherwise we think Domenic will be in great danger."

Angelina understood what her brother was saying to her and she answered, "Well tell me Simon, when will I have the chance to meet Domenic and tell him he must keep away from the farm and our fields, because he may be in danger?"

Simon shrugged his shoulders and said, "Well, for the time being, I need to go and see Giuseppe. Between us we need find a way for you two to meet secretly until all the problems have been resolved. For now we need to have some rest, and then I will go to the village and try to have a word with our cousin Beatrice."

Next morning Simon ran down stairs, looked all around to make sure nobody saw him leave the house, and headed towards the village. He needed to go to his aunt's house, to see Beatrice and try to find a way for Angelina and Domenic to meet, without his parents knowing anything about it. When he arrived at his aunt's house, Beatrice came to open the door. When she saw her cousin, she threw her arms round him and said, "This is just wonderful! I miss you all so much, but above all my dearest cousin Angelina."

Simon said, "Beatrice, I don't understand you... how can you say that, when you know we were all together in church yesterday. Above all, we were all so happy to hear the priest announce to the congregation the news of your marriage to Giuseppe."

Beatrice gave a sigh and said, "My parents and I were very tense. We really thought Uncle Renato would stand up and embarrass us all."

Simon said, "Mum thought exactly the same. She told my brother she was preparing a cocktail for my father with a bottle of our best wine and would make him drink all of it, so he would become drunk, not be able to hold himself up, and then he would need to go to bed. But Roberto thought she was out of her mind, and went to have a word with Dad to see what he had in mind. He was surprised when Dad said to him, "Son, I wouldn't do any such thing; I'm very angry, but I'm not so silly as to mess up my family in such a manner and risk being thrown out of the Church. So Roberto went back to Mum, told her about what had been said, and she began to feeling a little easier."

Beatrice laughed. Simon said, "Angelina is extremely happy for you both, that you will be able to get married with the blessing of your parents. She very much hopes one day our own parents will remember that when they were young their family where dead against their marriage for the same reason. Their parents also wanted their children to have a better future and hoped they would be prepared to wait until they found the right person, someone who would be able to support them financially and have a better future for their family."

Simon continued, "That was the reason why our father emigrated to America, like many thousands of people, because after the Unification of Italy, you couldn't be well off unless you were the daughter or son of the upper class like Dukes or Duchesses."

"Beatrice said, "I think my uncle and aunt live in an imaginary world yet, as Angelina said, they should know better. Now they are old, they should have a bit more common sense.''

Simon said, "I came here today because I wanted to speak to Giuseppe. I understand now, more than ever, that Angelina is truly in love with Domenic, and he with her, but because our parents make it difficult for them to meet each other, there is a chance that Angelina will become very depressed. I think she could easily do something very silly, which upsets me to even mention it."

Beatrice was shocked to hear that from Simon.

She said, "Yes, I think that even more now that I'm not with her. It's not easy for her to take all the stress that uncle keeps putting on her by herself. It seems that he will go to any lengths to prevent her having any contact with Dominic. It's about time that Uncle was less domineering with his daughter and gave her more freedom, because when the time arrives, she will marry Domenic whether he likes it or not. He can't do anything about it and he needs to understand that now, or he will suffer the consequences later?"

"Yes, I can see that." said Simon thoughtfully. "I don't need to go and speak to Giuseppe, but to both my parents and make it clear to them that they must stop pressurising their daughter with their silly ideas. Otherwise there's a chance that they won't be having a wedding with their imaginary rich man, but maybe an undertaker for the funeral of a very special daughter."

Beatrice began to cry loud enough for her parents to hear from the next room. They both came out and her mother asked, "Beatrice, what is going on?"

Simon and Beatrice didn't really like to tell them what the problem was, knowing that it wouldn't help Angelina's situation, but would aggravate it enormously for both families and that would achieve nothing at all. Simon knew Beatrice was much moved that Angelina missed her so much, and he thought he would ask his aunt and uncle if they would mind letting Beatrice go back with him to the farm house for just a few days, until Angelina felt better.

Giovanna agreed readily, "Of course Beatrice can come and stay with Angelina, as long as she likes or until Angelina feels better."

Simon was relieved. "Oh thank you auntie, for letting Beatrice come home with me. My parents will appreciate having Beatrice with us for a little while."

Beatrice went to her room and packed the clothes she needed for her stay with Angelina, and then she went round the house to tell her brothers and sisters that she was going back to the farm for a little while to see her beloved Angelina, but would soon return.

"What about Giuseppe?" Giovanna asked suddenly.

Beatrice replied, "I'll leave a message for Giuseppe. He will understand and anyhow, I won't stay longer than necessary, just long enough to see if I can speak to my uncle and auntie about Angelina. She needs help, and if they don't stop pressurising her they will be very sorry, and it will be too late for them."

"Oh, Beatrice," exclaimed Giovanna. "I don't know what reaction you'll get from the old man. I am very concerned for you. If there is any trouble you must come back home immediately."

Beatrice looked at her mother and laughed, "Oh mother, just because my uncle incarcerated Angelina to prevent her meeting with Domenic, doesn't mean he is a violent man. I can assure you he wouldn't harm a fly. I can't imagine him harming me, just because I'm there to defend Angelina. At the end of the day he loves us very dearly, and in his mind he only wants what is best for us. Unfortunately Angelina and I both fell in love with men that he doesn't approve of, and we can't help that. Mother, I tell you, when it is all over he will be the best granddad for our future children."

Giovanna shrugged her shoulders and said, "If it's as you say, then so be it, but just be careful, for your own sake."

Beatrice said goodbye to her mum and dad and all the family and left with Simon to go the farm.

When Mary saw Simon and Beatrice arrive she was over the moon, but couldn't understand why Beatrice had come. They'd only seen them the day before in church for the announcement of her wedding to Giuseppe. She couldn't help asking herself if there was something wrong with her sister or her family.

When Beatrice saw her aunt, her face lit up with a big smile. She ran to her and gave her a big hug.

"Auntie" she said. "It's so good to be here again even if it's only for a few days. I've spent all my life with the most wonderful auntie and uncle and cousins and I've missed you all so much."

While Beatrice was talking to her aunt, Angelina was just round the corner of the house and heard Beatrice's voice. She ran to her and threw her arms round her.

Then with tears in her eyes she said, "Beatrice you've risked coming here to see me".

Beatrice put her arms round Angelina said, "Yes! I came here to talk to uncle and auntie, and if they don't like what I have to say to them, they can throw me out of the house. I have to try and tell them that they can't force any of their children to do what they think is right for them. Whether I'm successful or not, this is important for me. I need to lift this heavy burden from my chest in order to get on with my life."

Angelina was flabbergasted. She would never have thought Beatrice had so much strength in her.

She embraced Beatrice and then said, "My dearest cousin, since I was a little girl I have been blessed to have you with me, not just as a cousin but much more like a sister. We grew up together and we became inseparable until, for no fault of ours, we've been sharply separated. But now we need to fight and start claiming our rights. We are only human and are nearly old enough to decide our own destiny without our parents' interference."

Beatrice said, "That's the reason why I'm here today and we should stand up to claim what is our right."

Angelina said, "Now tell me, how we do that?"

Beatrice replied, "Angelina please watch me!"

Then she went looking for her uncle Renato and her cousins Roberto and Simon and when she met them she asked them to make sure her aunt was present. She told them that they all needed to meet in their sitting room. When they were all sitting down she looked at them and said,

"Uncle, auntie and dear cousins, I came here today because I need to thank you all for the tender, loving care you have all given me since I was a little girl. When you asked my parents if they would let one of their little girls come and stay with Angelina, and my parents said 'yes', it was a privilege for me to come here and grow up with Angelina. Not for a moment did I think she was my cousin, but my little sister; and she still is my beloved and precious sister. It's no-one's fault that destiny has brutally separated us. But I came here today to say that we may have been separated, but we will always stand together, no matter what life throws at us, good or bad. Uncle and auntie, you know yourself that when two people are in love they need to get married and they need to see the priest, because before he can publish the banns in church, he has to teach the young couple all about matrimony and what it means, when two people are in love with one another. Matrimony is when God joins together one woman and one man with visible and invisible signs, giving them the Grace to have children and educate them in the Christian faith, and help them to grow up. But then they must remember God only lends the children to them to help them to grow up and follow what the church has told them. The parents must not interfere with them when they are old enough to know what is right and what is wrong themselves. They need let them follow their own destiny."

"I have been blessed because my parents understood the teaching of the Bible and I'm sure you are just as wise as them. Think about the birds in sky, they work very hard, they build a nest and have little ones, but when they are big enough they leave the nest and fly away. Like them, you also should give Angelina the chance to choose her own man. When she can achieve who she thinks is right for her, she will be like the birds. If you don't let her do that, there is a chance she might go into a deep depression and harm herself, and then you won't need to worry any more about wedding expenses, only those of the undertaker, because she's been hurt and resented for not being able to fulfil her dreams."

When Beatrice had finished her speech to her aunt and uncle, Roberto and Simon gave a cheer and clapped their hands. Her uncle just stood there, rooted to the spot without saying a word.

Angelina was left speechless to witness Beatrice giving such a long speech to her mother, father and brothers.

Beatrice then turned to Angelina. "Angelina, this is the reason I needed to come here today," she said. It was to remind auntie and uncle, especially uncle, that he is, without a doubt, the one who created all these problems."

Later, when Beatrice and Angelina were alone Angelina laughed, and said, "I think my father must have felt very embarrassed after the lecture you gave him today. He shouldn't forget what the priest said to them so many years ago and you reminded him that the birds in the nest must one day fly away. That must be the sternest lecture he has ever heard and he certainly wasn't expecting it."

Chapter 52

Beatrice said to her aunty and uncle, "I need to go back home. Can I take Angelina with me? It will be only for a few days and my family will be overjoyed to see us together again. Angelina's father looked at both of them and was speechless, then he looked at his wife, and she said. "Yes, of course. I'm sure my sister, Giovanna will be more than happy to see the girls both together in the midst of all her family."

Roberto immediately ran downstairs to prepare the carriage, and even the horse appeared happy to see the two young ladies jump into the carriage together. Roberto took up the horse's reins and the carriage headed towards the village. When they knocked on the door of their aunt's house, Giovanna came to open it, and when she saw Roberto there with Angelina and Beatrice beside him, she was very surprised, as she didn't expect to see her daughter so soon. Neither did the rest of the family but Giovanna rejoiced, and there was even more rejoicing when one of Beatrice's young brothers came in, saying he'd heard that the little village of Catailli was holding a big party and everybody was invited.

Beatrice said, "Well, Giuseppe must know all about it, being a postman in the district. Surely he will know where the party is and what it's all about. She called to her young brother Mario saying, "Go to Giuseppe and tell him I'm back home now and have Angelina with me for a few days. Ask him if he knows anything about the party and what it's for."

Mario said, "I saw Giuseppe today, and he asked me if I knew anything about when you would be home. I said I didn't know, but now you are here and I know he will be very pleased to hear that you are already home. Then I will ask him if he knows where the party is. As you say, he is the postman and he must know what is going on all round the entire district." And off he went.

He knocked on Giuseppe's door and his mother opened it. , "Oh, it's you Mario, is anything wrong?"

Mario replied, "No, but I need to tell Giuseppe that Beatrice is back home and she's brought Angelina back with her. She hopes Giuseppe will be able to come to our house for a little while.''

Giuseppe's mother said, "Yes I'm sure he will, I will go and tell him."

Giuseppe had already heard his mother talking to somebody and he came out of his room and said, "Mum, who are you talking to?"

His mother answered, "Mario is here, and he came to tell you that Beatrice is back from the farm and has brought Angelina back with her. She sent him to ask if you can come to her house for a little while."

Giuseppe said, "Mum, ask Mario to tell Beatrice I will be there as soon as I can."

Mario heard what Giuseppe said and ran off, shouting over his shoulder, "Goodbye." Then he ran back home to report to his sister what Giuseppe said.

After just a few minutes Giuseppe arrived and he was very happy to see Beatrice with Angelina. He said, "When Simon came here yesterday, he was very concerned about you Beatrice. He thought, if Beatrice thinks she can go to his house and tell her uncle what she thinks of him, knowing what kind of man he is, there is a chance Renato might throw her out of the house."

Beatrice said, "Giuseppe, I didn't care. I needed to go and tell him he had no right to prevent Angelina seeing Domenic. I'm sure that quite a few years ago, when they were young themselves, they went to the priest like we did, and the priest must have told them exactly what he told us! Well I went there and I gave them a lecture about the Bible. As I said before, knowing my uncle's temperament, he wouldn't listen to me, and he could easily have thrown me out of their house, but he didn't. After I'd finished my lecture about the Bible, Auntie, Roberto and Simon, clapped their hands for a long period of time, but

Uncle just stood there and he didn't say a word. When I asked them if I could take Angelina with me he didn't answer, but looked at Auntie, and, as you see Angelina is with us here today, and will be here for a few more days."

Giuseppe said, "Beatrice today you and Angelina will have a big surprise. This is pure luck for both of you, because you've both come home just in time for a big party. It will be held this evening at Francesco's house, and I need to be there because Domenic and I, with another couple of young men will be playing music. It's all because Eduardo is getting engaged to a beautiful young lady. She is the third of six sisters, and Domenic will have a shock when he sees you there. I'm afraid he will find it difficult to contain himself, and maybe he will find difficulty in playing his accordion, or his guitar; but I'm there, and I hope with my help he will get over the shock, and get on with the show. Without any doubt, you will have a chance to meet his family and they will be happy to see you at last."

After she heard what Giuseppe said, Angelina began to shake. She looked at Giuseppe and said, "I don't know if it is right for me to go there without being invited to Eduard's party. What will Eduard and his fiancé say when they see me there?"

Giuseppe said, "They will be very happy to meet you at last. I'm sure Domenic has already spoken about you many times to his family and now they'll have a chance to see what you look like."

Angelina added, "What if Domenic gets too excited and he will not play his music, then nothing will go as planned and his family will blame me for interfering with their party."

Giuseppe said, "Don't worry, the young couple, all her sisters and their boyfriends, will be too excited at their engagement and their beautiful sister getting married to such a good looking man. They won't take any notice of what is going on around them. In the end everything will go ok and for you it will be a day to remember. I'm sure when the time comes for you and Domenic it will be even better."

Angelina laughed, "I don't know about that, but I can assure you Giuseppe, after the lecture Beatrice gave Dad yesterday, I wonder how much longer my father will take to understand that the battle he has with me. He knows I will never give up Domenic and eventually he will have to come round to my way of thinking."

When she heard about the party, Beatrice's mother, Giovanna, said to both girls. "That's it! I will make sure that when you both enter the Francesco house this evening, the guests will turn round and ask themselves, who are these two beautiful young ladies?"

Both Angelina and Beatrice started laughing and Beatrice said "Mum can you make us as beautiful as they are?"

Giovanna said, "I'm sure they are very beautiful, but when you enter wearing evening gowns, with your hair done up and a beautiful tiara on heads, wearing a little make up, they will wonder who you are, and they won't stop admiring you both as truly lovely ladies. I'm sure Domenic and Giuseppe will be very proud of you both."

Angelina turned to her with her eyes shining and said, "Dear auntie, you are the best auntie, and mum in the world."

When Giovanna saw her two beautiful young ladies all done up and looking very elegant, tears came running down her face, knowing they were her two precious girls.

When Giuseppe saw them, he gasped. "Mrs Forino, who *are* these two beautiful young ladies?" he asked.

Giovanna said, "They are the two ladies you need to take care of this evening, and present to Mr and Mrs Francesco Di Gatto as their guests, and above all remember to tell them that you and Domenic are also the two precious young men in their lives."

Giuseppe then hugged his future mother-in-law and said. "I promise you that Beatrice will be my treasure forever. I will love and respect her and I will give my life to her forever. I'm sure Domenic will do just the same. We will do whatever it takes to make sure these two lovely ladies, Beatrice and Angelina, will lack nothing."

They hugged her again and said, "Now it's time for us to make a move so that we can get there before the party starts."

In fact, when they got there, the party hadn't yet started, but the guests were slowly arriving. Mr and Mrs Di Gatto came over to them and, with a big smile Mrs Di Catto said, "Well, well. We are honoured to have these two lovely young ladies with us this evening."

Then Mr Di Catto turned to his wife and said, "I think we will learn a little bit more from Domenic and Giuseppe about these two young ladies this evening."

Giuseppe and Beatrice asked Mr Di Catto where Domenic was.

"He is in the other room making sure all the musical instruments are all in good order for the evening show," he said.

Giuseppe and Beatrice went to look for him to tell him that Angelina was there, so he wouldn't have a shock. When they found him, Giuseppe explained the situation to him.

"We didn't have time to let you know about Angelina and Beatrice coming here this evening. I didn't know myself until an hour ago, when Mario came to my house and told me Beatrice had brought Angelina back home with her, so here we are."

Domenic had tears in his eyes. He said, "I'm very excited. I thought this would never be possible, knowing the situation with her father. Now here she is, and my parents have a chance to meet Angelina and I'm very proud and happy."

Giuseppe said, "Yes I know, but you need to be brave and behave like a gentlemen. Go and present your future wife to your parents and all your family. Have a good talk with your all your family, while Beatrice and I go round and mingle with the other guests."

Domenic gave Giuseppe a big smile and said, "You're my true friend, I don't know how to thank you. It's impossible to tell you how much I appreciate your help and your friendship."

Giuseppe and Beatrice started circulating with the other guests, leaving Domenic with Angelina and his family.

Mr and Mrs Di Catto called their son Eduard into a corner of the room, and his father said to him.

"Eduard, we all know this evening is your engagement party with Lina, but we must decide how to deal with this situation for Domenic. If everybody gets to know about Angelina this evening and we present her to all our guests as our future daughter- in- law, there will be fireworks, and a big war between our two families. There is already bad feeling between us, though I don't know why. It would be unbearable for us, if these two children, for no fault of their own, are caught between two warring families."

Eduard said, "I think I need to call Domenic and Angelina into the other room and explain to them why, this evening, we need to treat her like all the other guests until she is old enough to make her own decisions. Then the priest will be able to announce the banns in church like everybody else. Nobody can do anything about it until then so we need to keep quiet and get on with our lives. If Angelina's father gets to know she's been here this evening he will go crazy because he put her in the trust of his wife's family and he will blame his wife for letting her go to the village. This will create a bad feeling between Angelina's father and her aunt's family. That is a situation which could very well get out of hand and goodness knows what could happen then. I will need to explain, not just to Angelina and Domenic, but also to Giuseppe's family and we must be conscientious in keeping peace in the families."

Angelina was too naive to understand how older people could behave in such a manner when they've been young themselves. Why can't they get on with their own lives without creating a lot of trouble and unnecessary stress for everybody?

It was decided that it would be better if Angelina and Beatrice didn't mix with the other guests, to avoid any consequences in the days ahead. It might even be better if they stayed in the kitchen to help Domenic's family prepare the food to be served to the guests in the interval. Then they'd have the chance to be with Domenic and Giuseppe, while the guests sat down and had a chat amongst themselves.

When the party was over, Angelina and Beatrice waited until all the guests had left and then Angelina said,

"Mr and Mrs Di Catto, I speak for myself and my cousin in saying that we don't have any words to thank you and your family enough, for receiving us here in your house this evening. I also thank you both for understanding my position and I hope one day we will all be a very happy family."

They smiled and said, "We know the day will come when your family and ours, will sit together round a big table and raise a big glass of champagne to you and Domenic, and wish you all the happiness you both deserve."

Domenic and Angelina couldn't help getting very emotional, and with tears in their eyes they kissed all of Domenic's family, as did Beatrice and Giuseppe. Domenic and Giuseppe accompanied Angelina and Beatrice to Beatrice's home, and when they arrived, Beatrice said, "You both need to come in, otherwise my parents would be hurt. They will want to know how the party went."

Beatrice was right. As soon as Giovanna as saw them she was very anxious to know how the party went, and above all what impression they'd made on Domenic's family.

Beatrice said, "They were very impressed." Angelina nodded in agreement, and Beatrice continued. Actually we were the only ones dressed in evening gowns and with our hair done up. The guests were whispering to one another and we think they wanted to know who we were, so we went into kitchen and we ate all the best food that was there. We had a chance to be with Domenic and Giuseppe in the interval. When the party finished, we thanked Mr and Mrs Di Catto and all their family. It was such an enjoyable evening."

Beatrice didn't tell her mother that Eduard had said that it wasn't wise for Angelina to mingle with the other guests in case her father got to know, which would have caused a lot of problems between the families.

"After five days of pure enjoyment, being able to see Domenic every day in her aunt's house, Angelina knew it was time to go back to her home. Tears ran down onto her cheeks when she left because she knew she would find it very difficult not to be able to see Domenic. Her brothers had warned her of the danger if her father happened to see his future son- in-law near the house, or anywhere else as there was the possibility he could attack him, and that would be terrible.

Giovanna saw her niece crying and said to her, "What's the matter with you now?"

Angelina said, "It isn't easy to go back home when I know there is no chance for me to see Domenic. My brother has warned me that if Domenic is seen anywhere near our house there is a chance he could get hurt by my father. I can't understand why my father is so against Domenic and his family. They are a nice family, hardworking and honest; and I feel I'm privileged to fall in love with their son Domenic."

Her aunt took a handkerchief from her handbag to dry her tears and said, "Don't worry. It will soon be Beatrice's wedding and Domenic will be invited. We will arrange for you to be together, without anybody knowing, and remember, in six months' time you will be twenty one, and then you'll be free to marry Domenic without your parents' consent."

Angelina said, "I'm a fool. How could I have forgotten about that! We could even run way and then he can't do

281

anything about it because we are old enough to do just that."

Chapter 53

Three or four weeks later, Renato and Maria received the wedding invitation from their family-in-law for the wedding of Beatrice to Giuseppe, but there was a dilemma. Domenic was to be Giuseppe's best man, so Mary hid the invitation card away, until she could speak to her sons and find a way to resolve the problem. When they arrived home they saw that their mother was very worried. They asked her what was wrong.

She said, "We have received Beatrice's wedding invitation from your Aunt Giovanna and Uncle Mathew, but I'm very concerned about your father, because the best man will be Domenic and no doubt Domenic's family will be invited. I don't know how your father will react to that."

Roberto asked, "Where is the invitation now"?

"I haven't let him see the invitation before I had a word with the two of you, so I hid it. You see I don't know how to handle him. He will be furious."

Roberto looked grim. He said, "Mother, leave it with Simon and me. We will deal with him tomorrow while we are in the vineyard. You prepare a good lunch for us to take with us, because we shall be there all day if necessary."

The next day, Roberto and Simon went with their father to the vineyard. Everything looked in harmony with nature. The hedges were starting to turn green, the trees full of chattering birds and the air was fresh with spring just around the corner. Even their father appeared to be in a good mood.

After three hours of solid work trimming the vines, Renato said, "Come on boys, it's time we sat under that oak tree and have a break. He looked thoughtful. "Our village never changes," he said. "Yesterday I went to the village and there were a few women chattering away about everybody's business and I heard mention of Beatrice and

Giuseppe. I couldn't help listening to what it was all about. One of them said, "Do you know about the wedding? The other one answered, "What wedding? I haven't heard anything."

The first one said, "Well, it's the daughter of Mathew and Giovanna, the one who was brought up by her sister Mary. Unfortunately there is a big problem, because Mary and her husband became so attached to the girl that they planned for Beatrice and their own daughter Angelina, to marry men from well off families. Now Beatrice is to marry the postman, and if Angelina has her own way, she will marry the son of Mr Caccia Capo, the timber merchant. Renato is very disappointed, and there's a chance he'll be very angry. Who knows what he might do? He could create some big problems for the young bride and groom."

The other lady said, "Don't be silly now. He only wants the best for his girls. I tell you that he may not agree with the choice the girls have made, but he's not silly by any means. He will be as brave as the best when it comes to it and I can assure you, when these girls have their own children, he will be the best granddad ever."

The first lady said, "I don't believe it, but time will tell. Now it's late and I'd better go home and prepare tea for my family."

Roberto and Simon listened quietly, letting their father speak his piece.

Renato said, "That lady was right. I know I don't agree, but I can't do anything about it. The only thing I need to do is to make peace with myself and with my family. As that lady said, "I hope they will have a lot of children for us to spoil."

Roberto and Simon burst out laughing in relief. Then Simon said, "We hope that goes for us as well!"

Their father patted them both reassuringly, and said, "Undoubtedly, you will always be my precious sons, and in future whatever you say or do, I will not interfere, but one thing I need to do is to confess to both of you that I can't stomach Angelina's boyfriend."

The sons burst out laughing again, and Simon said boldly, "We know why. Because you think he can play music better than you do."

Renato glared at them and seemed annoyed. Then his face softened a little and he said, "Maybe so, but I didn't have the same opportunity and a good guitar like he has."

Robert said, "Dad, Simon was only joking, we think you play very well."

And when we think about the courage you must have had to emigrate to America, without knowing where that boat was taking you or what you were going to do when you got there, we know that you are a very strong person." said Simon.

Renato looked at his sons and said quietly, "Boys you're wrong .When I left Italy, so many thousands of other young men and even some women did the same, because the unification of our country gave us no opportunity to live on our own and make a reasonable living. Maybe that is why I'm so obsessive about wanting you all to have a better future, much better than we had when we were young."

Robert and Simon looked at their father and saw he had tears running down his face."

When they returned to the farm house, Roberto and Simon waited for an opportunity to be with their mother alone, and then Roberto said, "Mum, the problem has been resolved .There is no need to worry, for we think our father has now come to his senses and Giuseppe and Beatrice will be able to get married without any worries about our father."

Mary said, "I can always rely on you two. There is a proverb that says, 'Easier said than done' and today you two have done, and many other times too, what others just talk about. I want to thank God, for giving us such kind and clever sons. "

Two weeks later the church of Saint Antony was in great splendour, with many, many beautiful colours, ready for Beatrice and Giuseppe to celebrate their wedding, with all their relatives and friends, and without any disturbance from Beatrice's uncle.

Chapter 54

Renato had made peace with Beatrice and Giuseppe, but he just couldn't resign himself to the fact that his own daughter was in love with the son of a merchant and not a farmer like himself. He had a sister, Gillian, who lived near Milan and she wasn't well, so he wrote to her, saying,

'Dear Gillian, I know you are not well, so I think it would be good for my daughter Angelina to come and stay with you for a little while, to give you a helping hand until you recover.'

Then he posted the letter, and went to his wife saying, "Mary, I have received a letter from my sister Gillian saying she is very poorly. As she's all alone, I think it would be good if we sent Angelina to give her a hand until she recovers. It will be good for my sister and also for Angelina."

His wife immediately understood his true meaning. In his mind he thought that if Angelina stayed with his sister there was a chance she would fall in love with someone else, or better still, Domenic would fall in love with someone else. Renato knew Domenic played music every Saturday evening in the church club, and the girls flocked around him. In his mind he hoped he would fall in love with one of them and forget all about Angelina, then all the problems would be solved.

Renato approached Angelina, saying, "Angelina, my sister is not well and she wants you to go to her and help her until she's better."

But Angelina was cleverer then he thought. She understood completely, what her father was doing, and she answered, "Father, Auntie has three grown up daughters to look after her, why does she need me?"

He answered, "Because they have jobs and they haven't time to take care of her."

She went up close to her father and said, "Father, you really think I'm that stupid, that I don't understand what you're trying to do? Now you can write to Auntie Gillian and tell her that she needs to ask her daughters to help her because I have no intention of leaving my mother and brothers. I'm head over heels in love with Domenic and you can do whatever you like, but you can't make me go where I don't want to go, not now and not ever!"

Mary heard all the noise and said, "What is going on?"

Angelina answered, "Mother, did you realise that Dad wants to send me off to go and look after Aunty Gillian, just to get rid of me, because I'm a nuisance to him. Like Beatrice, according to him, we both fell in love with the wrong men. Luckily, Beatrice was able to return to her Mum and her parents not being as domineering as my father, allowed her to marry the man she loved. But that's not for me. If I want to stay, I have to marry someone I don't love to please my father, otherwise I must go to Milan so he's rid of me. He wants me to go and look after Auntie Gillian and my father thinks I can forget about Domenic. I know he hopes I will meet someone else and that will be the end of Domenic, but he is wrong, I will not! Before long I will be twenty one, and then nobody can stop me marrying the man I love."

And with that Angelina slammed the door and went out.

Mary was very annoyed with her husband. She said to him, "Renato, only a few months ago Beatrice came here and warned you, if you don't stop playing this game we will lose our daughter forever and then you will feel guilty for the rest of your life. You will also turn me, your family and the whole district against you, and serves you right! When you first returned from America, you were a very kind man and helped anyone in the village who was in need. Now in your old age your behaviour is not right towards me, or to anybody and indeed not to your family! Why don't you like Domenic's family, Renato? Tell me just who do you think you are to judge people and think you have more right than anybody else to feel so superior to Domenic's family? Now you go to look for your

288

daughter, apologise to her and bring her back home."

Two hours later Roberto and Simon returned from work and found their mother very upset.

Roberto said, "Mother, whatever is the matter with you?"

Mary answered, "Angelina is not at home and your father is out looking for her."

Simon came in from the other rooms and said, "I heard what you said. "Why is father looking for Angelina? What's happened?"

Roberto answered, "I haven't the faintest idea, just like you. We can both see that our mother is very upset."

After a few minutes Angelina came in and they could see she had very swollen red eyes. They look at each other and both asked Angelina what was going on? Angelina didn't answer them. She ran into her room and slammed the door.

Robert and Simon again, asked their mother what was wrong.

Mary said, "Don't ask me, ask your father?"

Roberto said, "How can I ask my father when I don't see him anywhere round here?" She replied, "He's outside somewhere looking for Angelina."

Roberto was mystified and couldn't understand what was going on in their house.

He said to Simon, "When our father comes back home, we need to ask him what is going on here. While we were in the fields working, Mother has had a problem with Dad and I wouldn't be surprised if it isn't the same problem as always, with Angelina. These two keep interfering with Angelina's life."

Two hours later, their father came home looking very worried and very weary. His sons took one look at him and knew there was something dramatically wrong with him. But neither their mother nor their father would say anything. So their sons gave up on them and agreed that they probably weren't going to find out the reason why these two were behaving in the way they were. They left their parents to themselves in the kitchen.

When the boys were alone, Roberto said, "It wouldn't surprise me if they've been quarrelling because of our sister's situation. Angelina come in with swollen red eyes and seemed very upset."

Simon decided to go back to his parents. He said to his mother, "We've worked very hard all day, then we come home and there's no supper. We're very tired, and now it looks like we'll be going to bed without anything to eat because of you two. Instead of behaving like two adults, you've been quarrelling about our poor sister. It's about time you left her alone to get on with her own life. Tomorrow will be another day, and then we shall find out the reason why Angelina came in with swollen eyes and a very red face."

Chapter 55

The next day Angelina was very quiet and her brothers wanted to know why she had been so upset when she came home the previous evening.

She said, "You would have been upset if you knew your father wanted to get rid of you, just because you can't fulfil his ambitions."

Roberto found it difficult to understand what his sister meant. He went back to his mother and said to her, "Mother, I'm very concerned about Angelina. She is mad, saying our father wants to get rid of her."

"Roberto", said his mother with a sigh. I'm afraid it is your father who is deranged. He told Angelina that he wants her go and look after your Aunt Gillian near Milan because she isn't well. But your aunt has three of her own daughters who can easily take care of her. Why on earth does your father think his sister needs Angelina to go all the way to Milan, when it's not necessary?"

Roberto said, "Mother, Angelina is not stupid. She understood the reason why he wants to send her to Milan. It's because he thinks and hopes, that while Angelina is in Milan, Domenic will fall in love with one of the girls in the church club, who crowd round him when he plays music. Father thinks that when Angelina returns from Milan she won't care anything about him, and will at last come to her senses and marry John. Then all his problems will be over."

Mary said, "That's just what she said and I agreed with her and that is the reason why she is very upset."

"Angelina has no need to worry," said Roberto, "Because we will not permit our father to do any such thing. We love her and we want her to marry the man she loves, whatever he says."

Roberto and Simon then went in search of Angelina. She was in her room. "You don't need to worry about our father," Roberto told her.

"Do you remember all the noise he made about Beatrice, but in the end everything was resolved, in the best way? We will have another chat with Dad and we can promise you that when the time comes, your wedding will be just as good as your cousin's, or even better, you'll see."

A few days later, when Roberto and Simon were working in the orchard with their father, Roberto said to him, "Dad, the other day I met Jimmy, and he told me that John's parents are over the moon, because he is engaged to a very beautiful young lady who works in an office of government administration and he thinks it will not be very long before they get married. Jimmy himself is very happy because he's been offered a job as a waiter in a restaurant in Rome and that will give him the chance to get out of farm work. Eventually he will settle in Rome with the hope of better opportunities in the city."

Renato looked at his sons in disbelief and said, "How can his parents permit their son to get engaged to a young girl who doesn't know anything about farming? And as for Jimmy leaving his father and brothers, with all the work they have ahead of them, just to go off to the city to work as a waiter? I don't believe you!"

Roberto and Simon laughed and said, "That's up to you Dad .If you don't believe us, just wait and see."

When they finished working and returned home, their father was very discouraged. He just couldn't believe what his sons had told him. Mary noticed that he was stressed about something and said, "Now then, what's the matter with you this evening. In this house, for one reason or another, it seems to me we just can't have a day without problems. I'm fed up! You'd better begin to understand that if you don't stop annoying your children, they will all leave us and then you will have something to moan about."

Renato looked at his wife, and said, "I love my children, and that is why I would like Angelina to marry a farmer, because she won't have any worries about food or anything else. Not just her, but also her family, and besides, she would also be near to us."

Mary shrugged her shoulders and then said, "I can understand that, but Domenic is a good young man, he is hard working and very kind to everybody. He's very well behaved, and all round the village people speak well of him."

Renato said heavily, "Ok Mary, I just don't like him," he admitted.

Mary laughed without humour and said, "There you are, "You don't like him, but your daughter loves him, and that is what's important!"

Roberto overheard their conversation and decided that he needed to go to the village and have a chat with his aunt and uncle.

Twenty minutes later he arrived at their house and when he knocked on the door, Beatrice opened it. Seeing her cousin Roberto, she immediately thought something had happened to Angelina."

"Oh, it's you Roberto. Please tell me Angelina is okay. I have been very worried about her. Giuseppe and I have achieved our dream, but my poor cousin is very unhappy because she loves Domenic and it's very difficult for them to meet one another."

Roberto said, "I know and you're right; she is very unhappy, because as you said, you and Giuseppe have achieved your dream. She is very happy for the two of you. Simon and I know when you were with us she could manage the situation much better between our father and herself. Now she thinks our father will never come to his senses. There is nothing she would like more than to have his consent, just like you and Giuseppe had from your parents. She wants to be able to marry Domenic in the same way."

Beatrice said, "Can you and Simon arrange for Domenic to meet Angelina when uncle is working in a place where he has no chance of seeing them. Or if he does, that you'll both be there to help them?"

Robert said, "That's easier said than done, but we'll try.

When I go home, I'll have a chat with Simon and then together we'll have a talk with Mum and see how we can resolve this problem once and for all. Beatrice, this must be between you and me. None of your family must ever know anything about it. Nobody from your family needs to know I have been here."

Then he embraced his cousin and left.

When he arrived home, he spoke to his brother Simon and said, "I went to the village to auntie's house, and had a chat with Beatrice. Later on, when I know there is nobody else around, we need to talk, but for the time being we mustn't draw attention to ourselves. I will explain later. It's a very serious matter and if we're not careful we could be in a lot of trouble.

"Simon said, "Goodness me! You're frightening me, what is going on?"

Roberto said, "Nothing we can't handle. As I have already told you, keep quiet and soon I will be able to reveal all to you."

Simon was worried as he didn't understand what kind of secret Roberto could be hiding, and how long it would be before he was prepared to tell him.

The next day Roberto said to Simon, "Listen to me, Simon, while our mother and father are out shopping, we need to speak to Angelina about something and if she agrees with us we can help her, but she needs to cooperate fully with anything we say or it won't work."

Angelina was in the rose garden when she saw her two brothers coming towards her. They smiled and Roberto said, "Angelina, we promise to help you and Domenic get married, but only if you promise you won't let us down and don't tell anybody what we plan to do."

Her face lit up and she said, "Yes, I will do whatever you both say, but I don't understand. How can you bring my wedding forward when I'm not even allowed to see Domenic. Both of you will be in danger if he comes near our house. Father won't allow it."

Simon himself was mystified, hearing Roberto being so

sure about whatever he was planning.

Then Roberto revealed his plan to them both. "Giuseppe will go to Domenic and tell him to come round to our farmhouse, but if our father sees him, he must just go away. We will be around if our father tries to attack him and we will make sure he has no chance of hurting Domenic. He needs to come as often as he can, and you should stop worrying. Later at night, Domenic can come with his guitar and sing a serenade to Angelina, beneath her bedroom window. 'Angelina, my dear, Angelina come down. I bring you my heart. It's weeping for you, etc.' We'll keep an eye open for our father, and in a month or two you can tell our mother you're expecting Domenic's child. I can tell you, Angelina that will really shock our parents. We'll stand by you and we shall see what will come out of that."

Angelina said to Simon "This is a very scary plan, but I will do it."

Simon went to see Giuseppe and explained to him what Roberto had suggested. Giuseppe agreed to go to Domenic and create a plan that would work, with a very happy end for both families.

That evening at eleven o'clock, Domenic went to the farm with his guitar and began to sing, 'Angelina. My dear Angelina, open the door because I want to come up. I have brought you my bleeding heart, you're my love.'

Angelina's father heard Domenic serenading his daughter. He quickly put on his trousers, went into his stable, picked up a big stick and went out to find Domenic and give him a good hiding.

Roberto and Simon were waiting for him and ran over to him. They grabbed hold of him, and Roberto cried, "Father! Stop at once. Whatever has come over you?"

Renato said, "My sons, can't you see that this hooligan has come here to disturb, not just our daughter, but all of us as well."

Roberto said loudly, "That doesn't give you the right to harm him, just because we've been disturbed. We hope this doesn't happen again."

But it did happen again, regularly, and without a break for some time.

Then Roberto and Simon decided it was time to move on. They told Domenic and Giuseppe, that it was time Angelina told her parents that she was expecting a baby.

"It will turn their stomachs up and down," said Robert, "But we can be sure they will immediately ask Domenic to arrange for the wedding as soon as possible."

A few days after that Angelina went to her parents and said she needed to have a word with them. They were very pleased, and for a moment they thought she was going to tell them that she had come round to doing what her father wanted.

Angelina drew in a deep breath and said, "Mum and dad, I've come to see you because I have very good news for you, and also for my brothers. I'm expecting a baby!"

Her parents stared at her. They were both in tremendous shock and nearly fell out of the chairs they were sitting in. Mary immediately went out to look for her two sons in the fields, not far away.

She said, "Boys come home at once. We need you now."

Roberto and Simon heard her call and both smiled. They knew all along that it was the day when the bomb would explode.

They put down their tools and ran towards their mother. They acted very properly, and Roberto said, "Mum, please calm down. Will you please tell us what's happened?"

Their mother appeared to be very frightened. The two sons went home, and found their father weeping, but Roberto and Simon couldn't understand if it was for joy or grief. They said, "Come along father, tell us what's happened?"

He look at both of them with his eyes full of tears and said, "You sister is expecting a baby!"

The sons jumped up and down. Both parents took their sons hands together and all four of them started to sing a lullaby, the one that was sung to them when they were born.

Angelina was very frightened, but at the same time she knew it was the only way she and Domenic could follow in Beatrice and Giuseppe's footsteps, so that both the cousins could realise their dreams.

She went into the room where her mother and father were singing the lullaby and she said, "May I join in? The family was extremely happy. But Robert, Simon and Angelina had a secret. What they said and what they did was a lie. Now they needed to get on with the publication of the banns in church and quickly take the wedding forward.

Renato was too much of a gentleman to support the gossip of people in the village so he would do whatever it took to see that his daughter would have a good wedding. Better than any they had seen in the area for a long time. He called his sons and said,

"If anybody had offered me a million lire, and told me to give permission for my own daughter to get married to the son of Mr Francesco Di Catto I would have said, 'No'!, but now the situation is changed. I'll shall present myself to Mr Francesco Di Catto and ask him if we can put aside our silly behaviour and be good friends. We must give these two children a chance to get on with their lives in a respectable way, for us, for them, and for our new generation."

Roberto and Simon were delighted to go to the village of Catailli and meet Eduard and Domenic to give them the good news. Domenic wept for joy and Roberto and Simon invited all the family of Francesco Di Catto to come and have dinner at the farmhouse with Renato Caccia Capo and his wife Mary. A few days later, Dominic said to Robert and Simon, "I don't know how to thank you both for all that you have done for us, but what we do now? We said there's a baby on the way, but this not true. What happens next?"

"Don't worry Domenic. Our parents do not want

anybody to know about it. Dad will be so embarrassed if gossip spreads round the village. We can assure you that before you know it, he'll go to see the priest himself about the wedding."

Two days later Renato and his wife went to the village and made an appointment to see the priest. The priest couldn't contain his joy, when he saw the man who had incarcerated his own daughter and forbidden her to meet with the man she loved, now here with his wife to arrange for the publication of their daughter's wedding banns in church. Angelina was concerned about going to church, when she knew that, to obtain what she and Domenic wanted, they'd had to lie.

Roberto explained to her, "In your case, Angelina, we're lying for a good reason, otherwise it wouldn't have been possible for you to get married and the pair of you would be unhappy for the rest of your lives. It's only because we've lied, that this wedding will be celebrated soon and we can assure you, it will happen very quickly, and everything will be alright."

Angelina said, "What will be happen to us after the wedding, when there is no baby?"

"Simon said, "We will spread the word that you lost the baby, and anyway, we hope it won't be long before you will have the real thing."

At the first publication of banns in the church, between Angelina and Domenic, all the people in the village began to talk about the wedding. They all knew Renato would take this occasion to show off, as he always did. They still remembered the celebration when they'd had the blessing of his farm about twenty one years before, so people knew it would be a big wedding for the people of the two villages. It would be talked about for years to come.

Mary asked her sister Giovanna to help her prepare Angelina's bottom drawer of fifty sheets; fifty pillow cases embroidered by the nuns, many woollen blankets, and all her personal wardrobe, beautiful furniture, etc. as well as frying pans, big and small, some of copper, and china.

The most beautiful wedding dress was prepared for her. Renato invited nearly all the people of both villages to celebrate his daughter's wedding, just as he'd done for the blessing of his Farm twenty one years ago. It was nominated, the wedding of the year!

The End

CPSIA information can be obtained
at www.ICGtesting.com
Printed in the USA
LVHW081430091220
673723LV00020B/169